Copyright © 2015
L. J. Thorburn
(pen name Blair Coleman)

All rights reserved, including the right to reproduce
This book, or portions therein
No parts of this book may be reproduced without
The written consent of the author
All persons in this book are fictional and any resemblance
To persons living or dead is purely coincidental
All illustrative material used has been purchased legally,
And with the right to use in such a manner as for, but not limited to,
The purpose of book cover design. Websites used
www.canstockphoto.com
www.kozzi.com
www.pixabay.com

First Published Sept 2015
ISBN: 9781091398672

Dedications

This book has been a long time coming, and before I thank the most important people in my life, I want to thank Sarah Lovett for introducing me to NaNoWriMo.

Graceful Damnation was always in the back of my mind, but I started writing it for NaNoWriMo after Sarah told me I simply had to sign up. And so I did… in November 2014.

Then my Faction series happened (which actually happened way before Graceful) and Graceful kinda got pushed back. I didn't touch it for about 8 or 9 months after I 'completed' NaNo.

And I have so many people to thank while I wrote and wrote like a woman possessed to get it finished and published before the intended October release.

Obviously, there is my family. My mum and my sister, especially because without their unconditional love and support, I really don't think I'd have the confidence to keep doing what I do. My dad and his partner, Leslie also, for always showing their support and buying my books and telling me I'm great!!

I want to thank my partner, Simon. I've neglected him once again to make sure I can present this piece of filth to you glorious readers in a timely manner.

I want to thank everyone that's ever offered words of support and encouragement, and I really can't name them all, or we'll be here all day and I know you're dying to start reading some classy smut, as one of my friends called it!

Needless to say, the names I will drop, as I always do because – one way or another – these people keep me grounded, sane, or crazy hehe. Luke, Annie, Elisia – I love all of our conversations and your 'words of wisdom' or just your general 'make me feel better' random talks. You guys are awesome.

Karen, Brenda and Shaz for promoting me and reading everything I pass to them for criticism. Karen especially, because I am absolutely sure she is literally glued to her computer, posting pimp posts on everything going. It's amazing! I don't know how she does it.

All the Betas that have helped make this story what it is… Brenda, Karen, John, Nadine, you guys are amazing! You put it all into perspective for me.

Every one of you rocks!!! And I appreciate all that you do for me. I am so grateful for your continued support, each and every one of you.

Preface

Graceful Damnation was always meant to be a three-parter, but I had a moment of realisation where – if I ended on the intended cliffhanger – it would be very difficult to bring it back round to the erotic genre. And that's what Graceful is – it's an erotic novel and I didn't want to change that.

So I came back to it, after an 8 month hiatus (well, not a complete hiatus, I was working on two other novels and one novella) and turned it into a standalone with the idea of writing a book for each of the characters.

I've had fun with this one as you can probably imagine. And my research took me in all kinds of directions, some great, some a little darker than I would usually delve, but all necessary to get this out there (and hopefully remain jail-free with some of the sites I had to visit!)

I hope this pleases you guys, because it's taken my blood, sweat and tears to get finished, and I will warn you now, the opening scene is NOT for the faint of heart, but please don't judge me – it had to be done.

Happy reading, guys and girlies!!

Graceful DAMNATION

By Blair Coleman

Chapter 1

London, August 2012

Grace

Walking into work, I keep my head down; my hair covering most of my face, while I head for the staff toilet.

"Afternoon, Gracie," my boss, Ivan calls from somewhere behind the counter.

I throw him a wave, but don't look up.

Shouldering my way into the bathroom, I lock the door behind me. Only then do I lift my head and look into the mirror above the sink.

The daft bastard has marked my fucking face - on any other day, he tries to avoid leaving bruises where people can see and question; calls them nosey twats for prying.

But what does he expect? If he punches me in the face for all the world to see, I'm gonna get the Spanish Inquisition from those close to me - which basically consists of my boss and the other evening waitress, Penny.

Delving into my bag, I pull out my foundation and dab it on my face, trying to hide the rainbow of colours coming through.

"Can I borrow you for a minute, Gracie?" Ivan's voice rings out from the other side of the door.

"Won't be a mo." Time to put my game face on.

Shit, that'll have to do - I can hide the majority with my hair and just hope no-one picks up on it.

Leaving the toilet, I follow my pudgy, bald-headed boss into the café, keeping the swollen side of my face out of Ivan's line of sight.

"What can I get you?" I stroll up to the customer Ivan points out and take my order pad from the pocket of my apron.

Looking at me, a smile breaks across his face, "What you offering, darling?" He places a rough hand on my lower arm and begins to stroke. I flinch at the contact, despite being used to his platonic affection.

"I'm offering not to break your fingers, provided you remove your hand within the next three seconds." I throw him my usual sugary-sweet smile and bat my lashes, even as I try to slow my erratic heart-rate.

The guy's a regular, always in here around this time and always hitting on either me or Penny. He doesn't take offence and always laughs at my quips, and tonight is no different.

"I'll take a coffee, thanks, sweetheart. Creamy and sweet, just like my favourite hostess." His grin widens.

Returning his smile, I cock my head, "Now, would that be me, or the other girl you salivate over?"

"Only have eyes for you, babe." He winks at me.

"Uh-huh, for tonight, at least."

*

It's nearing closing, and I know Penny's noticed my face – she's been staring at me on and off all night, and she'll be on me the moment I hang my apron up.

It won't be for a while yet, however, because a swarm of people walk in – fresh from last orders at the pub opposite, I imagine.

Running up behind me, Penny slaps my arse. "I have those papers you asked about. You up for a quick drink when we're done?"

She's giving me her code for, 'and we need to talk about your face, again', but I can't.

"I wish I could, babe, but I need to get back."

Pouting and running a hand through her cropped, blond hair, she murmurs, "Grace… ." She looks at me with large, brown, doe-eyes – a knowing expression. "Fine, we'll have a quick one here when we lock the doors, and I'm not taking no for an answer."

"Alright, but just the one; I have to be up early tomorrow."

*

Forty-five minutes later, the café doors are locked, Ivan's left and Penny pulls a bottle of vodka from her bag, smiling while she shakes it at me, motioning for me to grab two tumblers.

We each take a seat and she pours me a double measure, sliding it across the table to me. "What happened this time, Grace?" She doesn't look at me while she pours herself one.

"What do you mean?" I don't look up - don't want her to focus on my face, but I figure she's already taken a good look at it and that's why we're sitting here.

"You know what I mean, lady." She releases a heavy sigh, twirling the silver heart pendant she's wearing around her neck - I bought it for her birthday last year. "I have those documents you wanted." She knocks back the vodka and reaches for her bag.

My voice is barely a whisper when I reply, "Thank you, Penny. I couldn't do this without you." She hands me the forged travel documents and papers and I slide them down the side of my top, securing them beneath the strap of my bra.

"Grace Emery, sorry, Morgan; I'm going to miss you, ya know?" Her eyes sag with sadness and she bites the inside of her cheek.

"I'll miss you, too, babe." A tear falls down my cheek and Penny wipes it away with a half-smile.

This weekend, I'll be outta here - three days and I will be as far from London as humanly possible.

You see, four years ago, when I was twenty years old, my boyfriend, Garrett Phillips walked into my life.

After years of enduring a shitty upbringing following the death of my parents before I hit my teens, I ended up on the streets and a breath away from selling my body in order to pay for a decent meal. But then a thirty-one year old Garrett walked into my life and changed things for me. He offered me a place to stay and I moved in with him.

A week later, he fucked me up good. Blackened my eye, bruised my ribs and fractured two fingers because he thought he caught me eyeing up his cousin.

The beatings became a regular thing and you're probably wondering why I didn't just leave him.

He provided for me, took me off the streets and saved me from a hooker's life. He gave me a home when no-one else would. I didn't know any different, and, at the time, I feared leaving him would cost me more than one or two fractured bones. I know what Garrett can do to someone who crosses him. Over the years, I've watched him beat the living crap out of people he called friends. I knew he'd kill me if he ever found me.

I got my job working for Ivan at a local greasy spoon about two years ago. Garrett doesn't like it. Could be because I make my own money, but more than likely because guys can hit on me when he's not around. To appease him - or rather because he beat me for saying no – I've been dealing for him on the side. It's been a huge risk, because if Ivan found out, he'd have kicked me out of the place and I needed this job so badly. But it'll all be over soon.

Garrett's been taking the money for the drugs, and my wages - at least, he thinks he has been. For the past year, I've been lying to him about how much I make; keeping back my tips so that I'll be able to leave him and go somewhere he can't find me.

I'll change my name, my appearance, anything if it means I can get away.

By the time Ivan pays me at the end of this week, I'll have enough. I figure I'll go somewhere like Scotland, or maybe even Ireland - somewhere far enough away the lazy fuck won't bother to come looking for me.

I'll miss Penny. She's been a lifeline for me while we've worked for Ivan, but she knows I can't tell her where I'm going – she knows I will have to cut all ties from this life. I can't take the risk.

I stand and give her the tightest hug I can, crying into her shoulder and telling her how much she will always mean to me.

*

It's gone midnight by the time I'm stumbling down my street, but my brain's fuzzy from the vodka we knocked back in the last half hour, so I'm not too bothered right now.

I have a smile on my face because I've taken my shoes off, and the warm, rough pavement is providing a delicious massage to the ache in my feet. I'm struggling to keep my eyes open, though, when I turn into the shared garden of our apartment block – I'll be in bed before I know it.

Bending down to get a close-up of the lock, I slip my key in – making sure to be quiet – and walk into the living room.

Garrett's slouched, eyes lolling, in his favourite, brown leather armchair; that thing has seen better days – the leather's worn across the arms where he picks at it when he's high on his choice drug of the day. It's also full of knife holes where he's lost his temper more than a few times and took it out on the furniture.

His three-day old, brown stubble is showing the grey his shaved head doesn't and he's squinting his beady, green eyes at something on the TV, with a joint jammed between his thin lips.

Turning his listless, glazed eyes on me, he gets up – drowsy and stumbling – throwing what's left of the spliff to the floor and stomping it out.

"Where the fuck you been?" He spits his words through gritted teeth and my stomach plummets.

My eyes dart around the room, catching sight of two of Garrett's gang buddies – Billy 'Brass' Brassington and Garrett's cousin, Frankie Davis – on the opposite, garish orange, three-seater sofa.

They're both staring at me, sneering, decaying teeth on display while they knock back their cans of Carling.

Garrett's fist connects with my cheek and I fall to the floor, spitting blood. "Been fucking your way around Croydon, have you?" He gets in my face, nose to nose; his putrid-smelling spittle coating my lips and nose.

Leaning up on two hands, I turn my head toward him. "No, Garrett. I promise. We had a last min–"

He slaps me hard, despite his dazed state. "Lying bitch, I can smell the booze on your breath."

"Penny and I had one drink after work, after the rush." My voice quaking, I don't dare look at him this time, but I won't cry – I never give him that satisfaction.

The kick he launches into my ribs is clumsy, but heavy and he staggers while I drop to the floor again. "You better be telling the fuckin' truth, Gracie. You know what I'll do to you if you're dishing out pussy to every bastard goin'."

Brass throws a can at my head, "Fetch me another."

"Guzzling fucker," Garrett slurs, eyes half-closed, backing away and slumping in his chair.

Taking a couple of deep, painful breaths I clamber to my feet, clutching at the ache lancing through my ribs. I look between Garrett and Brass.

Brass – like Frankie – is disgusting to look at; both gangly and gaunt, in comparison to Garrett's bulky frame, but with receding hairlines and sunken eyes. That's what years of drug abuse will do to you.

Garrett reckons he's clever; only dabbles now and again in the 'softer' stuff, not the hardcore shit he deals – plus he's a greedy fucker, it would take a miracle for him to lose his timber.

I don't say a word to either of them; instead, I limp into the kitchen and grab another cold one from the fridge.

After a few minutes staring into the veiling darkness outside the kitchen window, I shuffle back in on the threadbare, cream carpet, dropping Brass's can on him – daft fucker is already half-asleep, doesn't even notice the can falling into his lap. Frankie's head leans on Brass's shoulder, drooling.

Garrett's dozed off, too, *thank fuck.* I spy the remains of some 'new' drug they've likely been smoking all night. With any luck, I'll manage a couple of hour's kip before Garrett crashes and decides he needs to get his dick wet.

His head falls back against the chair, mouth open, letting out soft snores.

Creeping out of the room and down the hallway, I dodge the squeaky floorboards I've committed to memory.

Entering the bathroom, I glare at the grime across the walls and floor, fags ends litter the sink and toilet and there is tin foil and baggies thrown across every available surface – some empty, some not.

Looking in the mirror, I note the purple and red bruise already forming against my pale skin, accentuated further by my bright, auburn hair and the charcoal rings circling my once-sparkling, baby blue eyes.

This would be another one of the times where Garrett's been too high to remember not to mark my face. I'm going to have to make up yet another excuse tomorrow at work. Maybe I'll just call in sick.

Light footsteps sound in the corridor and I peer out the door.

"Hey, Frankie." Garrett's cousin ambles toward me.

He doesn't say anything, just leers at me, shouldering the wall while he stumbles forward. I'm used to his stares, he's always glaring at me one way or another, often with a look that says he wants in my pants – I ignore it, lest Garrett accuses me of flirting again.

Closing the gap, his eyes narrow at me, his lip hitching into a half-sneer before he pushes me further into the bathroom, closing the door behind him.

"Gaz is sleeping, I'm gonna keep you satisfied tonight." His breath stinks of beer and stale cigarettes.

"Leave it out, Frankie." I go for the doorknob, my hand shaking.

Thrusting his hand against my chest, he shoves me against the basin and it hurts, jarring my tailbone and sending a shooting pain up my spine.

"Frankie, what the fuck, man?" Terror seeps into my trembling voice. I don't shout out though, I'll be the one paying the price for *my* 'infidelity' if I do.

"Shut up; let a real man show you how it's done." His rancid breath makes me want to wretch. "You're gorgeous, you know that?" He runs a scrawny hand down my cheek and I flinch.

Patting my face a little too hard, he moves, wasting no time unbuckling his belt. I'm shaking like a leaf, but I'm not standing for this – dealing with one piece of shit from this family is enough – *Frankie isn't having his way with me, too.*

I muster the strength to push him back with leaden limbs and try to walk past. He stumbles over his half-removed jeans, but reaches out for me.

"Whore!" he spits at me.

A shooting pain races through my neck when he grabs my shoulder-length hair and yanks me back.

Bile rises up my throat and he smashes my head in the mirror above the basin with an audible crack. Blinking back the sharp pain, I catch blurred sight of slivers tumbling from the frame and into the sink. I hold onto the basin, stumbling, nicking my feet on the larger shards that have dropped onto the linoleum floor, fighting for control of my watery vision.

Warm blood trickles down my neck before Frankie grabs the side of my head, turns me and forces me on my knees. He flops his limp dick out of his pants and grabs a fistful of my hair, angling my head toward it.

It smells like he hasn't washed the thing in weeks.

He growls and my stomach lurches when he hurls me against the side of the bathtub, and I hiss through gritted teeth at the agony while I clamber to my knees. It's that cheap, plastic shit; otherwise it could've done some serious damage. I blocked the impact with my shoulder, but it jarred my ribs all the same.

He drops down in front of me and spits in my face. Thick, stinking mucus slides down my cheek. "I been waiting on this for years. I'm gonna fuck you six ways from Sunday, bitch."

He grabs me around the throat and throws me to the floor, my heart pounding in my ears. I struggle against him – body stinging from the lacerations to my exposed flesh from the glass slivers beneath me. He tears at the shorts I wear under my uniform.

"You're gonna get it now, open those legs for Frankie." He leers over me, his lips curling up.

He painfully manhandles my breast, trying to pry my legs apart while I tremble beneath his weight. I open my mouth to scream, but he clamps a sweaty palm over me and I can taste the cigarettes on his skin.

My eyes bulge, staring at the grimacing shadow of his face, silhouetted by the light above.

Panic constricts me when his fingers probe the thin material of my knickers, my chest tightens and I grind my teeth into Frankie's hand. I feel the pinch of skin between my teeth and bite down, hard. Frankie yelps, removes his hand from my face and backhands me with it.

It stings like a bitch and I spit blood on the floor, clutching my cheek with one hand, battling Frankie with the other.

Kneeling on my wrist – his bone grating against mine with excruciating pain – he continues to rain blows down on my face, not just stopping at a few bitch slaps.

Frankie grabs me by the waist and yanks me down, making light work of ripping off my underwear. I try to scream again, but he cracks me another blow and my head snaps sideways.

The glint of a long, glass shard catches my eye.

The perverted tosser positions himself to shove his semi-erect cock inside me, pushing my legs further apart and jarring my hip bone. He thrusts forward, trying to angle himself in, but I don't give him the satisfaction.

I grab the sharp sliver – shredding my palm in the process – and ram the pointed end straight into the side of his neck.

The glass slices like a knife through butter.

Frankie's hand flies to the weapon. He pulls it out – blood spurting across the floor – and clamps his hand over his neck. Thick, dark fluid runs between his fingers.

I scramble back, feet slipping in the blood seeping from his wound. Quick jets spatter my clothes and face. I close my eyes and mouth – no way is that shit getting into my system; I've no idea what the dirty bastard's got swimming in his.

Frankie drops to the side, flapping and flailing like a fish out of water. Scurrying back on hands and feet, I watch his eyes roll back, his face turning ashen. Slick blood pumps from his neck while he tries to keep his palm over it. It pools beneath him in a deep, crimson puddle.

Spasms subsiding, his arms drop, limp. His bloodied face has fallen to the side and his tongue is half-hanging out. Vacant, glassy eyes stare at nothing.

Panic settles in my churning gut and the realization of my actions hit me like a sledgehammer to my stomach. On wooden limbs, I lurch for the tub and hurl over the polished enamel.

Wiping my mouth with the back of my hand, I rise on shaky legs, averting my gaze from Frankie's lifeless form.

Naked from the waist down – and past giving a fuck – I stagger down the hallway, uniform bunched around my hips. Pangs of agony shoot through my body and I remember the first creaky floorboard the moment it groans under my weight.

Shit! Standing stock still, I listen. I can't hear anything save for Garrett's bull-like snoring and the buzzing of muffled voices on the TV.

Ambling forward, I grip the doorframe and peer into the sitting room, leaving smeared, red handprints on the yellowing paint. Garrett is still sound asleep and Brass is muttering something incoherent to himself in between snorts and snores.

I swallow down a large lump of bile and lumber back down the hallway, noticing the dark drops and bloody footprints I've left on the grey carpet. *Fuck,* I don't have time to clean this shit up.

Passing the bathroom, I see Frankie's limp foot poking from behind the door and my legs give out. I drop to the floor, heaving; my body wracked with sobs, my head throbbing. I close my eyes and suck in deep breaths, my mind ticking over, scrambling for a coherent thought.

Clambering to my feet, I stumble into the bedroom, eyes darting about for clothes while pain lances through my neck and back.

Throwing on some track bottoms – my breath coming in intermittent gulps – I shuck off my pinafore, the envelope still tucked inside my bra, and pull on a hoodie, wincing, trying to ignore the torture surging through every bone in my body.

I wipe my hands and face with a top from the floor before I wrap the bloodied material around my palm.

I grab a backpack from the battered, old wardrobe and begin shoving clothes into it, along with the cash I've been hoarding in our beat-up mattress and a stash Garrett keeps hidden he thinks I know nothing about.

Tiptoeing down the corridor, careful to check Garrett is still out cold, I prize the door open with infinite slowness – sweat beading my forehead, limbs throbbing. I stagger out into the sticky, humid, summer air – thankful for the darkness – and head for the tube station, not once glancing back.

Chapter 2

Chicago, October 2014

Grace

"Fuck, you lucky bitch!"

Harley laughs at my outburst. She's just shot me in the head, again!

We're playing Call of Duty on two separate TVs in the same large, bare-bricked living room in our loft apartment, so I can't see when she sneaks up and offs me. She's too damn good at this game.

"You need to get some practice in, Gray." Her accent isn't Chicago; she's from Tennessee, and it's clear.

Scoffing at her remark, I smile. She's such a tomboy and I love her to bits for it.

Two years ago, I got lucky – very fucking lucky. Terrified the police would find me, I ran and ran, and I didn't stop until I reached Heathrow airport.

Using the fake documents Penny gave me, I booked a flight to Chicago – I'd literally closed my eyes in front of a map and jabbed my finger down on the sparkling city in Illinois. After what happened, Scotland or Ireland seemed too close to home.

The beauty captivated me the moment I stepped off the bus from the airport to the city – the tall buildings, the dazzling lights. The air felt clean and fresh.

Staying in meagre shelters across the city for the first three months, I worked in and out of bars for cash in hand. Everyone I encountered seemed so friendly, willing to help – a far cry from the calibre of people I associated with in London.

In my free time, I began creating sculptures from salvaged rubbish, used my money to buy paints and canvases, and started selling my work around local parks and in the bars I worked in. I found it therapeutic, and I gained quite a knack for the craft.

A little over a year ago, photographer Harley Lewis walked into my bar. She took one look at me and my work, heard my London accent, and would not shut up with her millions of questions about England and my life there.

Avoiding the obvious answers, we took to one another right away. She offered me a place to stay with her and her model roommate, Cameron Edwards.

Harley helped me set up my own website selling my sculptures and paintings, and I do well through it – a natural flair she calls it. I am so grateful for her and Cam.

Harley drops her controller and slides over the teakwood floor toward me. Her long, chocolate waves pool over her shoulders and cascade down her back.

She places a gentle hand on my shoulder, "You want something to drink?" she asks me, bunching my hair in her palm.

She's always fiddling with something, and she loves the colour of my tresses, so she's always playing with them – I'm not uncomfortable with it, I find it sisterly, the way she does it.

I shake my head. "I'm good thanks, babe."

"So, you picked anything to wear for Saturday, yet?" There's a smile in her words.

It's Harley's twenty-sixth birthday Saturday, and Cam has managed to score us tickets to some hot new club opening in town – God bless his good looks and model connections. Harley might be a tomboy, but she still loves to dress up all glitz and glam. I call her a geezer-bird in my common London accent and she laughs at me when I say it.

"Chill out, Harl, it's only Monday; plenty of time for that."

She giggles and I can't help but smile.

Placing my controller down, I switch off the games console just before our front door opens and I hear high-pitched squeals and giggles.

God give me strength, Cam has brought home a 'date' and it's not even dinner time yet.

He's got commitment issues, our Cam, and I accept that – I'm not exactly falling all over myself to enter another relationship... though if the right guy came along... but it kills Harley when he brings these empty-headed, bimbo tramps back to our apartment.

Her eyes are glued to the raven-haired doll – whose sole personality is, without a doubt, in her inflated chest – hanging off Cam's arm. Harl looks ready to cry – her eyes are welling up.

Cam doesn't know Harley is crushing on him big time. Ha, listen to me – fancies him. He could at least have some damn respect, though, and not subject us to his raucous fucking – this is a loft apartment, not a damn mansion – we can hear almost everything bouncing off the brick and metal-lined walls.

I glance at Harley and the longing in her eyes while she moves her stare to Cam.

Oblivious, he smiles at us both, grabs the chuckling, caked-in-make-up floozy by the hand, and drags her to his room.

I lift my arse off the plush, red sofa and walk up to Harley, placing my hand in the middle of her back. "Come on, babe, we'll hit Potter's."

Potter's Lounge is a bar a couple of minutes' walk from our apartment. It's decked out in dark wood floors, red and brown leather and low lighting. It oozes old-school Chicago appeal.

Harley doesn't need asking twice. She throws a leather jacket over her casual jeans-tank top combo and heads for the door.

I reach for my light blazer and rush out after her, grabbing the door keys.

"Why does he do it, Gray?" She links my arm and rests her head on my shoulder while we walk.

"Because he doesn't know you like him, hun."

"But why *those* kinds of women; they're vile?" She wrinkles her nose up.

"But they're easy, and he's clueless. You need to tell him, babe." I'm sympathetic toward her, but she really does need to man up and let it out.

"I'm not his type, though. I'm too *man-like*. He'll laugh in my face and our friendship will be ruined." She lets out a hefty sigh.

"Oh, Harl. Don't you get how fabulous you are? He'd be thick as shit to knock you back."

"But what if he does?"

I don't have an answer for her, but luckily we're just strolling through the entrance of Potter's.

We grab a seat at the bar and order two Turkey Clubs and beers.

*

An hour rolls by, and Harley and I have forgotten about slagging Cam's choice of women off and are busy giggling over the slightest of things – courtesy of the alcohol, no doubt.

The barman approaches us and hands over two more bottles.

"We didn't order these, barkeep," I giggle, falling into Harley's arm and causing her to burst out laughing.

"Barkeep!" she screams out, banging her palm on the dark, shining bar top and laughing out loud.

Thankfully, the barman, Dane, takes my unintended insult in good humour and smirks. He's cute when he smiles; it dimples his cheeks and highlights his blue eyes.

"Courtesy of the gentleman at the end of the bar." Dane grins at us, pointing to his left.

I glance over and a good-looking guy tilts his beer bottle in our direction.

Hmm, tasty. I can make out his dazzling green eyes from all the way over here, and his dirty blonde hair is a funky-styled mess.

I return his gorgeous smile and tip my head in thanks, taking a sip of the gifted beverage.

"He's yummy," Harley slurs, a little too loudly. The guy's smile widens. "You should ask for his number."

I throw my glance back in her direction. "Harley--"

"No, no, no." The drink is taking its toll on her. "I don't think I've seen you go on a date since you moved in and you need to get laid, girl."

I palm my head. This girl is unreal when she's tipsy.

Little does she realize, I *choose* not to date. It's not that I don't feel ready – enough time has passed for me to adjust – it's just that... well, I don't quite know for sure, maybe I'm just being skeptical... guarded, even. It's gonna take more than a couple of beers and a dazzling smile to win me over. I think.

"I agree," a male voice begins, "about taking my number, I mean; not that you need to get laid... I wouldn't know."

I turn my head and the hot bloke has moved closer to us. He is rather delicious and he smells of ginger, woody musk and spice - an inebriating scent.

"Grace." I offer the guy my hand in an effort to stop him stumbling over his words, and because I *might* be interested... in nothing more than a drink, mind. For now.

"Miles," he returns, collecting himself. His large, warm hand engulfs my petite one.

"Harley." She shoves her hand between us, almost spilling my beer over poor Miles. She doesn't apologize. "Why are you sat alone?" No inhibitions, this one.

Smiling, he looks to her, "I was with a buddy, but he left not long ago. I saw you gorgeous ladies and figured I'd worm my way in with a free beer. How am I doing?" He cocks a smile and winks at me.

"Fabulous." Harl takes a long pull on her gratuitous drink and gives Miles a thumbs up before the bottle pops off her lips. "Grace needs a man."

Closing my eyes for a quick moment, I envisage all the ways I could get the bitch back for this.

"Sorry about her." I jerk my head in Harl's direction. "She's a lightweight." I punch her in the leg.

"Ouch! Ho!" She counters with a jab to my upper arm, laughing.

"That's OK," Miles snickers, "I think she might be onto something."

"You think I need a man?" I suppress a smile and raise an eyebrow. I gotta hand it to him – he's got a knack for putting his foot in it.

"No! Shit, sorry. I didn't... oh, fuck." He averts his gaze and stares into his beer.

A laugh rumbles in my chest and I place a hand against his taut bicep. "It's OK, Miles. I get what you mean."

He tries for a smile while Harley giggles into her beer bottle next to me, her eyes squeezed closed when I try to throw her a wide-eyed glare.

I turn back. "Listen, Miles, we appreciate the beers, but this really is girl time, ya know?" I raise my eyebrows and cast him a quirky, half-smile hopefully conveying the universal indicator for, 'we're slagging off men'. "But give me your number and I'll call you."

He smiles at me, understanding I think, and jots his digits down on a napkin before handing them to me. His fingers brush mine sending a few tingles down south.

"Make sure you do, Grace." He recovers from his embarrassment before downing the remains of his beer and placing his warm, moistened lips against my cheek. I shudder. "I'll look forward to it."

Watching him - or rather his tight arse - walk out the door, I smile to myself.

"You shoulda hit that," Harley pipes up, curbing her amusement.

I laugh at her and tell her to hush before taking a sip from my bottle.

*

It's well past one in the morning by the time we stumble back into the apartment. Cam is sitting on the sofa watching *The Walking Dead* DVD Harley got him for his twenty-fifth birthday a few months back.

"Hey ladies," he chimes, turning to smirk at us and pausing his show.

"Barbie gone home?" Harley's voice takes on a honeyed tone while she bats her eyelids.

Cam jumps over the back of the couch and races up to Harley, grabbing her in a bear hug. "What's up Harbo, you jealous?"

Oh, the poor boy. He has no idea.

"Hell no! Now put me down, ya great buffoon."

Cam places Harl back on her feet and she smacks his chest, mumbling something under her breath that sounds like, "ass".

"Yes, *Candy* has gone home."

I snort. "You're fucking with us, right? Candy?"

Cam grins and shrugs his shoulders. Harley glowers at him. I really do wish she'd just tell him how she feels.

Despite his 'playboy' lifestyle – and admittedly it isn't *that* bad, maybe two or three girls every couple of months – he is an amazing person.

Yeah, he's a model, and he's nothing short of stunning with dark hair that falls over deep, chocolate eyes and a tall, muscled physique, but he knows it's not all about his looks. He volunteers at homeless shelters and entertains sick kids at the local hospital. He's a saint, but none of it goes to his head – he's so laid back and humble. It's easy to see why Harley likes him. But a guy's got needs, and Harley is keeping schtum over her infatuation with him.

"I'm going to bed." It's time I left Harley and Cam alone – not that anything will come of it.

Making my way down the hall to my room, I hear Harley rustling in the kitchen and Cam starting his DVD back up. I roll my eyes and shake my head, smiling.

I don't bother switching the light on, I just undress and throw myself into bed. I always used to like sleeping in my underwear when I was a kid because I loved the feel of the soft duvet on my skin.

When I slept like this back in London, Garrett would take the opportunity to fuck me – in any hole he saw fit – and I hated it. Keeping clothes on meant restricted access unless he undressed me, and – on the occasion he didn't beat me into submission or literally rip my clothes away from me – he usually didn't have the patience, or fell asleep before finishing.

It took me months after moving in here before I felt comfortable and secure enough to do this again, and I smile while I snuggle under the covers, appreciating the soft scratches of the fabric on my naked body.

The last thing I hear, before I shut my eyes to welcome oblivion is Harley scream, "Go fuck yourself, Cammy." Then her bedroom door slams shut.

Wonder what he said this time. I'll ask her tomorrow.

Chapter 3
Grace

My alarm goes off at six-thirty and I really wish I'd remembered to turn it off the night before.

My head is swimming a little from the previous night's beers and I take a minute for the room to stop spinning before I attempt to sit up.

Today is going to be busy – I need to fetch Harley's birthday cake, go dress shopping for Saturday and finish a project for a client who's commissioned me to do four Impressionist canvases for her law office downtown – business is good.

Leaning against the headboard, I inhale. I can already smell fresh coffee brewing, so someone is clearly more insane than I am to be up at this hour.

Stretching my legs out in front of me, I groan amid creaking bones and bedframe. Swinging over the side, I put my feet on the luxurious, beige carpet and ball my toes in the plush fabric. I've done this every day for a year just because I can.

I smile and get up, throwing a long T-shirt on before padding into the living room.

Cameron is rattling around the open-plan kitchen in nothing but a pair of track bottoms, and his banging is making my head pound.

"Cammy, you wanna keep the decibels down to somewhere near jackhammer level?" I moan at him, secretly appreciating his smooth, toned abs from the corner of my eye.

"Hey, gorgeous. Heavy night last night?" He grins at me and I throw the tea-towel beside me at his head. He catches it and sticks out his tongue.

"Your fault." I accuse.

He feigns insult and gapes at me. "I beg your pardon, missy? The way I hear it, you got yourself some action last night, too."

"I so did not!" I'll kill Harley when she emerges from her tomb.

"Not what I heard." His smile, and the waggle of his eyebrows, tell me he's pulling my leg, so I ignore him for now.

"What else did you and Harl discuss? She didn't sound too happy when she went to bed."

"No idea, Graybo," he shrugs, "I gave her another dig about her jealous streak; obviously I was joking, but she took it the wrong way, I suppose."

"Oh, Cammy." I roll my eyes at him and laugh.

"What?"

Shaking my head, I pour myself a coffee.

Ignoring his question, I ask him, "You going downtown today? I could do with a lift to pick up Harl's cake."

He nods, taking a sip of his drink, holding up his hand indicating he'll be leaving in five.

I take my coffee back into my bedroom to throw some clothes on, making sure to be ready when he is.

Exiting Cam's stunning, silver, Toyota FT-86, I turn to thank him. He waves at me before revving off to whatever shoot he's got going on today.

I step into the Bakery on N Wabash Ave and greet Bella, the chef who can perform pastry miracles, in my honest opinion.

"Hey, Gracie-Baby, you come for your cake?" She's so cheerful, it almost hurts my head.

"Sure am, Bella-Honey, thanks for doing this, you're a legend." I offer her my most appreciative smile.

"You're welcome, sugar. Here she is." She pulls a pink and white box with a white, rope handle from under the counter and shows me her masterpiece.

I love it, it's spot on – a PlayStation controller. Harley is going to freak when she sees it.

"This is perfect, babe." I take the culinary delight and offer endless thanks and appreciation before I leave.

My heads all but in the clouds; I'm stoked with Harl's cake. She's gonna love it so much. Crossing the road, I jump at the sound of screeching tires before a horn blasts from behind me. Sidestepping quickly back onto the pavement, I watch the black limo catch the side of my cake box and it goes flying through the air.

Everything slows. The car stops and the box lands on the floor where cake explodes all across the road and all up my clothes.

I see red, I am fuming. Before I've even thought about it, I grab a piece of the obliterated confection and I launch it at the limo. It thuds against the back window and detonates across the blacked-out glass.

"Stupid twat!" I scream, beyond giving a shit at the passers-by, stood staring at the fiasco. Not one of the fuckers asks if I'm OK, though.

The back-passenger door opens and a suited and booted leg exits, followed by the rest of what I can only describe as a light-haired, broad, muscled Adonis. A few muffled sounds filter into my subconscious – something about speeding, accident... I'm not entirely too sure because *Holy Hell!* I am left breathless. My almost-vehicular-manslaughter-er saunters over, going for imposing by striding over to me with purpose. I'm not giving him any leeway to berate me with his shit, though, when I see him open his mouth to say something.

"What the hell are you playing at?" I yell at him.

He slows, and eyes me up and down. "You're British," he points out.

Obviously. "No shit, dickhead," I yell, "and you almost fucking killed me."

I'm not clued up on all American accents, but he sounds like he's from Upstate New York, not Chicago.

Regardless, his voice is dreamy and for a moment I forget to be angry – I think my knees might be wobbling and I want to run my fingers over the light stubble on his defined jaw…

"And what about this shit?" I point to the mess at my feet. "How am I supposed to replace this? I had it custom made!" He might be fit as hell, but he's ruined my damn cake – I don't care if I wasted money on it, it's the time I don't have to get another made.

"Please, allow me to have that seen to, Miss… ?"

"I had to wait over a week for it, you can't just 'see to it'. I need it for the weekend."

"I can't apologise enough, Miss… ?"

I'm not telling him my name, he can come at it from every angle imaginable, but he's not getting it.

"Forget it." I throw my hands in the air and stomp past him. He's completely ruined my goddamn day, I'm not even in the mood to go shopping any more, and I'm still dressed in fucking cake!

*

Walking into the apartment, I see Harley in the living room playing Call of Duty – surprise, surprise. She pauses her game and turns to look at me.

"What the heck are you covered in, Gray?"

"Well, it's a sugary mixture of chocolate, shame and fury. Some arsehole almost ran me over in the street."

"You're kidding me, right?" Harley rushes around the sofa and comes over to inspect me – for injuries, I imagine.

"Almost, Harl. I'm okay."

"So, what is this?" She fingers some of the cake off my jacket, sniffs it, then pops it in her mouth, moaning her appreciation.

"It *was* your birthday cake," I answer her with a sarcastic smile and one raised brow.

"What?! Who was it? Who trashed my cake?"

"Aww cheers, Harl. I almost got killed, but so long as you plot your revenge for the cake, it's all good." I pretend to be offended and wipe a fake tear from under my eye, feeling only slightly better that some prat almost ended me today.

She laughs at me, swipes another piece of mushed up cake from my jacket, then walks back over to the TV to continue shooting up adolescent teen boys, apparently satisfied that I'll live.

*

I spend the next couple of days completing my projects, texting Miles to join me as my plus one on Saturday night and shopping for another cake for Harley's birthday – though, nothing anywhere close to the awesomeness of her last one and it pissed me off even more.

It's Friday morning and I am tearing my hair out over this cake fiasco when someone knocks at my door.

Annoyed that I'm being dragged away from my laptop, I'm even more so when I open the door and find no-one standing there.

"What the fu--," I falter, staring at the floor near my feet.

Sat on my doorstep, is a pink and white box with a rope handle. My stomach flips and I'm a little too afraid to open the package.

I look up and down the landing, but no-one's there. I run to the window and see the tail end of a black car turning a corner, but that's nothing suspicious- it's a busy street. So, I spin back to the gift box. There's a note attached to it.

Edging over – I'm still wary of whatever is in this thing, and who left it here – I bend down and pick the piece of white card off.

Grace – a pretty name, for a pretty girl

I apologize once again

- C

Now who would this be off? Who the hell is 'C'?

The only person who would know anything about this packaging is Bella, and that douche...

Sexy, Businessman Adonis!

I tear the box open and there, nestled inside – and intact – is a cake in the shape of a PlayStation controller. But how the hell did he know?

Shit on a stick, he went into the bakery. *Yes, fabulous detective work, Grace. You could be a top P.I.*, but how fucking dare he throw his cash around in the hopes of making things all better? And so what if it might be working?

Chapter 4
Grace

Finally, Saturday is here and Harley has not stopped going on about how fabulous tonight will be.

After the mysterious *C* dropped the cake off at my doorstep – which Harl screamed her love for, but which I neglected to inform her a stranger dropped off – my mood perked up enough to allow her to drag me round the shops for a new dress... and shoes and bag and accessories. The girl is relentless.

I ended up treating her – and me, after being pulled from shop to shop – to an afternoon of spa treatments at Elizabeth Arden. We indulged in a facial each and got our nails done. For a tomboy, I didn't hear Harley complain once about being pampered like a princess.

Cam's kinda been AWOL the last couple of days; he got called for a last minute shoot in Cincinnati and ended up staying over. But he's back here today for madam's birthday, and she's trying so hard not to look over the moon about it, but she can't hide it from me. Cam, as usual, is oblivious.

My girl is all smiles when she steps out of her room looking like a million quid in a short, tight-fitting, red dress and black platform heels, both of which accentuate her long, shapely legs. Her gorgeous, brown hair is curled and falls in sexy waves down her back. She's got minimal make-up on, just enough shadow and liner to give her deep eyes a smoky hue, and a quick swipe of matching red lip gloss.

Cam is looking rather dapper in faded jeans, a fitted white tee and a dark grey blazer with the sleeves rolled up. His hair is swept to the side and held in place with monumental amounts of gel and hairspray, no doubt. He knows he looks amazing, but he doesn't notice Harley almost drowning in a puddle of her own drool over him.

And I've opted for an azure-blue cocktail dress. It finishes above my knees, with thin diamante straps clutching at material that swoops down to gather at the small of my back. I've teamed it with killer, silver-lace heels and a matching bag. My flame-red hair is also curled, but gathered in a messy bun at the side of my head and I've coated my lips in a subtle, almost-nude Chanel lipstick.

I must admit, we look amazing.

We pose for a quick selfie before the cab pulls up downstairs and we pile out the building, intent on getting happily drunk and dancing the night away.

Miles meets us outside Club Knight – the newest spot on the outskirts of town owned by some rich, playboy-type called… wait for it… something or other Knight. I don't care.

Tacky name aside, however, the club itself looks spectacular. Strobe lighting highlights the huge, purple neon sign bearing the club's name, red carpet runs up white marble stairs and luscious, green topiary is positioned either side.

The queues are horrendous, and limo after limo after Bentley after Porsche pulls up outside the main entrance. There is a cascade of glitzy dresses, sparkling jewels and dangerously high heels on display, not to mention some pretty hot, well-dressed men.

Cam's tickets mean we can avoid the swarming mass of fashion statements and high-class escorts, and get right on in to begin our night.

The doorman glances at our invites and waves us inside.

My mouth hangs open at the sheer beauty of this place.

Soft, lilac and baby blue lighting illuminate the glass and chrome interior. White leather sofas line the outside of a sleek, soft-grey, marble dance floor. The bar at the far end is amazing – glass, silver, glistening black granite – it looks futuristically stunning.

The ultra-modern décor is set off with a tasteful amount of vibrant green palm trees and exudes an accidental (I think), aesthetic, tropical theme.

I catch the guys eyeing up the place with the same level of excited astonishment, before we manage to reel it back in and head to the bar.

Harl and I are straight on the exotic cocktails and Miles gets the first round in. Cam decides it's only proper we also indulge in a round of shots, and so orders four apple-flavoured Vodkas. We accept with large grins, toast our thanks and appreciation amid clinking glass, and set about downing them before sipping our Pina Coladas and beers.

I'm three drinks in and feeling buzzed when Miles asks me to dance, and I smile my acceptance. He takes me by the hand and I sway and shimmy my way behind him to the dance floor, followed by Cam and Harley.

Miles is looking fabulous tonight in black-wash jeans and a white shirt. They cling to his toned chest and sculpted arms in a way that has my insides clenching. His hair is that same styled mess from Monday night and I am dying to run my hands through it.

I settle for gripping his powerful upper arms when he pulls me into his hard body. His hands roam a lazy trail to the small of my back and we grind in perfect sync to Chris Brown's, Loyal.

When the song ends – changing to some remixed version of an R Kelly tune – Miles pulls me closer. His hands run up to my neck and he buries them in my hair, pulling me back a little. I can feel his erection against my thigh and, I must say, his size is impressive. It has my girly parts buzzing and excited.

When his hooded gaze catches my eyes, I feel his dick throb before he brushes his lips against mine – gentle at first, exploring, probing. His tongue flicks out to lick my bottom lip and I moan against him before opening to allow him to delve into the warm, moist recess of my mouth.

He tastes delicious – a heady concoction of citrus and honey – and I slide my tongue in between his lips, wanting more of the decadent flavour.

I'm shunted forward by some inconsiderate dick dancing far too close behind me. Prizing my lips from Miles's, I turn to give this arsehole a piece of my mind, but I stop before I've even uttered my first word.

Businessman Adonis is stood staring at me with a gleam in his eye and a smile pulling at his plump lips.

***

Colt

Against my will, I haven't been able to get that ruby-haired Goddess out of my mind.

Doesn't matter whether I'm on the phone with an entertainment coordinator, in a meeting with my finance committee or stood above the toilet taking a piss – she's there.

That morning, I'd left an investment meeting, and the moment we rounded the corner of N Wabash Ave, my driver, Jovan, swore something in his native Serbian and swerved the car while honking the horn.

The papers on my lap went sweeping across the vehicle and I grabbed hold of the door handle before Jovan skidded to a halt.

I'd craned my neck at the thud at the back window to find out who the hell possessed the damn nerve to throw something at *my* car.

Behind the chocolate mess, I saw her standing there, yelling and gesturing; her fiery-red hair rustling in the light breeze, gorgeous tits spilling with heaving generosity over a light jacket and white tank top, and she wore dark jeans that clung to her athletic frame.

Compelled to talk to her, I launched myself out of the car before she could disappear, collected myself and strode over – aiming for intimidating confidence, but failing miserably because it didn't affect her in the slightest when she'd asked me what the hell I was playing at.

My dick throbbed in my pants at her delectable British accent.

My mother is British; born and raised on a horse farm – hence the name, Colt and British women have always fascinated me and I can't even begin to explain why.

Even with this woman cursing and yelling at me, my insides tightened over her plump, lush lips and amazing, light blue eyes. *Sexy as fuck.*

She took no chances in giving me her name, though, but I am not easily deterred. If I want something, I will stop at nothing to get it.

The moment she stormed off, screaming about her ruined cake, I watched her sweet ass while she walked away from me. The sway projected vivid images of it naked, and positioned in front of me, her hands spread on my office desk while I pounded into her from behind.

I'm not a stickler for daydreaming, but hell, the things I could do to her...

Adjusting my hard length, I took one more look at her fine body before she rounded the corner. She didn't once look back, but it didn't discourage me.

I walked into the bakery – I knew that packaging well, my mother is a fan of their pastry delicacies – and I gave a simple nod to Bella.

"Mr. Knight, what brings you here today?" She'd looked flustered, face smudged with flour.

It's usually a Friday I visit to pick up something sweet for Mom.

I told Bella what happened and she cursed at me in Italian for ruining her hard work. I told her I'd pay double if she could reproduce whatever that feisty spitfire ordered and have it ready before the weekend. She swore at me some more, but promised her best efforts.

Walking in Friday morning before brunch with my mother, the angel handed me the box with her creation. I told her I'd deliver it if she would give me the address.

Grace Morgan.

Arriving at her apartment building, I didn't plan on knocking the door and waiting for her. No, I wanted the mystery, the chase almost. I knew she'd be mulling it all over in that pretty head of hers and I wanted her to think about me. I wanted her to know that I knew where she lived, and that I could turn up in front of her at a moment's notice whenever the need arose.

I saw the way she looked at me that morning; she may have been screaming profanities and acting aggressive, but I saw the fire in her eyes. She wants me just like I want her.

*

I plan on waiting until after the weekend before I step up my campaign to have Grace in my bed. My new club opened tonight and I need to have my game face on - a lot of important people will be putting in an appearance and the club is under the media spotlight because of it.

Lucinda Gould - my head of marketing and design (and one-time fuck buddy) - led a marvellous campaign to give this opening the hype it deserves. She may have only been mediocre in the sack, but her creative side always shines through where my PR is concerned.

I'm sitting in my office, nursing my second crystal tumbler of Martell and watching the banks of monitors displaying every angle of Club Knight.

I lean back and smile at my achievement - three years of hard work it's taken to get this club open and I'm proud of the effort my team put in.

Club Knight isn't the only establishment I own, though. I have a casino, two cocktail bars and a high-class strip club - catering for both men and women.

But this is my finest business venture to date and one I've achieved all by myself - none of my father's finances having been plunged in to it, not like the others - although, the strip club; not so much help there. My mother didn't approve and he's under the thumb. I love both my parents with everything in me, but he is pussy-whipped and it's not something I envy.

The club is already almost at capacity - I'm kept up to date with progress reports from the head of security; a brick-shithouse, no-nonsense Russian called Dmitry. He's worked for my family since my dad made his first million selling his computer franchise some fifteen years ago; I'd just turned sixteen and knew, then, that I wanted to be every bit as successful as him.

Now, Dmitry works for me managing a team of equally large doormen.

Downing my glass of Cognac, I place the tumbler on the table beside me. I'm just about to pour my third measure when a striking clash of color captures my attention.

Glaring at the monitors, my breath hitches.

Grace.

I can't believe my luck; the red-haired beauty is in *my* club, of all the places. And she looks exquisite. The blue dress she has on finishes above shapely legs begging to be caressed, and clings to her taut abs and tight ass.

She's dancing with some jerk with his hands all over her.

Using the laptop in front of me, I zoom the camera in on her perfect body. That dress is magnificent at accentuating her feminine curves, but would look much better, crumpled on my bedroom floor.

She laughs at something the jerk whispers in her ear and moves in close to murmur something back. I don't like it - it should be my body she's dripping off; me she's whispering to.

I imagine the kinds of things I'd love to hear her say to me - she wants to trail those delicious lips down my stomach, wrap her silky tongue around my cock, feel me buried hilt-deep inside her.

My dick throbs at the thought.

The idiot with his hands over Grace leans into her and places his lips on hers. I stand with rushed abruptness and my chair hits the back wall with a loud clatter. *No way, this is not happening; she's meant for me.* I want to feel those lips, taste her sweet flavor, roam my hands over every curve of her tight body. And what I want, I get.

Striding over to the stairs, I fly down them two at a time, smoothing my shirt and tie when I reach the bottom. Running both hands through my hair I open the doors and enter the main club area, heading to the dance floor with one thing on my mind.

*

"I'm so sorry, I wasn't watching–"

"You!" She half turns and cuts me off with a scowl.

My lips curl up at the look of recognition on her face. I note the flash of desire in her eyes – brief, but there.

"Did you get my gift?" I smirk at her, raising my voice over the music.

"Are you stalking me, now?" She tries to hide her grin, but I see it before it disappears and she furrows her brow once again while she continues to cling to the jerk in front of her.

I feign insult, "I would do nothing of the sort. I owed you a cake and I always pay my debts."

She turns fully and puts her hands on her hips, giving me full view of her amazing body. "So, why are you here?"

The asshat behind her is eyeing me up and down, one eyebrow raised. He'd do well to keep any comments brewing to himself.

"I own this club."

Both their eyes widen and Grace's hands drop from her sides. "You do?"

I ignore her question and hold my hand out, "Care to dance?"

"I don't believe we've been introduced," Jerk starts, "Miles Thompson." He holds his hand out for me; a rigid, non-impressed look across his stern features.

Grace doesn't give me a chance to tell the guy to fuck off before she adds, "As you can see, I have a date, but thanks." She turns away from me, moving to place her arms around Miles's neck.

I sidle up close, place my hands on her waist and whisper in her ear, "I could have him removed."

"Then I'll join him," she spits back, affording me the flash of a firm gaze.

"Have it your way," I wave to catch the attention of the nearest bouncer. Childish? Perhaps, but she'll learn to accept my infatuated selfishness when she's screaming my name and begging me for more of what I'm desperate to give her.

"You arsehole. Ya know what, don't bother." Her voice is raised, and she takes hold of Miles's arm. "You don't own me. You replaced a goddamn cake *your driver* obliterated in the first place. I owe you nothing, so kindly fuck off; you're ruining our night."

I love the fire in her eyes and the spark in her body language. She's attracted to me, she just won't admit it.

Fine. She can play hard to get, but I will have her.

I place my hand on her waist.

"Get the fuck off me," she yells, then turns and walks out after that dick.

Chapter 5

Grace

I cannot believe the nerve of that prick, I'm seething. I don't care that my body reacted to the heat of his touch – how dare he act like such an arrogant cock? The world does not revolve around him and his bullshit ego.

Stepping outside, I see Miles motioning for a taxi. "Wait," I shout after him.

He turns to face me, "Grace, you should go back inside. Don't let him ruin your night."

"He's already ruined my night, screw him. You wanna go somewhere else?"

Smiling at me, he apologizes to the cab driver and waves him off. "Sure, where you thinking?"

"Potter's?" I raise my brow and shrug my shoulders.

"Sounds like a plan." He offers me his arm and I link mine through it.

Deciding against walking with the drop in temperature – and my skimpy dress doing nothing to keep the heat in – we hail another cab.

Clambering in, my stomach flips a little when Miles grabs my hand in his large, warm one – although nothing like the reaction my Judas body put me through at the sight of what's-his-name Knight.

I push the thought aside – I won't contemplate anything intimate with Mr. Domineering.

*

Before long, we're sitting in Potter's Lounge chugging our way through our sixth beer. I've text Harley to let her know what happened, telling her to stay put and enjoy herself when she offered to join us -
I'm liking getting to know Miles.

He's twenty-seven - a year older than me - has an eighteen year old sister called Paige, who lives with their parents, rents his own apartment and works two jobs to put himself through medical school. It's a struggle, he tells me, but he knows the hard work will pay off.

In turn, I tell him snippets of my life, including how I met that fucktard from the club, but leaving out the fact I used to be shacked up with some drug-dealing gang member who saved me from a life of prostitution - although I use the term *saved* rather loosely - and that I murdered his cousin in self-defence. I tell him both parents are dead and a nasty experience with an ex forced me to leave the country to make a fresh start.

My attraction to Miles is blossoming and I can't help but find a little of my internal walls starting to crumble with each gorgeous smile he flashes my way. It's been a long, unsteady road for me; trying to open up to the possibility of finding someone I can actually hold a conversation with, who doesn't want to hurt me or beat the shit out of me. I should've noticed the glaring warning signs when I first met Garrett under the circumstances, but none of those alarms are ringing when I look at Miles. He's sweet and funny; something I've never found in my past. I find him so easy-going and a real joy to talk to, so when I tell him about my passion for art and he asks to see some of my work some time, I throw caution to the wind and offer a nightcap at my place. It seems the most logical thing to do and I've no fear even entertaining the thought. Even less so at his enthusiasm when he accepts.

Downing the remainder of our beers, we walk the few minutes to my apartment; the fresh air making my head spin - there are no lights on, so Harley and Cam are likely still out.

Before we reach the stairs to my level, however, Miles takes a gentle hold of my shoulder and turns me to him. He cups my face and looks at me with his dreamy, viridian-green eyes. My heart lurches into my throat when he leans in and places his warm lips against mine in a sensuous caress.

I don't even want to stop him. His lips feel silky soft against me and my body reacts in the most delicious of ways without even thinking about it. My legs weaken and I step into him for support, he clutches me against his hardened torso, his hands roving over my back and up my neck. I meet his feverish eagerness by running mine through his thick hair, parting my lips to allow his tongue deep exploration of my inviting mouth.

Moaning against me, he pulls me closer. That impressive shaft of his is pressed against my thigh and I can feel the pooling excitement in my underwear while he trails a hand down the side of my breast.

I'm not used to this level of intimacy; it's exciting, new, and a little daring on my part, and when we break away, we're breathless. I say nothing, but grab his hand and lead him upstairs to the apartment. There's a white note attached to my door and I grab hold of it while inserting my keys in the lock, but before I can read it, Miles turns me and presses me against the door.

The kiss he crashes to my lips is more desperate; our tongues colliding in a hot, moist assault while our hands wander over each other's bodies with reckless abandon.

Reaching behind me to open the door, we stumble through, still attached at the lips.

With a brief parting, Miles grasps at the hem of my dress, pulling it over my head. Again, I don't want to stop him, though my heart is racing ten to the dozen and my body quakes just a little. My nerves calm somewhat as he stands before me, a sexy, half-smile tugging at his lips while he admires my choice of black lace lingerie; my breasts spilling out of the netted bra and the opaque material of my panties leaving little to the imagination. I'm not used to someone looking at me with such unabashed lust and my body melts under his gaze.

A primal sound rumbles in his chest and he lunges for me, gripping my arse cheeks and lifting. I circle his waist with my legs while he trails hot kisses down my neck and collar bone, giving me goose bumps that sore across my sensitive skin.

Rounding on the sofa, he lays me down, hovering above me, his heated eyes drinking me in.

His eyes devour every inch of my body while I unbutton his shirt, my hands brushing his hard, masculine chest. Draping the garment over his shoulders, I pull it off and throw it to the floor.

He straddles me, bending down to slip his tongue between my lips. My hands make light work of his jeans and they follow his discarded shirt.

He's commando.

His remarkable length is hot against my stomach and throbs against me with every plunge of his tongue. Butterflies dart around my stomach and I can't tell whether it's nerves or excitement – it's probably both, but nothing in me is screaming at me to stop this.

Snaking one leg around his waist, I grind my sodden sex against his thigh. He groans and trails his hand down my stomach. My muscles tighten when he reaches the rim of my intimates and he runs an unhurried finger down the crease of my thigh.

My body quivers against his touch, but a delighted gasp escapes me when he slips his finger behind the flimsy material.

"Fuck, Grace. You're so wet," he whispers against my lips and I respond by taking his bottom lip between my teeth.

Growling, he slides two digits deep inside my aching pussy. The sensuous assault is alien to me and beyond immense. I moan against his lips, arching my hips for deeper penetration while he continues to draw them out before plunging back in with relentless ambition.

My toes tingle while heat sweeps my body, a thin sheen of perspiration beading my forehead. I close my eyes against Miles's continuous onslaught, throwing my head back and clutching at his hair while he litters my neck with frantic kisses and sweeps of his slick tongue.

He thumbs my responsive clit.

"Shit!" I come apart, all too soon while his fingers continue to milk me of my release.

Orgasms from masturbation are nothing like this and I can't stop the stupid smile from spreading across my face while my body buzzes with the most deliciously heated tingles.

Miles runs his free thumb across my bottom lip as he pulls out of me and already I feel empty.

My eyes flicker open and, once my fuzzy sight is restored, I see Miles hovering above me; a smug, satisfied smile on his face. But before I can return any favours, we hear giggling coming up the stairs to the apartment.

"Damn it. Harl and Cam are home." I scramble to put my knickers on while Miles grabs his jeans. I'm still high on sexual tension, though, because I can't stand up straight.

He throws me his shirt – which just about covers my arse – and buttons his jeans up when the door swings open.

After a short pause while he assesses the situation in the living room, Cam slurs, "Ooo, Graybo, you dirty slut," trying to keep his balance while he squints at Miles.

My face heats and I pull the shirt closed around my breasts.

"You naughty girly, Gray-Gray." Harley stumbles into Cam and they begin another tirade of fitful cackling.

After affording them a sheepish smile, I look to the floor before grabbing Miles's hand and leading him to my room amid a chorus of 'oohs', 'aahs' and choice names.

Miles backs me against the bedroom door, closing it, with one hand supported on the panel behind. He smiles against my mouth while he presses his lips to mine and, with the deft fingers of his free hand, removes his shirt from my body.

His jeans come off next, and both items end up somewhere on the floor.

Taking the lead, I back him toward my bed, my lips still tasting his, hands pushing against his chest. It's now or never and, while part of me is hesitant, the majority of me wants this. If his fingers can work that kinda magic, then I can only imagine what the rest of him can do, and my body is aching to find that out.

I move to take my heels off.

"Keep them on," Miles growls and I oblige him.

Miles reaches for me, turns me and pins me on my back on the bed beneath him, parting my thighs with a groan before trailing his hands down either side.

Placing his warm lips to the flesh of my inner right thigh, he creates a lazy trail of kisses down until he is hovering above my sex-drenched panties. I can feel his hot breath against my pussy and the heat sends me dizzy with desire.

"Mile... ," I breathe, fisting his hair while he blows light flurries on my slick opening.

He hooks two fingers in the waistband of my lace underwear and slides them over my thighs and down my calves, kissing, licking and nibbling every inch of the tortuous way.

Kneeling before me, he grabs my waist and pulls me toward his waiting tongue. He flicks the tip over my aching bud and I grab the bed sheets beside me, raising my hips in sweet response.

Slipping a finger inside my clenching core, he presses against my sensitive clit; the sensations coursing through my body, igniting me from the inside. His circular motions hit all the right spots, sending my body bucking and writhing beneath the erotic invasion.

He places a hand over my pelvis and pushes down.

Bunching the sheets beneath me in a tight fist, I cry out, "Oh, fuck... Miles... I'm gonna... ." My slippery cleft clamps down and, for the second time tonight, his skilful digits bring me to an exploding climax.

With heavy, rasping breathing, I barely register Miles lying down next to me. He circles the pad of his forefinger around my pierced bellybutton and I keep my gaze fixed on the ceiling,
controlling each laboured breath.

Moving to kiss me, he slips his tongue between my parted lips. His arousal presses against my thigh and I graze my splayed hand down his chest, past his torso to grip his pulsing member.

His dick is hot and solid and he releases a jagged breath against me while I tighten my hold, sliding my hand up and down his thick shaft. With each pull, I pick up speed and his kisses become more forceful the closer he gets to his climax.

He weeps at the head and I trace my thumb across the tip, using his juices to rub the ridge of his length.

Taking in a breath, he breathes out, "Don't stop," against my lips.

His dick swells in my hand the faster I pump, and his fingers clutch at the back of my head as he plunges his tongue in deeper. His body tenses against me and he moans his arousal before he shoots his hot load across my stomach.

"Fuck." His voice quivers and his legs shake against mine.

For long moments, he rests his forehead against me, his eyes closed and his breathing deep. His fingers are still tightly tangled in my hair, and I couldn't move even if I wanted to.

He kisses me again and releases me, turning and lying on his back, his eyes still shut and a smile pulling at his lips.

Sitting up, I grab some tissue from the bedside table, but he takes it from me and mops up his release from my belly.

Looking up at me he grins. "Sorry."

"That's OK," I chuckle; surprised at the tenderness with which he cleans me.

Sliding off the bed, I remove my heels before digging in my drawers for some bottoms and a sleeveless tee, "Do you want to stay the night?" I query, dragging the bottoms on over my legs and lying beside him

I purposely avoid the question of taking this further – satisfied that I've battled at least some of my demons tonight... satisfied being the operative word.

He replies, "Sure do," nuzzling into the side of my neck before he drapes his arm over my stomach.

A small part of me is awash with relief, but the rest of me is still buzzing from the spectacular orgasms I swear I can still feel tingling in the soles of my feet.

Within minutes, I hear his soft snores, his breathing evens out and his body relaxes against me.

Chapter 6
Grace

The usual scent of coffee rouses my sleepy state and I stretch out the aches in my body. I reach out a hand, but touch only empty space.

Turning my head, I notice Miles has disappeared - he's left a note on a piece of paper on my pillow;

Sorry, had to dash, have brunch with parents. Call me when you wake, Sleeping Beauty xxx

I smile, but I leave my phone on the bedside table - I'll call him when I feel more human. Right now, my head is banging and my mouth feels like some creature crawled in and died inside.

Perhaps the alcohol helped lower my inhibitions – as well as my walls – last night. Maybe, and maybe I acted a little out of character and perhaps a tad slutty, but I'm a little bit proud of myself for taking the plunge.

I've never been touched by a man like that before and a small part of me thought I never would. All I've ever known is pain and abuse and it feels kinda like a small victory against my past that I was able to just let go; even for a little while.

It's a step I'd always been scared to take - and probably even more scared to admit - but it's a necessary one and I almost feel like I've conquered the whole world this morning.

Until I move.

I've no choice but to get up slowly because my vision is a complete blur and my head is pounding. The room spins slightly and I close my eyes. It doesn't help. In fact, it only makes things worse and I take a few deep breaths to quell the nausea swirling in my stomach.

Slipping my legs over the side of the mattress, I plant my feet firmly on the floor and curl my toes through the carpet before making my way to the bathroom. If I'm expected to function past noon, I need to revitalize myself with a hot shower while trying to keep the contents of my stomach exactly where they are.

No sooner have I stepped out my room, then Harley is on me.

I hold a hand up when she opens her mouth, "Not yet, need shower, need caffeine."

She gives me a knowing smile and saunters off toward the kitchen while I lock myself in the bathroom. If she's got any sense, she'll be fulfilling my caffeine requirements.

I turn the shower on to 'scolding' and undress.

Stepping under the scorching heat, my skin reddens in an instant. Steam has already shrouded the room, but I love it this hot. I scrub at my face and body with soap before washing my hair.

Rinsing off the soapy suds, I stand under the gushing flow and close my eyes, the aches ebbing from my muscles, leaving behind a dull tingle.

While I would love to remain under the warm spray, I really do need to move.

Turning the shower, off I grab a white towel, wrapping it around my body and securing it above my breasts. Retrieving a robe from the back of the door, I drape it over my shoulders and head back to my bedroom.

Today is a day for casual track bottoms and a hoodie - which is exactly what I dress myself in before heading to the kitchen and my waiting cup of coffee Harley has poured me.

Putting my mug on the coffee table, I slump down next to her on the sofa.

"So," she starts, not taking her eyes off her video game, "good night?" Her face widens into a dirty grin and I'm totally envious that she doesn't even appear to be suffering anywhere near the level I am – despite being a drunken mess last night.

"Was alright." I shrug, containing my own small smirk.

"Sounded better than alright, Gray-Gray." She shoulder bumps me and my face heats.

"Someone got their rocks off last night!" Cam's booming voice makes me jump before I cringe from the shame, I feel Harl tense beside me. "Enjoy yourself did you? In fact, don't answer that, I heard for myself."

Ground, swallow me whole, please!

"You're a fine one to talk," Harl snipes at him when he joins us on an opposite chair and I'm a little surprised at her unprovoked outburst.

He fakes shock, eyes widening, and places a hand to his heart, "Whatever do you mean?"

"Piss off, Cameron. You know only too well we hear all the shit you get up to with those sluts." Harl hasn't even taken her eyes off the TV.

Cam's face drops.

Even I am a little taken aback by the vehemence in Harley's choice of words.

Cam is staring wide-eyed at Harl like she just sprouted two heads. "What the hell, Harbo--"

"And stop calling me that ridiculous fucking name." Harl throws her controller on the coffee table and marches off down the hall, slamming her bedroom door behind her.

"What's her deal?" Cam turns to me, shocked and a little pale.

I feel his concern – Harl would never leave in the middle of a shooting spree, but I shake my head; it's not my place to tell him how Harl feels about him. I hold my hands up, "PMS?" I offer.

"Fuck me. Please warn me when you're due to turn into a raging psycho; I don't think I could handle it."

My smile is forced. "She'll calm down."

***

Colt

I can't believe she left with that fucker. Oh, yes I can; because I acted like a macho dick and that obviously doesn't turn her on like most of the women I encounter. I find it a little displeasing that this will take a lot more effort on my part. I'm not used to it and I don't like it, but I can't fight it either, because I want her wrapped around my cock. I want that delectable vixen in my bed where I can screw her senseless all night long.

I'll be sure to see if I can tip the balance in my favour somehow. Dmitry is looking into Mr. Miles Thompson for me. I'll get him out the picture, somehow - legally, of course.

An arm unfolds from under the duvet and lands across my chest. *Shit* - Lucinda.

After Grace left my club with Thompson last night, I felt horny as hell at the sight of her, and mad as sin after she took off. I relieved both frustrations with Lucinda and now I have to deal with the consequences because I can't learn from past mistakes, it would seem.

I should've known better. She hangs around me like sores on a leper, but her infatuation is all one-sided - last night will not have helped matters.

"Morning, sweetheart," she utters, turning to face me and smiling.

I'm in no mood for pleasantries, because I made a mistake last night, and it won't happen again. "You need to go," I tell her, avoiding her gaze, "I have a meeting to prepare for."

Her arm tenses across me, but I ignore it, instead, moving it off and getting out of bed. I put some shorts on and place Lucinda's dress on the bed, hoping she'll get the hint.

If she does, she doesn't move, she only sits up against the headboard. She stares at me, clutching the duvet around her thin, naked body, her long, blonde hair sitting in disarray on her shoulders.

"I have to go soon," I repeat, affording a quick glance at her open-mouthed expression before I walk into my private bathroom to wash.

Before I switch the shower on, I hear hurried rustling, minutes before the door slams shut. Heeled footsteps echo across my polished-tiled, lounge floor and the front door crashes closed - guess she's pissed at me.

Unconcerned by her mood, I turn my shower on, ditch my shorts and step under the hot spray.

The moment the water trickles down my body in wet rivulets, I imagine it's Grace's tongue. She dips into the hollow of my neck, trails down my chest to swirl the moistened tip around my nipples, licks and kisses her way down my abs and circles her tongue around my enlarged member, lapping up the pre-cum seeping from my swollen head.

My dick throbs, the pressure building while I grab the base in a tight grip, stroking the shaft with mastered finesse.

Tightening my grasp, I think of Grace spreading her legs for me - sliding a finger around her glistening cunt before slipping two, slender digits inside. I pump faster, a hand shooting to the wall for balance. The tension builds until my balls tighten and still I continue to fist my length.

Dick swelling, I close my eyes, body jerking before I cum with a groan, shooting my load and watching it swirl with the water down the drain.

My legs grow heavy and I lean my head against the cool sensation of the tiled wall.

Taking a breath, I loosen the grip on my cock, wash myself off and step out of the shower.

I pad through to my room, naked, heading for my walk-in closet.

I do have a meeting this morning with my bank manager - I've bought a property in Kenosha and he's dealing with the sale. I will also need Lucinda's expertise as Head of my Design team to kit it out. That won't go down well, but she needs to remain professional; she's always known I'm not into serious commitment - two months, tops, and I'm ready for the next conquest.

Opting to grab a coffee on the way, I throw a jacket over my black shirt and jeans combo and head out.

Graceful Damnation

***

Grace

"Baby, what's wrong?"

Harley has her back to me, lying on her bed, hugging a pillow and gazing out the window at the afternoon sun.

"Grace, I can't stand this anymore." A quiver in her voice tells me she's been crying.

Sitting beside her, I place my hand on her shoulder, "Stand what, sweetheart?" Though, I'm sure I know the answer.

She turns her tear-stained face to me. "He was all over some tramp last night, about to bring her home until I told her he had an STD; she soon bolted." Harl smirks, but still looks doe-eyed.

Smiling back at her I ask, "So, why did you two seem so happy when you came home?"

"I downed a few more shots," she explains, "and I was just glad the tart left."

"Oh, Harley. You have to tell him, babe; you can't keep putting yourself through this."

She returns her gaze to the window, "I can't, Gray. It could ruin our friendship."

"And what do you think it's going to do if you carry on snapping at him like that?" I sympathize with her, I really do, but she can't keep driving herself insane over it. "Think about it, darling, OK? You might be surprised."

She nods, but doesn't say anything else, so I leave her to it and head to my room. Cam has gone to a shoot, so I'm on my lonesome for the next hour or so while Harl pulls herself together.

I fired off a text to Miles earlier in the day, telling him I enjoyed last night, have almost recovered and look forward to seeing him again.

His reply flashes on my screen when I swipe at my phone - he enjoyed our time together, too, and wants to take me for a meal; a proper date, this Friday.

Smiling after I type my acceptance, I chuck my phone on the bed and grab my laptop, settling back against the faux leather headboard of my bed. I have a couple of emails via my website requesting the cost of paintings and such like. One in particular catches my eye - Lucinda Gould - she wants quotes for several paintings *and* sculptures for a house in Kenosha; this could be lucrative, so I spend some quality time looking into it for her. I offer a coffee morning to show her my portfolio in the hope I can gauge a better understanding of what look she's hoping to attain.

She and her boss will meet me Tuesday morning for breakfast.

A light tap at my door rouses me from the nap I must've slipped into.

"Yeah?" I glance through groggy vision at my alarm clock - 4:04pm.

Harley tiptoes into my room, "Sorry, didn't mean to wake you."

"It's OK, babe," I smile at her, "I didn't even realise I'd fallen asleep. I need to get up; I'm starved."

I've been asleep for the best part of three hours and my stomach rumbles in protest.

"You wanna grab something at Potter's?" Harley half-smiles at me, her face still a little puffy around the eyes.

"Let's order pizza instead. Capri's?" I waggle my brows at her - she loves the place.

Capri's pizzas are amazing - gooey cheese, fabulous, rich sauce and for about $20, me and Harl will be able to pig out on a family sized with everything, and still have some left over for later.

Harley smiles and nods - the most enthusiasm I've seen from her all day, despite being asleep for most of it.

Cam's going to be away most the night on his shoot, so this will be a good opportunity for some girl time, but just in case, I send him a text to tell him to either stay out if he plans on extra-curricular activities, or come home alone. He'll wonder what I'm going on about, but I hope by ignoring his response he'll get the message.

With one extra-large Capri special, two large french fries and a helping of garlic bread on order, we pick out some comedy DVDs, crack open a bottle of wine and park our arses on the sofa.

A knock at the door signals the arrival of our junk food and I tell Harl to stay put while I grab my purse.

Handing the delivery guy some cash, I spy a white piece of card on the floor near the telephone table - the card attached to my door in the early hours of this morning; I'd forgotten all about it once Miles's lips were on mine.

I pick it up and turn it over:

Grace - you're wrong

You owe me a dance

- C

I officially have a stalker. I can't believe he came to my apartment while I'd been out with Miles - what would've happened should I have been at home?

My pussy clenches at the thought - traitorous whore that she is.

"Come on, Gray, I'm wasting away over here." Harl's exclamation stuns me from my musings.

Shoving the note in my back pocket, I kick the door closed - the pizza guy having long gone - and wander over to the sofa.

*

Lying in bed, gorged on girl talk, pizza and fries – followed by a tub of Ben & Jerry's – I keep thinking about that note. I still don't know this arsehole's name, so I grab my laptop and type in Club Knight.

Bringing up a page full of professional glitzy photos, I click the different options to find the details I'm looking for.

Proprietor – Colt Knight. And there's a picture.

Wow! Yes, I've met the guy, and he has to be every woman's wet fantasy, but having the opportunity to take a closer look at his picture with his gorgeous chestnut eyes and light, toffee-coloured, classically tapered hair, firm jaw and high cheekbones, I'm all but ready to cum on the spot.

My core clenches at the sight and juices seep through the thin material of my panties. My body is betraying me, and I seriously need to do something about it before I burst. *Ugh, how he is doing this to me?*

My pussy wins this round, and I'll berate her later for making me feel like I'm betraying whatever it is I have with Miles by getting off to another guy.

I can't think about that right now. Right now, I am throbbing so hard it's a wonder I haven't already exploded and so I set the laptop aside and slide my hand into the sodden lace of my underwear. I am so turned on it hurts, and I react in an instant to my touch – my sex pulsating, sending intense waves crashing through my heavy limbs.

With a gentle touch, I trace my slick opening. I'm drenched and I can feel the heat emanating from my pulsing core. I tease my entrance with the tip of my index finger, moving in circles before using two fingers of my other hand to massage my swollen clit.

A hiss escapes my lips when I dip my finger inside my slippery cleft. I'm hot and needy, and my head falls back, eyes close and I arch my hips while I rub with desperate fervour against my sensitive bud.

Pushing deeper into my dripping cunt, I curve my finger to hit my sweet spot, toying, teasing the quivering ridges with pressured strokes and I groan out loud before slowing my pace.

With gentle brushes both inside and out, my body begins to buck under the pressure. Heat blankets me and my flushed skin breaks out in goose bumps.

I remove my finger from between my wet folds and use the moistened digits to stroke my clit. My body reacts in quick success- my legs quiver and I writhe beneath my sexual onslaught, trying to suppress the moans escaping between my dry, parted lips.

All too soon, I come apart, rubbing out the last vestiges of my body-shattering orgasm before my hand stills and I turn my head toward my laptop, chest rising and falling with each laboured breath – Colt's face still stares at me, all smiles, charm and raw sex appeal.

Bastard.

Chapter 7
Grace

After a couple of racy texts back and forth with Miles, I didn't hear from him at all Monday.

I don't know how I feel about that. A part of me is a little hurt because I gave him something I considered sacred – I gave him my trust. Yet, the logical side of my brain is telling me that he didn't know – he doesn't know about my past and all the insecurities I've battled because of it. He's a man, and sometimes men just want one thing, and they will tell you everything you want to hear until they get it, and then they'll fuck off and shatter what little confidence you thought you had left.

Maybe he's busy – it's only been a day, after all.

And maybe he's acting like a typical bloke.

Well, fuck that. As confused as I am, I'm not letting another man get the better of me.

I can't afford to concern myself with it right now. The main point is, that I took that step. And, while he hasn't hurt me in all the ways I'm used to, I can't let that fester away inside me. He helped me overcome a barrier, and I guess I should thank him for that.

Fucking Neanderthal pig.

I shake myself off, though, because today I have my meeting with Ms. Gould and her boss and I should be super excited... I *am* super excited – this could be a flourishing endeavour and I need to keep my shit in check.

Smoothing down a knee-length, charcoal pencil skirt and adjusting my black, chiffon blouse – tied at the neck with a bow – I check my appearance in the mirror. I scream professional business woman; my patent, red pumps adding a daring splash of colour matching my glossed, ruby lips.

Piling my hair atop my head in a styled, messy bun, I snag my black, leather bag, hanging it from my arm while I slide my portfolio under the other. Heading for the door, I dip to reach for my keys from the telephone table and leave to grab my waiting taxi.

Twenty-five minutes later, the cab pulls up outside Brunch, in time for their seven a.m. opening. Our meeting isn't until half past, but I want time to prepare and get my portfolio together.

I order a latte from the waitress and gather my papers.

Tapping my pen against my bottom teeth – engrossed in my designs – I'm startled when an exaggerated cough sounds from beside me. Looking up, mouth still open, I catch my breath and my pussy clenches on sight at the grey-suited, slick-haired God before me.

Colt.

Of all the fucking clients. Of course it would be him, because why they hell not?

And Ms. Gould – I presume – standing next to him in a blue, wrap-around dress. She holds out a thin, matching-manicured hand, "Ms. Morgan?"

Clearing my throat, I rise to my feet, brushing down my skirt and extending my hand, "Yes. Please, call me Grace."

Colt's lip twitches into a smirk, "Grace. Lucinda praises your work. I'm looking forward to seeing what you're made of." He raises a brow.

Oh God! This cannot be happening. *Must remain profession... must remember, men suck.*

"Thank you for the compliment, Mr. Knight." I force my best smile, clasping my hands in front of me in an effort to stop them from shaking.

"You remember me?" The smirk reappears.

"It would be difficult not to." I don't return this smile; I'm pissed and he needs to know it.

Lucinda looks between us for a moment before grabbing the attention of the waitress, "Two cappuccinos." She reverts back to me, "Have you eaten, Grace?"

"No, I'm good, thank you." A caffeine fix is all I need to get me through the morning – although something stronger wouldn't be turned away right about now. "Shall we begin?" I am eager to get this meeting out the way now I'm under Colt's sparkling scrutiny.

I can see him – from the corner of my eye – staring at me, chin resting on his knuckles. Against my wishes, my body tingles under his gaze, my panties moistening.

"As you can see, Grace." Lucinda has opened up plans in front of me. "We're going for a Colonial look in the kitchen, while the rest of the house needs to ooze South-western appeal."

Nodding my head, I listen, offering my input while she spends the next painful hour discussing paintings and sculptures.

Colt spends that time throwing hooded, lust-filled looks my way, touching my hand whenever the opportunity presents itself and brushing his knee against mine. I spend the sixty minutes alternating between qualified professional, and horny teenager – the latter somewhat begrudgingly, maybe.

Colt finishes a third cappuccino and licks his lips with purposeful slowness, staring into my eyes. When he winks at me, it is my undoing.

"Excuse me for a moment. I need to use the ladies room," I offer by way of explanation.

Scurrying off with my tail between my legs, I enter the pristine, white-tiled bathroom and head straight for the sink. Clutching the porcelain, I take deep gulps of air. *What the hell is wrong with me?* Five minutes I've known the guy, and already he's invading my thoughts and my underwear – emotionally speaking.

I can't get his scorching gaze out my mind. I should be mad at him – stalking aside, he chased my date away because I told him no. He's an arrogant arsehole. They both are. I hate men. But the panty-dropping looks he keeps flashing my way are sending my sexual urges into a tailspin.

Oh, God, I want him.

I want him buried deep inside me, making me claw at him, suck on him, bite down on him – I want to scream his goddamn name! The thought causes a heated flush and a nervous flutter in my belly. *Where the hell is this coming from?*

Fine – I want him, or at least my body does. That doesn't mean I need to act on it. I have will power and control, I can resist him. I don't even like him – how can I want to fuck someone I don't even like?

"Grace."

My legs buckle.

Holy shit, his timing could not be worse. Colt stands in the doorway of the ladies bathroom,
one elbow braced above his head against the frame, the other hand on his hip.

Fuck, I am in trouble. I am in *so* much trouble.

Releasing the sink, I try to stand unaided. I manage it – just.

"What are you doing in here?" *Phew*, my voice doesn't quake.

"You were gone a while, so I came to see if you were okay." He removes his arm from the doorframe and steps into the bathroom, the door closing behind him.

"I've been two minutes, Mr. Knight." I point out to him, standing my ground, hands on hips.

"Please, Grace, call me Colt."

"You understand you're in the women's toilet?" I cock my head and raise a brow. He knows it... I know he knows it, and he knows I know he knows it... or something. *Oh fuck,* I'm babbling inside my own head. *Get a fucking grip, woman.*

He comes closer, my hands fall to my sides and I position my back against the sink – primarily because I can't go any further in my attempt to back up.

I place a hand on his hard chest, asking, "What are you doing?" I can't look him in the eye; instead I focus on my fingers, and try to keep my breathing under control.

He strokes my hand and a blasting ball of heat rides me straight to my core. I pull back, raise my chin and look into his chocolate eyes. He's staring at my lips and I lick them without a second thought – both them and my throat bone dry.

"Colt… ." My voice is all but a whisper.

"Say my name again." He leans into me, his lips brushing my earlobe.

My breath falters and my body prickles.

Snapping to my senses, I push away the hand trying to cup my face, "Mr. Knight, kindly respect my space and afford me the same professional courtesy I have afforded you." I push him back and make a hasty exit.

By the time I reach Lucinda I'm a quivering wreck, perspiring from every available pore. I try to act like nothing happened while I sit back down and finish my latte.

"Grace, your work is impeccable. We will definitely be in touch to discuss the pieces and prices quoted." Lucinda stands, offering her hand to me once again. I'm thankful she doesn't mention the sheen that must be evident across my face.

I don't get up to return her shake, my legs won't hold me. I remain seated while I grab her hand and I don't care if she thinks it's rude of me. "Thank you, Lucinda. I look forward to hearing from you."

A hand brushes my shoulder, "Grace, thank you for your time today. I eagerly await our next meeting." Colt's words tickle the skin on my neck when he leans in and I hold my breath.

"Yes, of course, we will need to arrange a viewing of the building for you in the next day or two, so you can take more accurate measurements and decide on the best positioning for the pieces."
Lucinda explains. "Your time and travel expenses will be compensated, naturally."

What?! I need to go to his home? I pray to God he won't need to be there, but I've a feeling my wish won't be granted.

"Sure," I croak out.

"I'll call you," Colt glares at me, lifts a brow, then whispers, "now that I have your number."

He smiles one more disgustingly sexy grin, his eyes narrowing when the corner of his lips curl up and pout, then he leaves with Lucinda.

Motherfucker, I collapse back into my seat, letting out a long breath, watching them clamber into the waiting limo before it drives off.

My phone beeps within minutes and I swipe the screen – a text from an unknown number;

> I'd love to spend hours between those gorgeous legs of yours
>
> C xx

My nipples tighten and my pussy throbs – damn my two-faced libido.

I am in so much fucking trouble.

Chapter 8
Colt

She knows how to play hard to get, but I'm a master at the game and I'll have my auburn-haired pawn on her back with her legs spread wide for me. And only me.

I pocket my phone – I would have loved to have seen the look on her face while she read my text – and instruct Jovan to take me home, after dropping Lucinda at her apartment. I put the privacy window up and stare out onto the streets of Chicago.

"Colt...," Lucinda whispers in my ear.

Placing her hand on my thigh, she traces a path up my leg, glaring into my eyes when I turn to stare at her, her nostrils flaring, lips pouting. How is she even still interested after the other morning? She must be desperate.

Before she reaches my unresponsive cock, I swat her hand away, averting my gaze.

She bores me, but it doesn't deter her – she tries again. I should just fuckin' fire her, but she does a good job and she knows the needs of my business.

Kneeling before me, she parts my legs, running both hands up my thighs this time.

A large part of me wants to put a stop to this – she doesn't interest me and I don't want her thinking otherwise – but I'm a man and I have needs, and a less than steely resolve when it comes to my cock and women who want to worship it.

Seeing Grace today, touching her, pressing my body against hers ... hell, it damn near undid me. The thought of her causes my dick to throb and Lucinda misreads the situation.

Flinging her blonde hair to one side, she leans into my crotch and trails kisses across my pulsing member. Despite the heat from her warm breath, I want to stop her, but I'm wound so fuckin' tight and I need a release.

Fuck it.

Grabbing the back of her head, I make light work of unzipping my pants before I slam my swollen dick in between her parted lips. I don't care if she loves or hates the force at which my cock hits the back of her throat – she wanted this, she'll fucking take it as it comes.

Her grip on my thighs intensifies with each thrust of my hips, but she continues to suck me off like her job depends on it.

Looking down at her feasting on my length, I can think of nothing but Grace *fucking* Morgan and how much I want to pound hilt-deep into that sexy body of hers.

I have to throw my head back, close my eyes and picture Grace's plump, red lips wrapped around my shaft, but all I can focus on is the fact Lucinda is on her knees and I'm feeling a little disgusted at myself for enabling her salacious behaviour.

Pushing her off me, I adjust and shove my vanishing erection back in my pants right before the car pulls to a stop.

Jovan's voice sounds over the intercom, "Sir, we have arrived at Ms. Gould's apartment."

"I'll see you tomorrow." I don't look at her, but I know she's on her ass on the floor of my car.

Piecing together what's left of her dignity, she grabs her bag and exits the vehicle, smoothing down her dress in the process. She slams the car door with force and I watch her stomp through the front door of her building.

"Home, sir?" Jovan's voice resonates.

Sucking in a deep breath, I release before addressing my driver, "Actually, Jovan, there's one more stop I need to make."

***

Grace

After another coffee or four, I left Brunch – head still in the clouds.

Walking back into the apartment, I throw my keys into the bowl on the telephone table. Harley is in front of the TV glued to her game – girl has a serious addiction – and Cam is either in his room or out.

Slumping down next to Harl, I let out an 'I need to talk about my day' kinda sigh – you know the sort; the heavy, over-exaggerated 'oh woe is me' sound you make when you really, really need the listener to get the hint and pay attention to you while you moan about the most trivial of things.

"What's up?" She may not have taken her eyes off her game, but at least she got the message.

"Remember the cock barrel from the club?"

"You mean the owner?"

"Yeah, him."

Harl nods, affording me a quick glance, inviting me to continue.

"I saw him again today. He's gonna be using me to deck out his new place."

Throwing down her control pad, she turns, crosses her legs beneath her and leans closer, giving me her undivided attention. "Spill."

Facing her, I bite my bottom lip, unsure of where to begin. "His Head of Design contacted me for a meeting, I get there, she turns up with the asshat in tow. I didn't even know; she never mentioned a name."

"OK, so what happened?" Harley rubs her hands together, a slight smile pulling at her lips – she's loving this.

Letting out a deep breath, I tell her, "He cornered me in the toilet, tried to kiss me then sent me a rather honest text." I hand her my phone and her eyes widen while she reads.

"Holy shit, Gray, this guy is hot for you."

"*This* guy is an arrogant, insufferable arsehole, after one thing, and one thing only." I roll my eyes at her, clucking my tongue and avoiding telling her how I'm not falling victim to another man's needs so soon.

"So... love him and leave him." Shrugging, she holds her palms up like it's the most natural answer in the world.

Love him and leave him? Can I do that? Can I act so brazenly man-like and treat him like I feel I've been treated? It's tempting, but no. I don't even know Miles's story, yet, but I do know that Colt is an arsehole. Besides, I don't think I have it in me to act that way.

I texted Miles on the way back home, but still haven't heard anything – I don't want to come off a slut, though; getting fresh with two guys so close together would be unusually promiscuous of me, and it's just not something I could bring myself to do.

Unfurling my feet from beneath me, I lean back against the sofa. "You made friends with Cam, yet?"

My change of subject is met with silence, before Harley picks her game controller back up. "I'm fucking everything up."

"I didn't realize you had a plan to fuck up."

"No plan, just our friendship."

Attempting to make light of the situation, I turn to her, "So, you can't do any worse if you just tell him how you feel now, then."

My smile isn't reciprocated, but a knock at the door saves me from any awkward tension.

Getting up, I pad to the front door, throwing it open with my usual heavy-handedness.

Colt.

Holy fuck, does this guy know when to quit, or what?

"What do you want?" I brace my body against the door, tapping my foot while I wait for an answer.

"I wanted to thank you for your time today by taking you for lunch."

The dimples courtesy of his smile are giving me butterflies, but I'm learning to fight against my body's urges.

"No thanks, me and Harl have plans for lunch." I hook a thumb in Harley's direction.

"I'm not hungry, Gray, you go ahead." There's a smile to her words and it would be so easy to throttle her for it right now.

Colt is half-smiling with one arched eyebrow, a look that has my panties moist in seconds. "You won't be disappointed." His low tone oozes sex.

God, my body is pulling me toward this gorgeous, tall, muscular man and my power to stop it is waning. "Maybe another time," I manage to squeeze out, trying desperately to remember the inner battle with myself mere moments ago.

"Promises, promises, Grace."

"I said, 'maybe', Mr. Knight." I go for sarcastic condescension, but I'm breathless, so it's almost a sensual whisper.

I'm rewarded with his bewildered glare, however, when I close the door in his face.

"What did you do tha–"

"What the fuck, Harl?!" I'm getting in there first before I wrap my hands around her neck.

"Puh-lease, Gracie. You are so into him, it's written all over your googly-eyed face."

"I don't look googly-eyed," I huff, crossing my arms over my chest.

"But you are into him."

Seeing an opportunity, I sit next to her with a smirk on my face. "I'll make you a deal... I'll go out with Mr. Arrogant Ego, if you tell Cam how you feel about him."

"What? Forget it," she furrows her brow, "It's no skin off my nose if you don't go out with him." Well, that backfired. "You know for a fact he's into you, it's only yourself you're spiting if you keep turning him down."

"Harl, he tried to stake a claim on me... while I was out with a date."

"So? So he's an alpha male; I think that's hot."

"You go out with him, then." I turn away from her, arms folded again.

"I would if he would." The corner of her mouth turns up into a smirk and I think I feel a little bit jealous.

***

Colt

She's driving me wild.

When I have her – and have her I will – she's not going to know what hit her. She thinks she's got control of this situation, but I know she'll give in before long.

I'm not one for pursuing women – especially the few who don't show interest – but she *is* interested, and my body is aching to hold her; I can't explain it.

These games she's playing are only turning me on, making me more determined to get her into my bed. I've never experienced this much trouble before – most women beg me to fuck them – but the chase is firing me up in the most delicious way.

Standing outside her door, I listen to her friend try to knock sense into her. Their voices are muffled, but it's clear when I hear her declare my alpha male status – she has no idea.

I'll be back, Grace Morgan.

Exiting her building I slide into the back of my car, instructing Jovan to take me home.

*

Entering the secured parking bay below my apartment building, I tell Jovan to take the rest of the day off - I don't have any further plans to go anywhere and I can drive my new Merc AMT GT should the need arise.

I swipe my keycard over the I.D. mechanism in the elevator.

I have a couple of charity events to set up at my clubs - I'm holding a Bachelor Auction and fundraiser at Club Knight for Bear Necessities Paediatric Cancer Foundation and a 007 Casino night in aid of raising money for Chicago Adventure Therapy.

On top of that, I have paperwork to sift through regarding my property in Kenosha and a plan to concoct to make sure only myself and Grace are present when I have Lucinda arrange the viewing.

I haven't heard from my Head of Design since this morning, but she will still be pissed at me for my behaviour toward her.

It's nothing new, she knows I don't want a relationship - as much as she keeps begging for it through her methods of seduction. I don't understand why she cares - she's fucking some PI from Naperville who she met after her wayward husband cheated on her several times during their seven year marriage.

I'll call her later this afternoon to get her to set up the meet with Grace.

Thoughts of the flame haired beauty cause my dick to twitch and I adjust myself in the elevator before the doors glide open on my penthouse apartment floor.

Stepping into the humidity-controlled foyer, I remove my brown, Armani loafers and hang my charcoal jacket in the sheltered coat rack before traipsing into the front room.

Shoving my hands in my pockets I stare out the glass-fronted building across Lake Michigan. The views are spectacular and I can see the marina from here - the glistening waters, the collection of boats and luxury yachts bobbing lazily on the water.

I love spending time on my yacht, the *Aurora Rose,* when the sun gleams over the waters and the air reaches a comfortable ambience - much like today.

I will take Grace out on the lake - we'll take *Aurora* to Kenosha in a day or two, once Lucinda sets up the viewing.

Reminding myself, I dig my phone from my beige, Gucci slacks and instruct it to call her.

She knows it's me, but she still answers the phone with the same level of professionalism. "Lucinda Gould."

"Set up the meet with Grace for Thursday morning, have the team leave the site; I don't want any disturbances or anyone getting in her way while she surveys the place. Tell her to meet me at the marina at eight."

"The marina?" I hear the perplexity in her voice.

"Yes, we'll take *Aurora* to Kenosha."

"You're taking her on your yacht? But--"

"Set it up, Lucinda." I end the call, pocket my phone and head to the bar for a sparkling water.

I would normally use my PA, Felix for such menial tasks, but Lucinda needs to be kept in the loop since she is heading up the design team. It makes more sense to have her arranging any meetings involved.

The only reason she's questioning my actions is because I've never taken a woman aboard my yacht - including her - save for my mother and sister. It's my own personal space - somewhere to escape - and I don't know why I feel comfortable, inviting Grace aboard, but something inside me wants to show the fiery fox a small part of my world. I want to watch her face light up when she sees the glittering city of Chicago from the serenity of the water - something tells me she will appreciate its beauty.

***

Grace

I'll admit; part of me is a little gutted I didn't accept Colt's lunch offer. But I know what he's after - the same thing all powerful, rich, alpha males are after - no strings sex, and, despite Harley's casual 'fuck 'em and chuck 'em' attitude; I'm not sure I can do it.

If he wants me, the fool is going to have to fight for it – whether or not I go ahead with the 'do and dump' him response to his advances, I can still have a little fun leading him on. He's stalked me and threw me out of his club - sort of - so I'll be sure to enjoy giving him something to chase.

After Colt left, and Harley began to sulk over her feelings for Cam again, I came into my room to do some research for Lucinda's project ideas.

I'm about to start sketching when my phone trills three times to indicate a text.

Grabbing it from the bedside table, I see it's Miles, even before I've swiped the screen.

A small smile dances across my face until I open the envelope;

> Hi Grace, sorry I've not been in touch sooner. Listen, I really enjoyed our time together the other night, but I don't think it's a good idea to see one another again. I've gotta buckle down with my studies, so I don't have time to delve into any kind of r'ship. I hope you understand x

Fucker! And I can smell bullshit a mile away - studies my arse - the guy's a player; got what he wanted to a certain degree and now it's time to fuck me off.

Bollocks to him, then. I don't need someone who's only goal is to get in my knickers - and that now includes Colt Knight.

Throwing the phone across my bed, I decide an early night is in order. I'm far too fired up to contemplate any other human activity and I need to sleep off my shattered confidence and remind myself – with a clear head in the morning – that it's his loss, and that I am a better person than he is.

Stripping down to a large tee, I get under the covers when my laptop signals an email. I'm not particularly in the mood to bother with anything more tonight, but it could be work related and I don't exactly live comfortably carefree enough to turn down a paying commission.

Lo' and behold, it's Lucinda, confirming a date for Thursday to take a trip to Kenosha. I'm to meet Colt at… the marina?

Oh God, what has he got up his sleeve this time? I ignore the fluttering of my stomach (because men suck) while I close my laptop and bury myself beneath my duck-feather duvet. I'm pissed at all men, so I quell the smile edging to break free.

Chapter 9

Grace

Thursday soon comes around and, to be honest, I'm looking forward to getting out of the apartment.

The tension between Cam and Harl is reaching stupid levels - when they're not working, each are going out of their way to avoid one another and I'm starting to get a headache from the glares Harley keeps giving the clueless boy.

I'm always seconds away from just blurting out the truth just to make my life easier, but Harl throws some of them daggers my way every time I go to open my mouth, so I figure I'm better off out of it.

Gathering my sea legs, I grab my bag and portfolio and head out the door.

Colt has sent his driver to pick me up and a beefy-looking, bald man in a black suit is waiting for me by the open car door when I exit my building.

"Ms. Morgan, my name is Jovan. Please, if I can do anything to make the journey more comfortable for you, let me know."

He has an accent, but I can't place it - his English is pretty damn good, though.

Ten minutes later - and I really could've caught a cab for all the time I would've spent in it - we're pulling into Burnham Harbour. The crystal waters reflect the dazzling skyline and the warm, autumn sun is beating down on the buzzing activity of those privileged enough to be members of the on-site Yacht Club.

Jovan informs me Colt will meet me at the entrance and walk me to his boat.

Pretentious dick.

Coming to open the door for me, Jovan steps aside and allows me to exit. I smooth down my skin-tight jeans for effect and ensure my blue and white striped, quarter-sleeved jumper is wrinkle free. I've teamed my nautical look with a navy blazer and a pair of white pumps - if I'm going to be spending the morning on a yacht, I'm going to look the part.

With a slight breeze coming off Lake Michigan, I throw my blazer over my shoulders and slip on my white-rimmed aviator sunglasses, securing my hair in a messy tie.

Gathering my belongings, I make my way toward the Harbour entrance where I see Colt leaning with casual aloofness against a wooden post, one foot tucked behind the opposite leg, hands buried in the pockets of his black-wash jeans.

I have to admit to myself, he looks delectable. He's wearing a salmon and white striped polo shirt with beige loafers and rimless sunglasses - he looks model perfect and I hate him for it.

Composing myself, I stalk up to him and hold my hand out, "Mr. Knight."

"Grace," he drawls, "how many times must I insist you call me Colt?" He takes a gentle grasp of my hand and brings it to his soft lips to brush them across my sensitized skin in a delicate caress. "You look good enough to eat." He raises a brow and looks straight into my eyes.

Fuck in a basket, I am so in trouble.

"Thank you," I manage.

"Come, my yacht isn't far."

Linking my arm, he leads me down the boardwalk, passing numerous mooring piers until we reach dock F.

Standing in front of the *Aurora Rose,* I am speechless. The boat is striking. At least thirty long meters of sleek, glossy luxury.

From the corner of my eye, Colt casts me a quick smile before helping me aboard.

Entering the middle deck, I find myself standing in a lavish, gorgeous room with LED lighting, beige carpets and plush, cream sofas big enough for at least four people a piece. There's a glass-topped bar with cream, leather high-chairs and a monstrous home-theatre system set aside an elegant dining area and marble-topped, mahogany wood kitchen.

The whole area reeks of money and, while I am in awe, and very much out of my depth here, I can't help but think of the commission on what I can only assume will be an equally opulent holiday home.

"Can I get you something to drink, Grace?" Colt leans into me, his words tickling the skin on my neck, causing a shiver to run down my spine and explode in my core.

I shake my head, removing my glasses, "No, thank you."

He takes my bag and portfolio, placing them on a nearby, oak table. "It's going to be a good couple of hours to Kenosha, are you sure I can't tempt you with something." His hand finds the small of my back and my body jerks in response.

His touch is glorious heat, pooling in my belly while I try to retain the use of my legs.

"I'll have a glass of water, then, thank you." I can't look at him. If his touch melts my legs, his gaze will most definitely spark a fire in my loins only he could douse.

Stepping away from the contact, I sit on one of the sofas, sinking into the soft cushions like they're a bank of fluffy clouds.

I resist closing my eyes and caressing the fabric - albeit it only just.

Striding over, Colt sits himself next to me, his thigh brushing my own, and hands me a crystal-cut glass of water, his fingers tracing a whispering path across mine. He takes off his sunglasses and looks right into my eyes.

Fuck me, he's messing with my head and he knows it. In fact, he's messing with a little more than my head and I almost hate him for it... I am trying so hard to hate him for it.

"So, Grace, is this 'another time'?" His odd choice of question confuses me and he continues, raising a brow at my furrowed one. "You told me I could take you out 'another time'."

He smirks at me, a gorgeous half-smile dimpling his cheeks.

"I also said 'maybe'," I remind him with a straight face.

Leaning even closer, he tucks a stray hair behind my ear, his touch scorching my skin. "What can I do to persuade you?"

Swallowing past the lump in my throat, and the tingling in my pants, I utter, "Mr. Knight, might I remind you of the request to respect my personal space and professionalism. This is a business venture, and needs to be treated as such."

Fuck, even I'm impressed with how strong and profound that came across.

Sliding off the sofa, but still smiling like a cat that got the cream, he offers me a hand. "Come, I want to show you the view across the water."

This man baffles me, and I can't explain it, but I want to play into his little games. The thought gives me a buzz - knowing he wants me, but not quite having his way. I admit, I'm getting off on the power and it's making me feel sexy as hell.

Slipping my hand into his, I allow him to lift me from the sofa and lead me up the stairs and on to the open flybridge.

It's magnificent.

Ocean blue-padded, diner-style chairs surround an oval, oak table to my left, and in front of me, a large, covered Jacuzzi.

To my right, a speed boat is secured to the stern and at the bow, just past a white-gloss, wood-topped bar is the pilothouse.

Stowing my marvel, I turn to Colt, "Very nice, Mr. Knight, I'm impressed."

"I didn't bring you here to showcase my wealth and good taste." His hand finds its way to the small of my back once again, "I bought you here to admire the views. I love looking at how the light catches every angle of beauty."

He hasn't removed his hand, nor his eyes, which are penetrating my very essence under his hooded, heated gaze.

Someone clears their throat behind us, "Mr. Knight, are you ready to set sail?"

A tall, handsome man with high cheekbones and a wide, firm jaw stands before us. He's dressed like a naval officer, so I can only assume he's the captain.

"Grace, this is Captain Michael Goodyear, he'll be taking us to Kenosha this morning." Colt walks up to the captain and offers him a firm handshake, which he accepts with a genuine, wide smile. "We're ready to go when you are, Michael."

"Very well, sir." Michael tilts his head and leaves us alone again.

Colt's ringtone pierces the otherwise awkward silence on my part and he moves further down the boat to sit at the oval table. He doesn't motion to me, but I take a seat opposite him either way.

"I said seven, Felix; the doors need to open for seven. The CEO will be arriving sometime after six and we need to have her prepped in time for the auction at nine."

His brow knots while he contemplates whatever Felix is telling him, then he stares at the screen on his phone and cuts Felix off. "Felix, I have to go, Farrah is on the line... no, I don't care if she's waiting on line one, my sister is calling me, she will have to continue to hold."

Colt swipes his screen and his tone changes from stern businessman to something much softer. Placing the phone back to his ear, he turns to the side - like that's going to muffle his voice - and lowers his tone, "Hi, Farrah, is everything OK?"

He smiles, but this is different to the half-curled, sexy pout I've been witness to. This is warm, genuine. It reaches his eyes and if they could sparkle, I swear they would right now.

"Yes, sweetheart, I will be there this weekend. I love you, too, tell Mom the same." He tries to cover his words with his hand, but I hear him - mostly because I'm not deaf.

Colt ends the call and turns to me while I try to hide my smile.

He moves away from the table, "If you'll excuse me for just a moment," he begins, "I need to make final preparations for tomorrow's fundraiser."

Strolling further down the bow, he fixes his phone to his ear again and this time I struggle to hear his words. We've begun to move and the wind is whistling around the flybridge.

This man is full of surprises, and my traitorous body is doing her internal "happy dance" because now she doesn't have to feel bad about wanting to bed a rich arsehole - he does have a tender side, and she considers this a victory over my apprehension to fall victim to his charms.

Well, she can put it back in her pants - I'm still not mixing business with pleasure.

Chapter 10
Colt

I love my family to the ends of the earth, my nineteen-year old, baby sister is my world, but Farrah has the knack of calling at the most inconvenient of times.

The smile Grace is trying to hide softens her features, highlights her natural beauty with such genuine conviction and for a split second something sparks inside - dances around my chest like a thousand flickering fireflies and I panic.

Shaking off the foreign sensation, I hang up my second phone call to Felix and reclaim my seat in front of Grace, while she tries to hide her smiling eyes from me.

"I'm sorry about that, Grace. I have an engagement with my family this weekend and my sister feels it necessary to remind me every few hours." She goes for a professional posture, straightening up and clearing her throat. "I also have a couple of charity fundraisers I'm trying to organize and my PA can't seem to function without me for one morning."

"If you need to postpone, Mr. Kni--"

"Of course not, Felix can hold the fort; it'll be a learning curve for him. If he can't manage for a few hours, then he is not somebody I need on my staff and he'll be fired for his incompetence."

Her eyes widen at my blatant disregard for my expendable team, but I told the truth - if Felix fucks this up, he's gone. And besides, I have Grace in my crosshairs now and I'm not about to let this opportunity slide.

"Perhaps we can go over some of the designs for your property". She moves to retrieve her portfolio from downstairs, but I offer to fetch it for her.

Returning, I lay her leather-bound folder on the table alongside two crystal-cut champagne glasses of Krug Brut Vintage 1988 – a perfect champagne to indulge in without the necessity of a preceding meal.

"Mr. Knight, I'm not sure alcohol is appropriate this early in the morning." She looks between me and the champagne with a raised brow.

Smiling at her, I push her glass closer, insisting, "We can call it a celebration for a successful business venture." I copy her when she takes her glass and holds it up. "To a lucrative relationship." Our glasses chink and she takes a demure sip of her beverage.

Placing her flute back on the table, she looks at me, "Wow, I've never tasted anything so heavenly."

Agreeing, I take the seat next to her, inching close enough for our thighs to brush - I feel her trembling beside me, but I pretend not to notice. It's damn difficult, though, because knowing I'm having this effect on her is driving me wild. I want to rip her clothes off and take her on this very table – and my throbbing dick agrees. But now isn't the time.

We spend the next hour going over her research and images, and I have to admit, I am impressed with her level of creativity. I'll hand it to Lucinda - she did well in her selection.

"Do you mind if we go indoors, Mr. Knight; I'm starting to feel the cold up here?" Grace shivers against my body and it takes everything in me not to wrap my arms around her.

I nod, "Of course. A late breakfast will be served shortly, anyway."

Making our way down to the dining area, I see that my staff has already laid the glossed-mahogany table with a selection of fruits and pastries. I pull out a cream-leather chair for Grace and she accepts, thanking me.

"Help yourself to whatever teases your taste buds."

This girl is not shy about her food. She fills her plate with all manner of choices, and I find myself watching her, not because she's beautiful - which she is - but because she isn't intimidated by my brashness like most.

She doesn't hide who she is - she's not fake and she possesses a fierce independence, unlike the majority of the women I have been associated with in the past.

This has become about more than just the chase - I want to understand what makes this woman tick.

***

Grace

Breakfast is delicious and I'm ravenous. I make no excuses for that fact and I do exactly what Colt suggests - I help myself.

After discussing some of my ideas for the Kenosha property, I have a good idea where I'm going to go with it. I can't wait to see the property - despite my earlier reservations - because I am committed to this job.

My easiest bet - since I've recognized his subtle attempts at flirtation - is to just ignore Colt's advances. It's a simple equation - men suck, Colt equals man, therefore he sucks and I will not be dragged into his game; or, more importantly, his bed.

For the remaining two hour trip, we delve further into his interior concepts and just how many pieces he requires. I do wonder why Lucinda isn't here to discuss the prices and lead-times, but I don't voice my concerns - I figure it's Colt's house; he must have a fair idea of what he wants and how much he's willing to pay for it.

Looking across the sparkling waters, I notice us pulling closer to the Marina. Gathering my belongings with Colt's assistance, I follow his lead down the two short steps to the main salon. The boat judders and I lose my footing amid the most girliest screech I think I've ever let slip through my lips.

Turning, Colt throws out his arms to halt my fall, but the force is too much and we both crash to the floor; him beneath me.

Heat creeps into my cheeks under his smouldering gaze - his lids are heavy and his breathing hard. His hand slips to the small of my back and his growing erection throbs against the crease in my thigh.

"Shit!" I exclaim, clambering up. "I'm sorry, Mr. Knight, I lost my balance. I hope I haven't hurt you." I stand with clumsy haste and notice the large bulge in his trousers. I lick my lips before I realize I'm doing it.

He's not even concerned by my obvious staring while he remains on the floor.

Oh crap, have I hurt him? "Please, let me help you up." I offer my hand, but he pulls me back down.

"I preferred it down here," he whispers against the flushed skin of my neck.

"Ahem." The exaggerated, sugary tone has me scrambling back to my feet again before I glance at a pissed-looking Lucinda - arms crossed, face scrunched into a scowl.

Colt rises to glare at his Head of Design, "What are you doing here, Lucinda? I asked for privacy."

Oh, he did, did he? "I apologize for that display, Ms. Gould, I lost my footing when we docked." I scurry to collect my scattered belongings.

"Yes, well, you must be careful next time." She switches her stare to Colt. "I'm here to oversee *my* project."

Colt's jaw tenses, "You mean *my* project, Lucinda. After all, this is my property we're viewing."

"Of course, but I need to be kept up to date, so that I can keep everything running smoothly and on time. You're a busy man, remember?" She turns on her heel before Colt can utter another word.

Angry - and seemingly without thinking - he grabs my hand and damn near pulls me off the yacht. I have no time to revel in the serene beauty of Southport Marina before I am hauled into the waiting limo.

Lucinda is already sitting inside, her long legs crossed, red sheath dress riding up her thighs. She holds a hand in front of her and inspects her nails from several angles, ignoring us while we get into the car.

Placing her hand over her knee, she stares out the window before we set off.

What's her problem? I got the impression she could likely be a bit of a bitch from our first meeting - sharp with the waitress, no nonsense attitude, straight to the point - but I failed to see why she'd take on this snarky demeanour all of a sudden... unless... she fancies Colt.

Oh, it's obvious to me, now. She wants him - or she's already had him - and she's jealous of his flirting.

While the thought amuses me that this woman is envious of Colt's one-sided infatuation - *big lie* - I will need to play it safe. She is still my boss, in theory; though I have no doubt Colt would still keep me on if she decided to change her mind.

Nevertheless, I swore a professional approach.

Five minutes later - still on the coastline of Lake Michigan - we pull up alongside a tree-lined avenue. Jovan parks the limo outside a gorgeous, two-storey brick, Georgian Revival home and Lucinda exits the very moment she can.

Chancing a peek at Colt, I notice his jaw is still firm and his nostrils flare while he watches Lucinda sashay up the paved walkway. I take the initiative and follow. He can stew in his limo with his best laid plans in tatters - I have a job to do.

It's well into the afternoon before I finish taking measurements and discussing positioning with Lucinda.

Colt spent the majority of the morning sulking in the vast garden at the back of the property and, at one point, went out for coffees and lunch. He returned in a better mood and I figured a breath of fresh air did the trick.

Finishing a sushi lunch, Lucinda's phone echoes through the empty abode. She excuses herself to answer it on the veranda.

I'm a little uncomfortable when Colt turns his attention to me, "I'm sorry for the intrusion today, Grace. Lucinda was supposed to leave you to your work."

"It's OK, Mr. Knight. I expected her to be here considering she's leading up this project; it's been no bother. In fact, I've preferred it. I have a clearer idea of what I can offer you now."

He raises a brow, but doesn't look too impressed.

Lucinda re-enters the kitchen, "I'm afraid I have to go, there's an issue I need to deal with back at HQ. Please excuse me." She holds her hand out which I take.

"It's been a pleasure again, Grace. We shall be in touch regarding the final proposals." She turns to her boss, offering him a toneless goodbye with one nod, "Colt."

No sooner has she walked through the front door, then Colt's whole moody persona disappears. "Come, Grace. We have work to do."

He leads me to a wing of the house I've yet to step foot in, and leaves me to continue my measurements and initial groundwork.

Floor to ceiling windows line an otherwise white room with original dark, hardwood flooring. The view across Lake Michigan is nothing short of spectacular. Golden rays give the expanse of water a crystal glimmer, disturbed only by the odd passing boat or a quick gust of an aquatic breeze.

I jump when a hand brushes my arm.

"I didn't mean to startle you," Colt breathes next to my ear.

Turning to him, his gaze has settled on the view. I turn back, "It's stunning."

"Yes," he simply utters.

"What made you choose this house?"

I don't know where the question came from, but something about this house, this setting, it doesn't scream arrogant business man to me and my interest is piqued. My inner slut also wants to know; considering she's still rubbing her hands in delight at his softer side.

He doesn't take his eyes off the view, "We grew up in Kenosha, before my dad sold his franchise and had me carted off to a New York boarding school."

"We?" For some strange reason, the thought of this man having a family, being a normal human, having a normal childhood, I find it... strange, despite already knowing he has at least one sister.

"Me, my brother and our younger sister."

Curiouser and curiouser.

"Do you have family?"

My breath catches in my throat at his question and I freeze.

"Grace?" He places a hand on my arm and I jump. "Are you OK?"

My whole body turns icy, I'm shivering, and I shrug off his touch. "I should get back to work."

He doesn't follow me when I go to grab my tape measure and sketchbook, but I feel his eyes on me. They stay on me while I make note of the lengths and widths of what I need because I probably look like a woman possessed – hurrying through everything and fumbling with my equipment.

"Could I have a glass of water, please?" I need to get his roving gaze off me for a moment.

"Of course." Taking one last look at me, eyes squinting in confusion, he leaves the room and retreats downstairs.

Letting out a deep breath, I lean against the wall, running my hands over my face. I don't know why I reacted the way I did. I have no family - my mother and father died before I hit my teens. But his question brought my past screeching to the forefront of my mind and my blood frosted over.

I've lived in paranoid fear of getting caught for two years. I know it's unlikely that the authorities are after me, given the length of time - I checked the UK news daily for a consistent twelve months and discovered nothing about Frankie's murder - but Garrett will be out for my blood, and the thought terrifies me.

I moved continents, so him finding me is damn near impossible - hopefully - but it doesn't stop me from looking over my shoulder every now and again.

Colt comes back in with a glass of water, ice and lemon. I thank him and gulp half of it down before taking a breath. He looks at me, his eyes open wide, searching for any indication as to what just happened. I force a smile and turn back to the window.

"I'm sorry if I worried you. I don't talk about my family; my parents died when I was young and I had no-one after that. You just reminded me, is all."

"I'm sorry, Grace." He places his hand on my shoulder, but there's no sexual tension to it this time. "I didn't mean to upset you."

"You didn't know. Forget about it." A curling half-smile pulls at my face, but soon vanishes.

He doesn't move his hand, but I can feel him hesitate over something – his body language is tense. "I have something for you." His free hand goes to the back pocket of his jeans and he pulls out an envelope. "Two tickets for tomorrow's fundraiser; I'd like you to come. Bring a friend."

Furrowing my brow, I ask, "Why?"

Staring at me for a moment, he opens his mouth to say something, then seemingly changes his mind with a quick shake of his head, replying instead with, "I appreciate the effort you've put into this job so far, and it's my way of saying thank you."

A sharp pang of disappointment hits me and I utter, "Thanks." I won't attend, but I appreciate the gesture all the same.

Chapter 11
Grace

Colt kinda stayed away for the rest of the afternoon. He sent me back home in the limo while he hung back to finalize some plans for his fundraiser tomorrow night.

I don't know how I feel about what happened today. We shared a moment, an actual moment devoid of all the arrogance and sass, but then I freaked out and it turned weird.

I'm still thinking about it when Harley comes into my room. "Hey girl, what's this?" She's got a large, toothy grin on her face and she holds up an envelope.

Colt's invitations. I left them on the kitchen side when I came in. "It's nothing."

"It's embossed with Colt's emblem; this is not nothing, missy. If you don't tell me, I'm gonna open it and find out for myself."

Ugh, she can be such a pain in the arse at times. "Fine, it's two invitations to his Black and White Bachelor Auction fundraiser tomorrow at Club Knight." I roll my eyes. "But I'm not going."

Letting out a high-pitched squeal, she jumps on to my bed. "Like hell we're not. Oh my God, I can't believe you didn't tell me. We can go dress shopping tomorrow morning, what's the dress code? It has to be glamorous. Can you just imagine? It'll be a gorgeous night."

"Breathe, Harl. I don't want to go. Things are... weird with Colt." I let out a sigh.

She tilts her head and smirks, "Weird how?"

I tell her about his flirtatious behaviour and the fact that I do want in his pants, but don't want to jeopardize our professional relationship. I divulge my musings over Lucinda's position and Colt offering information about his family unprovoked.

I skip over the part about me freaking out - she hasn't questioned me over my family or past life since learning of their deaths - and she puts a reassuring hand on my knee. "Grace, you're over-analysing this. He's given you tickets, he's not asked you on a date; we probably won't even see him, he'll be too busy running the night."

Perhaps she's right, maybe I am overthinking things.

A knock at the front door shakes me from my reverie.

"I'll get it," Harley offers.

She comes back in moments later, handling a pearl-white box with cream and purple-trimmed ribbon.

"What the hell is that?" I lean against my headboard and point at the package. Harl must've indulged again - she has a habit of spending money she doesn't have on things she doesn't need.

"It's addressed to you; it's from the Vera Wang boutique, Gray." Her eyes are wide, and imploring me to just open it already.

I sit bolt upright. "What?"

Shrugging her shoulders, she hands me the box and I pull the ribbon off and carefully lift the lid, sifting through pink and white tissue paper to be met with beautiful white chiffon material. "Oh my God." I pull the ball gown from the box and stand, holding it against me.

It pools at my feet with one draped layer emerging from a banded waistline. The large, silky bow around the waist rises to form a thick, one-shoulder strap encrusted with diamante detail.

It is exquisite elegance and I'm floored.

"It's from Colt." I turn at Harley's words to see she's holding a piece of white card. "It says 'A beautiful gown, for a beautiful woman. I look forward to tomorrow night'. Grace... "

So much for trying not to over think a situation. "Harl, I can't... this is too much, I... "

I don't know what to say or think. What the hell happened in that house that I blinked and missed?

***

Colt

The desperate, jealous bitch is lucky I didn't tear her apart, piece by piece. I cannot believe Lucinda defied my strict instruction and showed her face. The only reason she still has her job, is because I can't actually fire her for doing it. Even if her ulterior motive happened to be coming between my bedding Grace; her pretence is solid and there isn't anything I can legally do.

Something's shifted, though. I sensed it when Grace fell into my arms on *Aurora*. I can't explain it - don't want to - but holding her there twisted my insides. Her warm body against mine caused an instant reaction - an explainable reaction; I'm male - and if Lucinda didn't walk in at that moment, I don't know what would have happened. But it excites me to think about, more than it should.

The moment we shared in my house stunned me. I've never discussed my family with anyone - brief as it was - but for some reason it slipped out, and I didn't find it uncomfortable.

Until her reaction.

She intrigues me - I didn't mean to upset her, but I wonder what's happened in her past to cause her reaction.

When I handed her the fundraiser tickets, disappointment scoured through me when she didn't immediately confirm her appearance. I didn't help matters by falling all over myself and telling her they were a thanks for her work. *Why can't I just be honest?* Because, I *honestly* don't know what the fuck is going on in my head. All I know is that I want Grace at the event.

I called Vera Wang the moment she left and instructed them to deliver their latest piece to her home immediately - I just hope I guessed her size right. If a gorgeous evening dress doesn't sway her to turn up tomorrow, I am at a loss as to what will.

Why do I care so much?

Shaking myself off, I exit the car Jovan has parked in the underground HQ garage. I have a couple of things to sort through this afternoon and I need to make sure Felix hasn't broken down over the course of the last few hours.

The moment the elevator doors slide shut, my phone rings out. I swipe the screen to answer before looking at whoever it is, "Yes?"

"Colt?"

Her sweet tone rolls through my ears - she called me Colt. My dick twitches and I have to adjust when I reach my floor. "Grace?" I loiter around my personal reception area.

"Yes... listen, I... ."

She's received the dress and she doesn't know what to say.

"You're welcome." My lips curl into a full smile.

Stuttering over her words, she tells me, "I can't accept it... I mean, I appreciate it, don't get me wrong, it's stunning, but it's too much. Why would you buy me it?"

Taken aback, I need to ask myself the same question. "I... ." I'm going to go with honesty, this time. "I want you to come, Grace." Silence ensues. ... Grace?"

"I'm still here. Listen, Mr. Knight," she resumes her professional dialect and I can't help but feel a twinge of disappointment. "I need to remind you of our professional relationship." She says the words, but they lack the conviction from before.

"I understand, Grace, but I want you to accompany me as my business associate." *Fucking hell, here I go again,* but I need a positive outcome to this. "It would be a great opportunity for you to network."

"Oh." Her response sounds disheartened. "Well, perhaps I will see you there."

It's not a definitive answer, but my stomach lurches at the thought. *What the fuck is wrong with me?* "I look forward to seeing you." I hang up before she can say anything else and before I'm given the opportunity to put my foot in it further.

Walking up to my scrawny PA, Felix, behind the teakwood workstation, I wait while he picks up an incoming call, "Knight Entertainment, please hold." He presses a button on the switchboard and turns his attention to me, "Mr. Knight, Ms. Gould is waiting for you in your office."

My jaw tenses at her name. *What the hell does she want now?*

Nodding to Felix, he continues his call - I'll check the progress of tomorrow's event with him after I've dealt with Lucinda.

Walking through the double, oak doors of my vast office, I spot her sitting on one of my black, upholstered couches. She's facing the floor to ceiling windows overlooking the expanse of the city.

Hearing my entry, she turns her attention to me.

"What do you want, Lucinda, I have a lot to do this afternoon?" I turn from her, heading toward my large, cherry wood desk and I take a seat, lacing my fingers while I lean back and wait for her answer.

"I've been doing some research for the Kenosha project--"

"You were brought back here to specifically look at the Dawson proposal. Care to explain to me where you found the time to delve into my personal venture?"

Pursing her lips, she flicks her tongue across her teeth in agitation. "I discussed the proposal with Mr. Dawson and he is quite happy to proceed. I took it upon myself to see where I could save you money, and I found another artist that ca--"

"Lucinda, I am quite happy to spend good money on quality work," my voice peaks, I've reached my limit and I stand, placing my palms on my desk, "and I am equally happy with the work Ms. Morgan has done so far."

She pulls a sheet of paper from the folder tucked under her arm, "Yes, but if you'll just look, I think--"

"I don't pay you to think," I begin, walking around the desk to stand in front of her, "I pay you to head up a design team with a project of *my* choosing. You did your research, you chose well. Revel in that fact."

"Colt." She places her hand on my chest and looks at me from under her lashes. "I think she wants a little more from you than your money. I don't trust her morals." She steps closer, brushing her small breasts against me, leaning in and aiming to litter my neck with kisses.

Taking firm hold of her hand, I remove it from my body. "No, Lucinda, let me tell you what it is you don't trust." I look into her deep-green eyes. "You don't trust that *I* don't want her in my bed, because you have some one-sided infatuation with me and you're jealous."

"I beg your pardon." She backs away from me, scowling. "Don't be so conceited, Colt."

"Care to explain your behaviour, then? Hanging around me like stink on shit, throwing yourself at me in my limo--"

"I didn't hear you complaining." Her hand returns to my chest.

Grabbing her shoulders, I get in her face. "I'm not interested, Lucinda. You were a quick fuck, a means to an end, someone willing to put out when I needed a release. That. Is. All. Who I want to fuck from hereon in, or whoever wants to fuck me, is absolutely none of your business. Do I make myself clear?"

Tears well in the corners of her eyes and she prizes herself from my grasp, heading for the door. "You're an egotistical asshole," she grunts at me before leaving.

*

Managing to get the majority of my affairs in order, I buzz through on the intercom to Felix.

"Yes, Mr. Knight?"

"Can you come in for a moment please, Felix."

"Of course."

Knocking on the door, he waltzes in at my say so. "How can I help, Mr. Knight?"

"Tell me about this morning. You had a conversation with Kath?"

Shifting his footing, he glances down at his fidgeting fingers before running them through his messy, brown hair. "I'm sorry about that, Mr. Knight. She was adamant it was you she wanted to speak to, until I told her I knew all about the event." He raises his head to look at me. "It's all sorted now though, the caterers will be there at two after the decoration committee has finished; they'll be arriving at eight."

"Thank you, Felix." He takes that for his cue to leave and closes my door behind him.

A commotion from the corridor has me standing to attention and striding toward the doors to see what the hell is going on.

Lucinda is standing at the end of the corridor arguing with a sizeable man. She's crying and gesturing at him to leave, saying something about how she'll be fine, will deal with it.

The tall, broad-shoulder guy turns to face me. "Is that him?" He turns back to Lucinda. She nods and the stranger comes barging toward me, his face is red and his chest is heaving.

"Colt Knight?" he yells at me. I can see Lucinda smiling behind him, her lips twisted into an evil grimace.

"Who the hell are you?"

He responds to my question by punching me in the jaw.

Stumbling back into my office, I regain my footing and round on him when Felix rushes by with security.

Two large doormen manhandle the guy while he tries to resist. "You fucking touch her again and I'll break your fucking legs," he snarls at me, kicking out, sending Felix careening into the wall.

"Put this fool in holding and call the police." My security guys strong-arm him through the doors amid yells and profane insults.

Felix watches while Lucinda follows the dick and the security detail into the elevator. He turns back to me once they're out of sight, wide-eyed and pale. His wrist looks red and swollen and he has a drop of blood on his pressed, white shirt from a small laceration above his eyebrow.

"Are you OK, Felix? Call for medical."

"Yes, sir. I'm sorry, sir, he jus--"

"It's OK, I'm not blaming you. Who the hell is he anyway?"

Avoiding my gaze, he clears his throat, "Mr. Russell Alcott. I believe he is an acquaintance of Ms. Gould."

Ah, her PI fuck buddy. Explains everything but his outburst, and her snarky smile before the guy launched his fist at my face.

I won't press charges because I don't need to draw attention to the business, but he can stew downstairs on his own for a while before I throw him out of my building. Lucinda I'll deal with after the weekend.

Chapter 12
Grace

I'm screwed.

Colt wants me to attend his fundraiser for my own benefit. I want to go because I'm attracted to him, but I don't want to go because I am attracted to him. Harley wants to go because she gets to buy a new dress. I feel like I have to go because Colt's bought me a new dress.

And I am completely fucking confused over who has feelings for who right now!

I'm not going to be able to get out of it, though, Harley will drag me by my hair kicking and screaming. She's got this 'match-maker' aura surrounding her, and thinks tonight will end up some fairytale romance where the hot, rich, muscled guy sweeps the damsel in distress off her feet.

While my stomach still flutters at the notion, I don't dare to think about it any further – or at least I don't over-think it. Much.

I haven't dragged myself out of bed yet, but looking at the clock I know it won't be long before Harl comes rushing in, pulls me from my pit and takes me downtown to shop.

7:02 flickers and what d'ya know? Harley comes racing in.

I've never been an early bird - I couldn't give two fucks about the worm - but living in Chicago means being shaken from my slumber at un-Godly hours.

Seeing my open eyes, Harl bounces on the bed and squeals at me to get my arse up and ready for a shopping expedition. I have an overwhelming sense of déjà vu, but I am not treating her to another spa day! If anything, she owes me one.

*

One hot shower, two large Starbucks cappuccinos and a cinnamon bun later, we're outside 900 North Michigan Shops and Harl's eyes are near enough popping from her skull with the excitement of hunting for glitzy attire. Tomboy my arse.

She drags me around for a couple of hours before we end up back at Bloomingdale's - the second department store we looked in - where she picks up a gorgeous Tadashi Shoji dress with a black lace, illusion bodice and vampish, tulle skirt covering her feet.

It's cost her about two photography sessions she hasn't done yet, but it's beautiful.

We spend another hour looking for accessories and I choose a simple, pink pearl earring and necklace set, while Harl opts for Zirconia drop earrings and a matching bracelet.

My budget won't stretch to shoes, but I have a wardrobe full and besides, my dress covers my feet. Providing Harl is up for a pedicure after lunch, I'll be fine.

***

My stomach is lurching and I swear I need to be sick. I keep wringing my hands and tapping my foot throughout the whole taxi ride to Club Knight. Not to mention checking my purse several hundred times to make sure I picked the tickets up.

"Will you calm down, Gray," Harl laughs, shouldering me.

It's easy for her to say. I have no idea what tonight holds in store and I am a full on nervous wreck. I might not even see him - he'll be too busy running the event and fending off swarms of desperate women. Or not, and he'll have one draped off his arm.

Oh God, the thought makes me sicker.

Taking a few deep breaths, I try to pull myself together. Grace Morgan does not do neurotic mess. Never have and I'm not about to start now.

Until I see us pull up outside the club.

I'm not about to showcase my anxieties any further than I already have, so I grab my purse - alongside my brass bollocks - and exit the cab.

Flashing our tickets, we're ushered inside by a tall lady with blonde, cropped hair. She's dressed in some adorable, white pantsuit with a shimmering, black sash around her waist. The suit's plunging neckline showcases her bony chest and the slight outline of her small breasts. Regardless, teeming the outfit with a black trilby and sharp-pointed, black patent heels, she looks killer.

The foyer of the club houses a large banner declaring the Black and White Bear Necessities Fundraiser and highlighting the focal point of the evening - the Bachelor Auction.

Harl and I have a decent amount of cash with us, but I doubt it will be enough to purchase any of the hotties for sale tonight. I don't care, providing it's enough to get me a little tipsy.

The lady takes us through the main floor - memories coursing through my brain of the last time I decorated their dancefloor - and up a set of stairs to an exclusive VIP area with a very limited audience.

Stowing my surprise, I take in our surroundings - low lighting, oak bar with a black, marble top. Chrome and black leather seating and charcoal, slate flooring give the room a lavish appeal. There is a dark, suede curtain at the far end, pulled back to showcase table upon table of gourmet delicacies.

"Mr. Knight will be by shortly to offer you a personal welcome to tonight's event," the hostess purrs. "Champagne is complimentary and there is a selection of meats, cheeses and vegetables through the banquet suite. Enjoy your night." She saunters away with a practiced smile.

On any other day, my stomach would be screaming at me to load up on free food and booze, but she just said Colt would be by any moment, so my stomach has gone on strike and, instead wants to vacate the rest of my body.

Turning to Harley my eyes bulge. "I didn't think I'd see him."

"Seriously?" She cocks a brow. "He bought you that gorgeous dress, and you don't think he wants to see it on you? Or off you, but, ya know... ." Her top lip curls into a half smile and she winks at me.

"But you said--"

"Yeah, but I needed you to shut up." Laughing, she turns away from me.

I think I hate her right now. I need booze and lots of it. Walking over to the bar, we each take a flute of champagne. It isn't the same exquisite notes as the one aboard the *Aurora Rose*, but it's still delicate and flavoursome and it'll do the job if my stomach stops knotting.

"VIP, Gracie! We're part of the elite, now."

I can't help but laugh at Harl's enthusiasm, in spite of my shredded nerves and the fact that she's enemy number one at this moment in time. She's got the knack – she's not even trying to loosen me up, but I feel myself relaxing just the same.

Then Colt walks in and my stomach plummets.

***

Colt

Spotting her right away, I am blown away by her beauty.

Gone is the sassy, fiery spitfire of my fantasies and in her place, a stunning, elegant, fine young lady.

"Fuck." I see her mouth to her friend, while she stares right at me.

OK, so not all of her sass has abated, but I don't mind - her smart mouth is what drew me to her and reminds my pulsing cock that her foxy persona still lurks underneath.

The dress is perfection on her - the pure colour brings out the copper tones of her loose, wavy tresses - she looks like a Goddess.

Her friend nudges her and whispers something in her ear. Grace makes her way over to me and I can see the nerves etched in her wistful gaze. "Mr. Knight." She holds out a hand for me and I accept it without a moment's hesitation.

Bringing it to my lips, I brush a soft kiss across her knuckles, feeling her tremble under my touch. "You look stunning, Grace. And please, for tonight, at least, let's drop the formalities."

"You must be Colt." Grace's friend flings her hand at me and I place a chaste kiss across her fingers.

She, too, looks amazing in Tadashi Shoji couture, if I'm not mistaken. Her dark hair is swept up into a mass of curls and diamante pins.

Beautiful she may be, but she doesn't hold a candle to Grace in my eyes.

"Charmed, Miss... ?"

"Harley, my name's Harley. Grace hasn't mentioned me?" She turns to her friend and jabs her in the ribs, smiling.

So this is Harley, a face to a name finally.

"Well, can I get you lovely ladies a drink?"

Downing the remainder of her glass, Harley hands it me, nodding with a mouthful of champagne.

"I'm good, thanks," Grace replies, showcasing her half-full flute.

Grabbing Harley another drink, and one for myself, I make my way back over, handing her the beverage. "Are you bidding on anyone tonight?" I look at Grace.

She offers me a shy smile, not quite returning my gaze, "I don't have that kinda money, I'm afraid. Are you participating?"

Her eyes meet mine and I think I see hope in them - hope that I am, or hope that I'm not?

"Yes, unfortunately. As host I'm honour bound." I roll my eyes and grin.

It's hope that I'm not - her smile starts to fade with my answer.

"Oh," she whispers, "well, good luck." She takes a few long sips of her champagne, averting her stare.

"What happens if you get some wrinkly, old hag?"

I can say one thing for Harley, she doesn't mince her words.

Affording her a soft chuckle, I tell her, "There isn't much I can do about it, I'm afraid. Besides, it's for a good cause." I laugh again as she shudders. "It isn't an escort service, it's a date; we don't bed them at the end."

"Bet it don't stop 'em from trying," Grace utters, but I hear her loud and clear.

"Perhaps we can have a dance, once the auction is over?"

Trying to act aloof, she answers, "Sure, why not?"

I consider this a small, personal victory.

"If you'll excuse me, ladies, I have an auction to prepare for." I turn to Grace, "I'll see you later." Throwing her a wink and quick smile at her flushed face, I leave the girls to their night.

*

To say I'm disappointed Grace won't be bidding for me is an understatement. I wouldn't have expected her to, in all honesty - there are a lot high-rollers and big spenders here tonight, and many of them hold this charity close to their hearts. Money will be getting thrown around left, right and center for the cause.

Nevertheless, I still beam at her when I spot her in front of the stage.

"Ladies and Gentleman, if I could please have your attention," Kath, the CEO of the Foundation addresses the large audience gathered before the podium, "First and foremost, I want to thank each and every one of you for turning up tonight to support such a rewarding cause. The money raised tonight will go toward funding our new wing, and I, for one, cannot wait to broadcast the finished project to show you fine people just what your generosity has accomplished.

But for now, without further ado, I shall pass you over to our gorgeous, benevolent host, and first bachelor of the evening, Mr. Colt Knight."

There's a stark round of applause while I walk up the three steps to the stage, followed by a swift bout of wolf-whistles.

I stand in front of the microphone, "Beautiful ladies, honourable gentlemen. I would just like to extend Kath's thanks for your attendance tonight." I see Harley whisper something to Grace, they both smile. "I won't delay the inevitable any longer, I know you women are all dying to get your hands on a prime piece of fine-cut steak," a chorus of laughter rings out, "so I'll start by saying, that what you see before you is a thirty-one year old entrepreneur with a dazzling smile and personality to match.

I enjoy fine dining, sailing and I am a bit of a history buff with a penchant for travelling. One evening with me, ladies, will leave you breathless above water."

More whistling resounds around the large main floor and Kath takes over to begin the bidding at a thousand dollars.

Escalating to three and half, I watch Grace, but her gaze is focused on someone else and Harley is frog-marching toward said target.

I follow her line of sight and spot him. I catch a breath – Miles *fucking* Thompson. Shit.

Chapter 13
Grace

Before the auction begins, Harl and I down our champagne, grab a fresh glass each and head downstairs.

I'm not sure why I think it's a good idea to put myself through this torture, because I don't particularly want to see some rich-bitch, floozy bid on a man I've finally admitted I want. But he looks so delicious in his pressed, black tux with white shirt and wine-coloured cummerbund - I have to get another glimpse.

Positioning ourselves near the front of the stage, we listen to Colt introduce himself - Harley makes a comment about his flaunting arrogance and flattering charisma, making me smile.

The moment the auction begins, women are screaming out ridiculous numbers. I might've said we brought a decent amount of cash, but it's nowhere near the figures these girls are throwing around.

Over three thousand dollars so far and still going.

Harley nudges my arm, her eyes wide, nostrils flaring - she looks pissed. I trail her gaze and I see why she's fuming.

Miles stands a few feet away. And he's bought a date.

I shouldn't care - she could be a one-off thing; like me, a piece of eye-candy on his arm for the fundraiser. I don't have much time to contemplate it, though, because Harley is already power-walking over.

Grabbing for her shoulder, I miss, and she storms over to Miles.

Spotting an irate brunette stalking toward him, he turns and blinks once before Harley reaches him.

I hear her yell, "Well, hello, Miles. Long time no see. Who's this? Your sister, perhaps?"

The mousy-haired waif on his arm extends her hand. "Claudette, his date. And you are... ?"

"An old friend." She ignores Claudette's outstretched greeting and flashes her wide eyes and tense jaw back at Miles, "Isn't that right?"

"I'm so sorry," I rush my words, directing them at Miles when I stand alongside Harl. Grabbing her arm I tell her, "Please, Harl; this isn't the time or the place."

"Fuck that, Gracie." She shrugs me off. "He takes you to bed, fucks you off because he's not after anything serious, then turns up here with some tramp. What the hell are you doing here anyway, you game-playing prick?"

"Excuse me?" Claudette exclaims, releasing her grip on Miles.

"No-one asked you." Harley doesn't take her glare off Miles, instead crosses her arms and tilts her head in wait for an answer.

"I volunteer at the hospital, I was invited."

"And the tart? Pay for her company did you, considering you've no time for dating?"

"You cheeky bitch." Claudette launches for Harley, but I step between them, throwing my hands against the slender woman's chest.

"You wanna control your *date?*" As much as I try to stop it, my voice drips with sarcasm in Miles's direction.

He's stood, pretty much ashamed throughout the whole exchange, but when I put my two-pence in, he rounds on me. "Screw you, Grace, and your friend. I'm not going to be made to feel bad for something your *boyfriend* instigated?"

Straightening up, I still. *What the hell does that mean?* "My boyfriend?"

"Yeah, the acclaimed Mr. Knight." His face is beginning to redden. "He paid me off to stay away from you and swore me to secrecy. But I'm not gonna stand here to be made a fool of over it."

"WHAT?!" Harley screams above the continuous racquet of the auction.

Floored as I am by the revelation - and I'll contemplate the truth behind it very soon - I have one question, "And you fuckin' took it?" I grab Miles by the lapels and back him against the wall, thankful no-one comes over to chuck us out, but also a little surprised. Can't be every day that a woman in a posh, expensive gown is trying her hand with a bloke much taller than her.

"Going once, going twice... sold to the charitable Ms. Webb for seven thousand, five hundred dollars," the auctioneer's voice echoes in the background.

"I'm up to my eyeballs in debt, Grace." Miles's eyes widen, but he doesn't try to loosen my grip. "I didn't want to; I liked you, I still do, but I couldn't afford my tuition, and dropping outta med school is not an option for me, or my family."

I can't believe what I'm hearing. I don't know whether to be monumentally pissed off with Colt, Miles or both of the no-good, dickheaded losers. I mean, what the actual fuck?

"Grace!" A hand rests on my shoulder and I turn to stare into the desperate eyes of Colt.

I don't know what to do, words fail me - I'm still trying to process everything I've just heard.

Harley reacts for both of us when she slaps Colt across the face. "You disgust me, you senseless pig. Stay away from Grace or I swear to God, it'll be more than a slap you get."

"Let me he explain," he begs, still glaring at me while a nice, red hand print appears on his cheek.

Getting in his face, I yell at him, "Save your goddamn breath, I don't wanna hear it. I knew my gut instinct was right. You're an arrogant, self-centred twat who sulks when he can't have his own way." My blood is boiling and I clench my fists. "Well I don't fucking belong to you, so goodbye, Colt."

Grabbing my arm, Harley pulls me toward the exit. I spy Lucinda by the main doors, leaning, arms folded, eyes squinted with her devious smile. "You're welcome to him, manipulative fucker." I don't know whether I'm directing that title at her or him, but I don't give a shit anymore.

My main concern, while Harl bundles us into a waiting taxi, is trying my damned hardest not to cry.

"Grace, wait. Please!" His shouts echo behind me.

Closing the door, I glance out the window to see Colt at the top of the stairs, his arms slumping to his sides in defeat.

*

"Fucking prick, how could I be so blind, Harl? I mean, what the fuckin' hell? Paying someone to stay away, why? Because I turned him down?" I'm almost screaming when we walk through the apartment door and I'm fighting for breath by the end of my rant.

"Fuck him, Gracie. He's playing games, but he's the loser in all this."

"Arrgghhh!" I yell at the top of my lungs. How could I be so stupid? I must remember my 'all men suck' mantra and not let my traitorous feminine parts control my rational thinking. Though, I doubt it'll be that difficult any more. I am a raging ball of ready-to-explode fire and I still can't even get my fucking breathing under control.

Throwing my purse on the table, I slump down on the sofa, my gown billows at my feet. "I've gotta get outta this bastard thing."

My phone beeps through a message when I stand and I retrieve my bag, grappling inside for my mobile and sitting back down.

"It's Miles," I announce, turning the screen to Harl in case she feels the impending need to look at his name blazoned across it.

Harl sits herself next to me. "What the hell does he want?"

I recite, "'Grace, I'm really sorry for everything, and I'm sorry you had to find out like that. The guy is no good. He offered to cover my tuition fees in exchange for leaving you alone. I was stupid to accept, but I felt I had little choice. My family needs me to provide for them, and I need to earn my degree in order to do that. I wish things were different - I really like you, I enjoyed our time together. I can only tell you how sorry I am, and advise you to stay well clear of that slimy motherfucker. Miles xx'"

Screaming again at how fucked this situation is, I launch my phone at the wall where it smashes to pieces. "I'm getting out of this fuckin' dress."

Storming toward my room, Harl shouts something about a bottle of wine that sounds rather appealing right now.

Sitting on my bed, I try to wrap my head around the night's events when there is a knock at the apartment door.

I pull the zip down on my gown and step out of the slippery material.

"Oh, hell no! You can fuck off, right now; she doesn't wanna see you." Harley's voice sounds down the hallway and I poke my head out my door in time to see Colt, calling my name and scouring the passage for my room.

Backing up, I search for my short robe, grabbing it, but I don't slide it on in time before Colt comes bursting into my room. "Get the fuck out," I scream at him.

Pausing, he drinks in my near-naked appearance. "Not until you listen to what I have to say, Grace."

Harl is stood behind him, hands on hips, and nod my head at her before she disappears somewhat hesitantly. She'll likely kill him and I think a little part of me wants to hear what he has to say for himself. A *little* part of me.

Turning back to Colt, I hiss at him, "I heard plenty about what you have to say. Where the hell do you get off paying someone to stay away from me? I *do not* belong to you."

"I wanted you."

"Well, I am not a piece of fucking property. You might be a rich-bitch, multi-club owning piece of shit, but I am not for fuckin' sale. Do you get that?" I launch one of my pillows from the bed at his taut body.

"Grace, please. It started out selfishly, I admit, but I..." He hangs his head.

"You what? You realized I'm not the easy lay you're used to? Realized your own self-importance before it blew up in your face? Too late, arsehole. Now, get out." I throw something else at him, I'm not entirely sure what - it could've been a note pad, coulda been my alarm clock - whatever it is, thuds against the wall when he ducks.

He's not getting away with it though - before he can right himself I throw a shoe and it hits him in the chest.

Anger consumes me and I throw myself at him, pushing, yelling, trying to get him out the door.

He grabs my wrists, twists me round and slams me against the wall. Raising my arms above my head, he crashes his lips to mine. I writhe, trying to loosen his grip, but he's too strong. I'm a victim of his carnal assault and I don't have it in me to fight.

He growls against my mouth and I moan out loud, my lips parting to allow his slippery tongue entry.

Letting go of my wrists, he forces my bedroom door shut, grabs my thighs and hauls them around his waist, pushing his hardened length against my heated sex. His wandering hands grasp my breasts and he uses skilled fingers to tweak the nipples beneath my white, lace bra. I groan my pleasure against his hot lips.

Circling muscled shoulders, I trail my hands to his sculpted back, digging my nails through his tuxedo jacket while I squeeze my thighs tight around him.

He cups my arse and lifts me up and I can feel the tip of his swollen cock pressed against my drenched core. With fierce haste, I tear the jacket from his body before ripping the shirt away from him, buttons flying across me while I tug it over his broad shoulders.

He lowers me to the ground, his sweet lips never leaving mine. I fumble for the button of his trousers and pull them down before he shucks them off.

Lifting me again, he turns, heading for the bed.

Placing me down, I whisper, "Colt," against the flesh of his neck.

He growls, "You don't understand what that does to me; my name on your lips. I've dreamed of hearing it the moment I saw you." He litters kisses down my neck, to my collarbone and my skin puckers under the feathery strokes.

Reaching my breasts, he teases first the left nipple. I pebble in an instant and he scoops me out of the thin material of my bra, flicking his silky tongue over my sensitive teat. I arch my back and moan his name again, fisting through his hair while he attacks the other nipple with equal excitement.

His hands trail down my ribs to the waistband of my lacy underwear. He slides them over my legs, licking his way down my stomach, circling the bar in my navel before dipping his tongue into the smooth V of my pelvis.

"Oh, God, Colt... please... " My voice is breathy and I throw my head back, closing my eyes.

Using two fingers, he parts the slippery folds of my pussy and slides his tongue up my dripping slit. I quiver in response and he thumbs my clit, taking another sweet taste of my honey before he plunges deep inside.

I cry out, my back arching further into his sensuous invasion.

He circles his thumb around my moistened bud and my body starts to convulse.

"Please, don't stop..." My cries are lost behind another rush of moans when he slides a finger inside my damp cleft.

Plunging in and out, his tongue works my clit, causing my body to buck. I pull on his hair, my feet tingling, heat pooling in my stomach, filtering to my throbbing core.

He slides another finger in and I come apart around him, my pussy clenching around his digits, coaxing every last drop of my release while my body floats somewhere ethereal.

Catching my breath I sigh, "Holy fuck, Colt."

Sidling atop me, he throws off his boxers and positions his heavy cock at my drenched entrance, teasing me with the bulbous tip. "I need you now, Grace. Are you...?"

"I'm on birth control," I answer his pending question in a whisper.

He slides in, inch by glorious inch, "Good," he utters on a breath, obscured by my drawn-out gasp while he buries himself to the hilt. "Fuck me, Grace, you're so tight."

He's huge, and my pussy hugs him something fierce while he fills me with magnificent heat.

Adjusting to his size, I wrap my legs around his and claw at his back when he pulls out and slams back into me. I cry out, the pain masked by the immeasurable pleasure blasting through my entire being.

Sitting on his haunches, he angles himself, so his dick hits my sweet spot and my body begins to quake again. He grabs the base of his shaft with one hand, stroking, and rubs circles over my exposed clit with the other. He looks fucking hot, handling his cock, his ripped body tightening with every thrust.

I throw my hands behind me, gripping my headboard tight with every plunge, arching into his deliciously dexterous fingers.

I cum screaming, Colt following moments later, after driving deeper and deeper into my satisfied, aching cunt, breathing my name before collapsing to the side of me.

I feel his chest rising and falling against my arm while I lay, prone beside him, our bodies' slick with sweat.

Feeling him smile against my arm prompts one of my own, before he nuzzles into my neck. He mumbles something incoherent and I turn to him.

"Amazing," he breaths, before light snores soon escape his parted lips and his breathing evens out.

I've waited a lifetime for someone to worship my body the way he just did, and it scares the hell outta me thinking about where we go from here, now that I've given him what he wanted.

And after I swore not to put myself in this position again.

Chapter 14
Colt

She's beautiful when she sleeps. I've been awake for a while, watching the slow rise and fall of her chest, barely believing that I am finally lying beside her, and shocked that I don't just want to fuck and run.

Some time in the night, we must've gotten under the covers, because she's drawn the sheets to just above her ample breasts. A light dusting of freckles dot her rosy cheeks, her russet hair is splayed across her pillow and her lush lips are slightly parted.

I can't explain what I'm feeling right now, but I know I don't want to fight it. Last night amazed me - I didn't think for one moment she would respond to my wanton attack on her; desperation took over, and with nothing left to lose, I threw caution to the wind.

The circumstances surrounding our coming together have been less than ideal, and I promise myself I'll make it up to her.

Not wanting to disturb her, I carefully slide out of bed, don my boxers and stroll down the corridor, headed for a coffeemaker I'm hoping she owns.

Pottering in the kitchen, a voice startles me, "Dude, who the hell are you?"

A tall, dark-haired guy rises from the sofa in the living room and stalks over to me. He's shirtless and I can almost appreciate his muscled physique - though not broad or bulky with it - as he tenses up, eyeing the stranger in his apartment. I do wonder who the hell he is and if Grace has fucked him. Jealousy is an emotion I'm not used to and I have to stop myself from balling my fists in a territorial display of anger.

"Colt. I'm... er... a friend of Grace's."

"I visit family for a couple of days and the hussies have already moved another male in here. Typical." He smiles before holding his hand out, "Cameron... Cam. Friend of the two lunatics who live here."

Phew, friend I can deal with. "I recognise your face; I think you modelled for Club Knight." He does have a familiarity about him.

His eyes widen, "Ah, the infamous Colt Knight. Yes, I did, thanks for the work."

"You're welcome."

Continuing with small talk, I don't notice Harley traipse into the kitchen until she stands beside me, glaring.

"Made up, did you?" Her voice drips with condescension.

I've never been one for feeling humble, but my cheeks heat under her scrutiny. "I wanted to apologise, to you and Grace. What I did was unacceptable and I will spend every moment I can making it up to you both."

"Yeah, well, you don't need to make it up to me in quite the same way." She shudders. "But if you hurt her again, I will rip off your balls and shove them down your throat. Clear?"

"Crystal." She scares me - and I'm not an easy one to intimidate – but I admire the fierce loyalty she has toward her friend.

Clearing his throat, Cam asks, "What I miss?"

I'm sure Harley will enlighten him while I go to fetch my phone that I can hear ringing from the pocket of my pants.

I'm thankful it hasn't woken Grace - she's still sleeping like an angel.

Smiling, I swipe my screen and answer the call, stepping just outside the bedroom.

"Colt, where the hell are you?" Lucinda. "I've had all and sundry screaming at me asking why you took off last night. You didn't... tell me you didn't follow her home."

"I had something *personal* to take care of, Lucinda; not that it's any of your damn business." It's too goddamn early for this shit.

"You left the fundraiser after being bid on to follow some *girl*, imagine how that looks, it--"

"Then I will discuss it with PR, and not my Head of Design. Where is Octavia, anyway, shouldn't she be the one hounding me over my disappearance?"

Sighing - or more whining - Lucinda answers, "She called me regarding the Dawson proposal and asked what happened last night. I told her you weren't feeling well and would call the very moment you could."

"Thanks." I hang up and instruct my phone to call Octavia.

Some moments later, I've managed to convince Octavia I must've eaten something that didn't agree with me - I felt ill and needed to leave right away. I inform her that I will apologise personally to Kath for my sudden departure, and make a televised, generous donation toward the opening of their new wing.

This appeases my PR agent and I end the call, trusting her to pass on the details to the Foundation.

Contemplating waking Grace, I decide against it for the moment - it's still early, but perhaps I can go fetch her breakfast while she sleeps.

After dressing, I re-enter the living room, noticing Harley stooped near the far wall, picking something up.

She spots me and informs me, "I'm collecting the remains of Grace's phone from off the floor, and possibly the wall. At least the SIM card is still intact." She shrugs, returning to the mess I now see scattered.

"I'm gonna go out to fetch breakfast, do you want anything?" I figure it polite to ask, considering she likely still hates me right now.

Tilting her head back in my direction, she smiles. "I could murder a mocha and a bacon, egg bagel."

"Consider it done."

Heading for the door, I turn the key, pulling it open and come face to face with what is largely becoming the bane of my existence.

"What the fuck are you doing here?" Miles's face scrunches into a scowl while he stares me down.

***

Grace

Opening my eyes, I strain my ears; certain I just heard raised voices. I look to Colt, but he isn't there and for a moment, I panic, fearing that I've been duped again. That is, until I hear the voices again.

"You best leave now, or I'll I throw you out." Sounded like Colt.

"What the hell are you playing at, Knight?"

Is that... ? *Oh, fuck no.*

I launch myself out of bed, grabbing my robe on the way out the bedroom door.

Cam meets me in the hallway - fresh from the shower - in just a pair of track bottoms. "What the hell?"

Voices can still be heard, yelling.

Shrugging at his question, I make my way into the living room, Cam following.

Miles squaring up to Colt stops me dead in my tracks. "What the fuck is going on here?" I yell above the commotion.

Turning to me, Miles scowls, his face red. "What the hell are you doing with this prick, Grace. After what I told you last night, I thought you'd have steered clear."

"Watch your mouth, Thompson." Colt doesn't touch Miles, but he doesn't have to. He stands above him a good few inches, and with his bulkier frame, looks intimidating just facing him off.

Miles isn't threatened, though. "Wanna tell me what you're gonna do about it?"

He moves closer to Colt and gets pushed back for his efforts.

"Stay outta my face, asshole," Colt snarls at him.

Harley steps between the two of them, urging them to stow their shit. She doesn't see Miles fist flying toward Colt - and neither do we - until it's too late.

Miles looks horrified – his eyes and mouth wide - when he catches the side of her face and she falls into Colt, then to the floor. I rush forward, seeing Colt seconds away from retaliating.

"Back the fuck up, both of you." I push them both further apart while Cam runs to Harley. "Is she OK?" I turn in Cam's direction, still fending off Colt and Miles from beating the shit out of one another.

"I'm good," Harl moans, clutching her head.

"You," I yell, digging my finger into Colt's chest, "sit down, and you," Miles's turn, "get outside. Now!"

Standing his ground, Colt utters in a low voice, "I'm not leaving you alone with that dick."

Miles goes for him again, but I use both hands to push him back. "Five minutes," I yell behind me while urging Miles toward the front door.

Closing the door behind me, Miles places a hand on my shoulder. "Please tell me you didn't, Grace."

Glaring straight into his eyes, I tell him in a stern voice, "I don't think that's any of your business, Miles. You dumped me, remember?"

His face reddens. "Because of that cocksucker, because he wanted to fuck you; add you to his ever-increasing number."

Miles has a point. At least, I think he does - I don't know how true it is until I speak to Colt, but from what I've gathered so far, it isn't going to be too far a stretch from the truth.

"You took money from him, though, Miles. You could've said no; you could've told me." I plead with him to understand where I'm coming from.

"I couldn't afford my fees, babe. I told you."

"You still could've showed me enough respect to tell me. You lied to me, you hid the truth. If he's a bastard for paying men to stay away from me to have me for himself, what does that make you?"

Hanging his head, he utters, "I'm so sorry."

I'm trying to be tactful about the situation - even though I'm the sucker in the middle of it all - so I place my hand on his arm. "You don't have the right to tell me whether I can or cannot sleep with him; you never had that right, but you only made things worse by lying to me, making me feel like a worthless piece of shit. I thought you dumped me because I didn't sleep with you. See it from my point of view, Miles."

Taking both my shoulders in his warm hands, he pulls me close. "I'm sorry, Grace. I don't know what else to say."

He clashes his lips against mine the moment the apartment door opens.

***

Colt

Pacing the apartment, I'm counting down the seconds. Five minutes is at least four and a half too long in my opinion, but Harley is still on the floor and there's an angry red mark already forming on her face.

I've applied a bag of ice to it, but there isn't really much else I can do. Cam is seeing to her.

Patience running out, I stalk toward the door, yanking it open to find *his* lips on *my* woman.

Launching at him, I grab the back of his collar the moment Grace tries to push him away. He lands with an audible thud against the wall.

"Colt!" Grace screams out.

Making a grab for me, she misses my swinging fist. I connect with Miles' face and a rush of pure satisfaction surges through me at the crack.

"Stop it!" she further cries. "What the fuck, Colt?"

"He was pawing at you," I spit through gritted teeth.

"Don't be so dramatic. He kissed me, I pushed him away. If you can't calm down you can go home." She's seething, her pretty face is red and her fists are clenched by her sides.

Before I can process anything further, Miles slams into me, taking us both down to the cold concrete.

Twisting my body, I come out on top. Grace is still yelling at us and I feel someone pulling me off Miles before I can get a punch in.

Landing flat on my ass, Cam stands above me, his attention directed at Grace.

"You're acting like a couple of fuckin' kids. Stop it!" she yells. "Miles, you need to leave. You dropped me for cash; I'm sorry, but that sucks." She turns her attention to me, and the smile I sport falls from my face. "You need to leave, too; you tried to buy my attention off and that's not cool either. I'll call you later. Now go, both of you... and no smacking each other on the way out or I'll fuck you both up."

"OK, like seriously, what have I missed?" Cam looks between us.

Rising, Miles walks up to Grace and it takes everything I have not to beat him back down when he touches her arm. "I really am sorry," he starts, "I wish I said no."

Tough shit, fucker - you did, now she's mine.

Grace nods, her eyes unmoving. He heads down the stairs and out of my sight.

"I'm not leaving," I tell her when she turns to me, "I said I was sorry, and I plan on proving it."

Taking a deep breath, she moves toward me, her hand grazing my arm. "Not right now, Colt. In case you missed it, Harley just got smacked in the face; I need to make sure she's OK. I will call you later, I promise."

My heart sinks a little, but she looks sincere when she tells me she'll call, and I believe her, because I'm just not ready to let her go any more.

Chapter 15
Grace

After spending some time making sure Harley is definitely OK, I retire to my room, sitting on the cushioned box in front of my window, staring across the bustling city.

It's starting to rain and I focus on the streaks of water while they cascade down my window.

I think back to my childhood and how I came to be where I am right now.

About sixteen years ago, I couldn't wish for more from my childhood, with two parents who adored me, great grades in school, a bunch of friends to get up to mischief with - as much as any usual ten-year old could, at least.

On my eleventh birthday, everything changed. I came home from school one afternoon and no-one was home. It happened sometimes - Mum and Dad would often have to work late at the hospital- and when it did occur, I would go next door to our elderly neighbour, Elsie's house.

She'd feed me and make sure I got comfortable in front of the TV with a blanket and hot chocolate before my parents returned.

This particular afternoon, however, Elsie didn't answer her door.

I sat outside our house for God only knows how long. Elsie turned up before dark and came running straight to me, her face red and swollen from crying.

I knew then that something had happened to my parents.

Elsie couldn't speak - too distraught. Only when my mum's sister, Aunt Candice turned up did I learn.

Mum and Dad finished their shifts together, they went to a coffee shop round the corner for a quick drink - I wasn't due home from school for another hour at the time.

When they were about to leave, a man barged through the door. He began firing off rounds from the gun he held - for no reason other than he was high, I later learned. Two of those bullets tore through my mum's neck and she died within seconds.

My dad hung on, he tried to throw himself in front of Mum and got three bullets in the back for his efforts. One went straight through his kidney, another in his lung. He lasted long enough to stroke my mother's face I was told, then, the moment the ambulance turned up, he died right there next to her.

My life ended that day.

I caused chaos wherever I went; I didn't care who I hurt because I suffered more than them. I would always suffer more. Nothing mattered to me and I started bunking off school, hanging out with teenagers, smoking, drinking.

Aunt Candice couldn't take it - I always considered her a weak woman compared to my vibrant, beautiful mother - and she shipped me off to a care home.

I didn't fit in there either. Foster home after foster home ended badly. I struck out, got bullied by the other kids, ignored by the parents. I was a damaged kid, and nobody wanted anything to do with me.

At eighteen, it became a case of fending for myself, only I didn't know how.

I began stealing, dealing drugs. But six years ago, I thought I'd be OK. Garrett put an end to my prostitution 'career' even before it began, took me from the shelter I'd housed up in, gave me a roof, food, and I appreciated him for that. Until the beatings started.

My time in care enabled me to grow a thick skin, but even Garrett would eventually tear through it. I numbed myself to the pain, ambled through life like a zombie, took the beatings, dealt his drugs, felt his sweaty, heavy body clamber on top of me night after night. He would never ask, he'd just take what he wanted- whenever he could get it up – and roll over and go to sleep.

The first night with Miles scared me a little. Don't get me wrong, I got caught up in the heat of the moment and enjoyed every minute of it. Miles pleasured my body in ways I didn't know existed. Garrett forced me into all kinds of lewd acts, but nothing intimate, nothing that rocked my world like Miles did.

And then there's last night.

Colt blew my mind. The man is magnificent - dynamic, dominant, gorgeous. I became putty in his capable hands and my body sang to his erotic tune.

Something changed in me last night. I knew I could give myself to Colt like no other man. His raw passion collided with a desire I'd long since buried. He woke me, roused the woman I knew resided somewhere within me.

But the display of possessive power this morning brought me right back to square one.

I know in my heart of hearts, he is not, and never will be Garrett. But this morning I considered him my saviour and everything came shattering back to earth with a resounding crash.

When I looked into his eyes before he left, I saw fear - mine and his - and I wonder if he really knows what he's letting himself in for. Probably not, because neither do I.

I just need to figure out if I'm willing to finally break free of the girl I once was, and embrace the woman I long to be.

A knock at the door makes me jump. "Come in," I mumble, collecting myself.

Harley walks in with the biggest bunch of roses I've ever seen. White and red, at least two dozen of each. They must've cost a small fortune.

"And so it begins." Harley smiles, but winces at the pain in her head, I assume.

Walking over to me, she places the large bouquet in my arms.

"Are these from Colt?" I pick out the small, white card nestled within and smile at the words;

Sorry is just a word.
Making it up to you is a responsibility.

- C xxx

Grinning, Harl grabs the card off me and reads; her face turning into a soppy mush with doe-eyes and a little pout. "That's so sweet," she tells me.

"You were his worst enemy five minutes ago, Harl," I remind her.

"Tut, please." She hands the card back to me. "It's been at least an hour or two."

Turning the card over in my hand, I ask her, "Should I call him?"

"Up to you, Graybo. I would, for what it's worth." She leaves me to contemplate her answer and I grab my phone, seek out his number and hover over the call button.

***

Colt

Leaving her - with that far-away look on her face – it's struck something within me.

Exiting the building, my chest aches. Adrenaline still pumps through my veins, but the need to be near her weighs stronger.

I spot Miles getting into a cab, he throws me one last hateful stare - eyes narrowed, jaw rigid and twitching. He slams the car door behind him and the taxi takes off.

A car horn sounds and Jovan pulls up beside me. Climbing in, I instruct him to take me downtown. I promised to make it up to Grace; to prove to her I'm after more than a quick fuck. I need to prove it to myself, too.

Stopping outside a florist, I head in and order the largest bouquet of roses they can deliver within the next hour or two. It's not much, I know, but it's a start and I hope she sees the gesture for what it is.

***

Walking out my gym - having vented the build-up of today's frustrations - I hear my phone trilling. A light buzz flutters through my stomach while I jog to retrieve it from the bedside table.

It isn't her, though.

"Hi, Mom," I sigh, lying back on my bed.

"What's wrong, sweetheart, you sound down?"

I roll my eyes, *trust her to notice.* "I'm fine, Mom, really. I thought you were someone else." *Shit,* that came out wrong.

Laughing at me she responds, "Thanks, Colt; I love you, too."

Rising on my elbows, I gush, "Sorry, I didn't mean it like that, I--"

"It's a girl, isn't it?" I can hear the smile in her words and I wonder how the hell she even knows this shit without me saying anything.

My mother wants nothing more than to see me settle down with a 'nice-looking, stable woman'. The thought made me shudder once upon a time - a committed relationship did not appeal to me; since finishing college I didn't have time to date women, make them feel special, take them home to meet Mom. I didn't want to. A couple of dates followed by a hot fuck any which way I could get it is all I ever needed – although, I omitted from divulging that to my mom.

But when Grace walked into my life - or more poignantly, my car - something in me snapped.

Don't get me wrong - the chase appealed to me; I wanted to fuck her senseless. But she resisted, and I loved it, more than I thought I would.

For Mom to pick up on my feelings so quickly, says something about the impact Grace has on me - she's never pointed it out before.

"Mom... ," I begin, sliding my hand under the pillow behind my head.

"It's OK, love. I won't hound you; I don't want to jinx the first woman my son is smitten over."

"I am not smitten." *Am I?*

"Uh-huh, sure thing. So, tonight... are you bringing your lady love?" The sound of her chuckling makes me smile.

"Mom! It's too soon--"

"So it *is* a girl? I knew it."

Clucking my tongue, I plead with her, "Change the subject, Mother. You called for a reason?"

She tuts back at me. "I don't need a reason to call my eldest boy, but now you mention it, I did want to ask you something."

"Fire away."

She asks me about the Kenosha property, how the renovations are going and when she can see it. She wants to use it for her yearly Christmas party and needs to know if it will be done in time.

"Everything's on schedule, you can have your party there. I'll have Grace create a few Christmas pieces for decoration." I smile at the mention of her name.

"Who's Grace?"

"Oh... she's the erm... she's a sculptor and painter, doing a few pieces for the property."

"Uh-huh." She's smiling again.

I hate the fact my mother knows me so well, even traits I don't express so often - she knows what I'm thinking even before I do.

"I'll keep you posted, Mom. I have to go; I have another fundraiser to plan."

"OK, darling," she giggles, "but make sure you invite Grace over for the party."

She hangs up before I can protest.

The phone rings again, I answer without looking, "Mom, I'll ask Grace; stop pestering."

"Ask me what?"

Holy shit! Grace.

"I... um... did you get my roses?" I rush.

"I did," her voice softens, "they're beautiful, thank you."

"You're welcome, and I meant what I said."

"What were you supposed to ask me, because I know it wasn't about the flowers?"

Double shit! Is it too soon to ask her to meet my entire family? Of course it is; she'll run for the hills.

"Colt?" she urges.

"Sorry, Grace. My mother wanted to ask you something, and you can say no, I will understand, but she will kill me if I don't at least ask." My words are hurried, I'm waffling. This is all new to me... and sudden; it's all so goddamn sudden and I'm shaking with anxiety. Me... fuckin' shaking over a woman!

"Colt, get to the point," she laughs.

"Will you accompany me to my parents' party tonight?"

There's an extended silence and my palms begin to sweat. I can still hear her breathing on the other end of the line, though, so she's not hung up. "Grace?"

Her next question waivers. "All your family will be there?"

Fuck, she's going to say no - this is too much, I knew it - she's going to say no.

"Erm, yeah, the majority at least, plus friends of the family."

Her breath catches before her answer sends my pulse racing. "OK, sure. I'll go with you."

Chapter 16
Grace

I'm not sure accepting is the best idea, but if I'm to embrace 'The Reinvention of Grace Morgan', then I need to dive right in, so to speak. I need to get rid of the stigma of my once shitty life and start pulling myself together. I've taken the first step, despite still being shit-scared because of it, but the guy still wants to know and that makes decisions like this easier.

It's been a fucked up few days, but I can do this. *Can't I?*

Meeting the parents is a big thing, but the *entire* family. I feel sick just thinking about it, but I'm doing it for me - it's time I lived a little.

I've been in Chicago about two years now, and I haven't gone on many dates - too afraid to let myself go and live in the moment because of Garrett's shadow hanging over me.

It's still fresh, but Colt is different... everything is different. He's a protector and when I overcome my insecurities, I'll feel safe with him - I know it.

I peel myself from the window box and pad through to the living room.

Cam and Harl are on the sofa; Harl playing Call of Duty while Cam holds a cloth full of ice to her head. He's not stopped fussing over her since this morning.

I park myself on the chair adjacent and Harl offers me a quick glance.

"Hey, girlie, you OK?"

Trying to nod, but still a little overwhelmed, I tell them, "Colt just invited me to his parent's party tonight."

Cam loses his grip on the ice and Harl drops her controller. They both turn to stare at me, wide-eyed and open-mouthed.

"Run that by me again," Harl requests, blinking several times in shock.

I bite my lip. "I called him, he thought it was his mum, and said she wanted to invite me. I--"

"His mother invited you?" I didn't think it possible for Harl's eyes to bulge anymore.

Nodding, I tell her, "His entire family will be there. I'm shitting myself."

Replacing the ice cloth to Harl's face, Cam pipes up, "You accepted, then?"

"Yeah, is that a good idea?"

"What's the dress code?" Typical Harley.

Shrugging my shoulders, I tell her I forgot to ask. I fire off a quick message to Colt to find out. No doubt Harl wants to drag me around more shops - my feet twinge in protest and I look back out at the rain – no way am I going shopping in this, so it best not be an occasion that I don't have suitable attire for.

My phone beeps to signal my reply and I reel off, "'It's going to be a garden party, so dress warm - smart casual usually. But whatever you wear, make sur--" I stop, face heating.

"What?" Harl's noticed my face; she's smirking at me from the corner of her mouth.

"Nothing." Shaking my head, I read the rest of Colt's message to myself;

> ...make sure I can remove it easily enough; there are one or two places I'm going to have to TAKE you! xxx

"What's with the goofy smile?" Cam throws a pillow at me.

I catch it and chuck it back. "Never you mind."

"Oh, no." Harl shakes her head and rolls her eyes. "It's started." She throws a cheeky smile at me and winks.

Ignoring the other sly smirks from them both, I embrace the moment and tap out my reply to Colt;

> Mr. Knight, are you going to take advantage of me at your parent's house? Whatever would they say? xxx

Sitting back, I tuck my legs beneath me, grinning at my phone like a goon.

It beeps back at me, only it's not Colt.

"Miles has text me."

"Apologising, I hope," Harl doesn't take her eyes off the TV, but her jaw tenses.

"'I'm so sorry about today, Grace. Please apologise to Harley for me, I never meant to hurt her, I feel like shit because of it--'"

"As well he fucking should," she throws in.

"'I meant what I said, that guy is trouble. I know what I did was terrible, but he's no better. Please be careful around him. I'm sorry again, I wish things turned out differently, but I understand how you feel.'"

"Ha, unlikely. Sounds to me like someone is jealous," she drawls.

Harl's perspective has done a complete one-eighty again since Miles punched her. She's not a huge fan of either right now, but a smack to the head has a knack of enforcing an opinion.

My phone beeps again and Cam makes a comment about my soaring popularity.

> What they don't know won't hurt them. Just try not to scream so loudly this time. Bring Harley and Cam – I owe them, too, and they can be our lookout xxx

Somehow, I doubt they'd be up for playing bodyguard for two rampant, horny adults while they fucked each other stupid, but they might enjoy the free booze - call it a consolation prize.

"You guys wanna come to the party? Colt's invited you both."

"Hell yes." Harl drops her controller and runs off to her room, I assume to try on anything and everything in her wardrobe.

I shout through to wrap up warm and she squeals something about not on my life before I turn to Cam. "You up for it?"

Nodding, he tells me, "Sure am, but I'm a bloke; I don't take so long to get ready."

Snorting at him, I reply, "Pfft, yeah right, you're worse than a woman, Cammy."

"Good point," he chuckles before retreating to his room.

***

Colt

"Oh, honey. Come and give your mother a hug." It may have been a request, but she leaves me little choice to comply when she grabs me around the waist and pulls me close.

"Hi, Mom." I step through the door when she releases her hold on me. "Is everybody else outside?"

"Sure are. Your dad's in the study, though. You should go say hi."

Giving her a quick kiss on the cheek, I head toward my dad's office. Retired he may be, but he still can't drag himself off his computer and away from helping the very people he sold his business to.

Before I can reach him, however, a force slams itself into my body and flings arms around my neck.

"Colt!" A delighted squeal escapes my sisters mouth and I turn when she slides from my back.

I pull her into a bear hug. "Hey, Faz. You look beautiful." And she does. Her slight frame is decked out in dark jeans, and a black turtleneck sweater underneath a brown, fur vest, zipped half-way; matching fur-trimmed, black leather boots on her feet.

"Mom tells me you're bringing a date?" She waggles her brows at me. "Is she hot?"

"She's beautiful, and she's strictly mine, so hands off." I deliver a soft punch to her arm.

"Hot friends?"

"Actually, yeah. She's bringing two friends; Harley and Cameron."

"Harley's a girl, right? Is she hot?"

Laughing at her brash attitude, I shake my head. She's just like Harley - speaks her mind. "Yeah, she's a girl, and yes, she is attractive."

Farrah clasps her hands together. "Fantastic." She giggles and runs back outside. "Love you, bro," she shouts in her wake.

For a twenty-year old, she's got the life and attention span of an energetic child.

Still smiling to myself, I stand outside the door to my dad's office.

Knocking, he tells me to enter.

He's sitting behind his French, pedestal desk and the glare from the laptop screen highlights his greying hair.

"Hey, Dad. What you doing? Shouldn't you be outside with everyone else?" I take a stand in front of him and place my hands on the back of the chair before me, while he takes a long sip of his usual brandy.

"I won't be long, lad. Jimmy's got stuck with the Layton package and needs a quick step-by-step."

Smiling, I roll my eyes. "I'll see you out there?" I head for the door.

"Sure. Oh, wait, you should know... er... Collette is here."

"What?" I grip the chair until my knuckles turn white. "Who the fuck invited her?"

He glares at me. "You watch that mouth around your mother, young man. Don't let me catch you swearing in front of her." He takes a breath and focuses back on the computer. "She's here with Donny."

"Still making her way up the food chain, I see."

Collette is a vulture. We went to college together and hooked up one summer. I bought her home to meet my parents - before I knew better, and she ended up sucking off my younger brother in the bathroom during dinner one evening.

I didn't find out until months later. He broke down in front of me, said he didn't know what to do; she cornered him and wouldn't stop.

I didn't blame him, I can believe it. Collette loves to screw - she likes to have her own way and if anyone says no to her, she'll make your life a misery. Something I experienced after dumping her.

She follows money wherever it goes. When I opened my first club, she got back in touch. I fucked her in my office, against my better judgment, but told her to piss off after I finished. She tried to have me shut down, but my attorney soon put an end to that.

Donny is my uncle's friend. He's a surgeon, so it makes sense she'd be hanging round him. He's twice her age, mind. But if they have money, she couldn't give two fucks. She's probably hoping he'll drop dead and leave everything to her. Won't happen - he's got three kids he dotes on and his estate will go to them and their mother - the ex-wife he's still in love with.

Praying I don't bump into her, I leave my dad's office to give Jovan a call, see if he's picked up Grace, Harley and Cam, yet.

My stomach flips at the thought of seeing her again so soon. It may have only been a matter of hours, but her beautiful face has been the cause of my distraction for the whole of today. It's welcome, but it's still unusual to me.

I tried to finalise the arrangements for the 007 fundraiser at Sovereign - my first casino. I got as far as confirming the catering, then left the rest to Felix because thoughts of my ruby-red minx occupied my every thought.

Jovan confirms he is a few minutes out and my stomach does another somersault.

Hanging up, I flinch when a hand trails a path across my shoulder.

"Colt, darling. Long time."

Fuck knows where the new, aristocratic accent came from, but there's no mistaking Collette's tone. I turn to her.

She's still the same curvy brunette I remember. Even in the midst of Fall, wearing a white, glittery top cut low enough to leave little to the imagination, and leather trousers that look sprayed on.

"Collette." I give her a nod. "I hope you're well."

"All the better for seeing you, handsome." She makes an exaggerated show of brushing imaginary dust off my shoulders before stroking down my arms and leaning in to plant an air kiss over each cheek.

"Where's Donny?" I don't return the greeting, instead I move away from her embrace.

She cocks an eyebrow. "Around."

"Well, if you'll excuse me, I'm expecting someone." I turn to walk away.

"You invited a date to your parent's house?"

I don't miss the note of surprise in her voice, and perhaps a hint of jealousy. "Yes, she'll be here any moment."

"Colt..." She sidles back up to me, her breasts pressed against my arm while her hand finds the small of my back.

A knock at the door has my parents' butler, Morris, stride forward to open it. I try to shrug Collette off my arm, but she's a leech, gripping onto me with a tight hold.

Grace walks through the door, laughing alongside her friends until her gaze lands on me. The smile drops and she scowls.

Chapter 17
Grace

The journey to Colt's parent's in Barrington takes a good forty minutes at least, and my nerves are shot to shit the whole way.

Cam and Harley tried to put my mind at ease, but I'm wound tighter than a sixty-five year olds' fourth face lift.

Pulling up outside a huge, gorgeous, brick and limestone house, my nerves vacate for a moment. I am in awe at the sheer size of it. And the outside alone is magnificent. A parking valet opens the door of the limo and we step out, facing the large, columned porch and double front doors.

Knocking, Harley exclaims, "My, my, how the other half lives. I wonder if his dad is happily married to his mother."

I snort a laugh as the door opens and I try to suppress my chuckle, and when I see some slutty brunette trying to shove her tongue down Colt's ear, I have no problems losing the smile.

"Uh-oh," Harl whispers.

Stalking into the parlour, I walk right up to Colt, take gentle hold of his face and plant a soft, lingering kiss on his lips. His body relaxes against me and he wraps an arm around my waist, pulling me in.

"Well, excuse me," the brunette begins.

Parting lips, I utter, "I did." Tilting my head in her direction I glare at her, giving her a quick, wide-eyed 'why are you still here?' look.

We're not going to get on, that much is obvious.

"Colt," she places a hand on his shoulder, "I'll leave you to it."

Taking hold of her hand between thumb and forefinger, I tell her, "You do that."

Looking me up and down, she wrinkles her nose, turns and walks away.

"Friend of yours?" I turn my attention back to Colt, satisfied that I've staked my claim.

"Collette? Not particularly," he starts, "C'mon on, I wanna introduce you to my mom."

And there goes my bravado - right into the pit of my stomach. I swallow past the lump in my throat and accept the hand Colt holds out for me.

"Don't panic," he whispers into my ear, sending delicious tingles to my now moist sex.

Walking through an immaculate, country-kitchen and opulent Edwardian dining room, we exit through sliding doors into the garden - Cam and Harl following. I am further amazed; their garden is huge. It's lakeside with a small pier running off a decline and a fishing boat tied off of it.

Further afield, I see a tree-filled orchard and in front of me is a large patio area lined with three-light, post lanterns, decorative garlands hanging between the fence posts and large, garden heaters dotted intermittently around white-clothed tables and chairs.

There are people everywhere, and I spot that snotty bitch from the parlour talking to an elegant-looking woman in a smart, black pant-suit. Her back is to me, her light-blonde hair swept into a stylish bun, but when she turns to me - prompted by a subtle nod from the tramp - I recognise her features right away.

Colt's mother. Has to be. And no doubt I've already been badmouthed. She walks over, a tight smile on her delicate face.

"Grace, I'd like for you to meet my mother, Delilah."

"Charmed, my darling." Delilah holds a hand out, pulling me in for one of those air kisses I've a feeling I'll need to get used to tonight.

"It's wonderful to meet you, Mrs. Knight. Colt didn't tell me you were British." I try so hard to stop my voice from shaking, but I don't think I'm all that successful. Colt squeezes my hand for assurance.

"Call me, Delilah. That's right, dear, I grew up on a horse farm in Dorset." She offers me a smile, but I think it's a little forced judging by the rigidity of her jaw. "What do you do for a living, Grace?"

"I'm a painter and sculptor," I swallow, bracing myself for the inquisition.

"Mom, I already told you; Grace is kitting out my holiday home," Colt jumps in, smiling through his words.

"So you did, darling." She resumes her assessment of me. "Is there good money in that, Grace?"

Colt tenses beside me, but I answer anyway, "I make enough to live comfortably, and it's something I enjoy doing."

"I couldn't imagine there being much in the way of profit for such a competitive market."

Wow, she's really digging here. "I work from home, so I don't have the added complication of renting a workspace and I have my own website that I promote through social media and word of mouth. It started a struggle, but I had help from two great friends." I look for Cam and Harl, but they're mingling, so I just point them out.

"That's very commendable, Grace. So, what brought you to America?"

Oh, fuck. The dreaded question. I feel Colt squeeze my hand again - he must remember my previous reaction.

"Mother, that's quite enough of the third degree, for now. I'm going to introduce her to Dad."

Delilah forces another smile before she takes a sip of the champagne she grabs from one of the servers. "Very well. I look forward to getting to know you better, Grace."

"You too, Delilah." I follow Colt back into the house. "Fuck me; I don't think I can go through that again with your dad."

Chuckling at me, he plants a gentle kiss on my forehead. "He's not as protective of his first-born, but perhaps I can relax you first." He smiles against my skin before pulling back and looking into my eyes with a devilish wink and a pouting smile.

"Colt--"

"Ssh." He puts a finger to my lips. "Save it. I want you calling out my name just before I make you cum."

Too late! I'm about ready right now and he's only spoken to me. I swipe my tongue across his finger before taking it into my mouth. Colt growls, grasps my hand and drags me toward a large, curving staircase.

***

Colt

When my finger disappears into her warm mouth, I make the executive decision that I'm going to fuck her right now.

Pulling her toward the stairs, I take them two at a time and Grace struggles to keep up while she giggles along the way.

Striding down the open-space hallway, I open the door to my old bedroom, careful to be quiet when I close it behind us. I back her against the door and waste no time. Grasping her hands behind her back in one of mine, I lift her chin with the other, crushing my lips to hers. Her tongue sweeps across my lips and I push my body tight against her.

I part her thighs with my leg and she moans into my mouth before I pull back. "Don't move your hands," I instruct, releasing my hold on her and dropping to my knees.

"Colt... ," she exhales.

"Ssh, try to be quiet." I smile, knowing it'll be difficult for her in a few short moments.

I remove her tan, calf boots and place them to the side. Reaching up, I unzip her pants, trailing them down her soft, creamy legs. Goose bumps pucker her skin and she leans her head back against the wall.

Helping her out of her jeans, I place my hands on her hips, breathing in the musky scent of her sex through her black, satin panties. She's ready for me and I am so fuckin' hard for her because of it.

Through the thin material, I lace my tongue up her quivering mound. Her body bucks and she goes to grab a hold of my head, until she remembers my command. Instead, a soft mewl escapes her lips and her legs dip while she tries to still her trembling body.

Stroking one hand from her hip to her pussy, I slide her underwear aside, blowing light flutters across her glistening cunt. She can't suppress her moans, though she's trying to keep them as quiet as possible. When I dip my tongue into her moist slit, her resolve crumbles. She can't hold back any longer and her legs buckle before a more audible groan rumbles in her throat and slips between her lips. Her hands fly to my hair and she holds me against her.

Stopping, I stand. "What did I tell you, Grace?"

"Please, Colt... ." Her head remains against the wall, her eyes closed.

Cupping her ass, I lift her, her legs wrapping around my waist. I carry her to my four-poster, oak bed and lay her on the powder-blue, damask sheets.

"Don't move," I direct, while she stares at me through hooded eyes.

Stalking toward my wardrobe - where I keep spare clothes in case I stay over - I open the doors, pulling out two of my red ties; the color will accentuate her fiery mane.

Returning, I clamber on the bed, straddling her beautiful, half-naked body. "Give me your arm."

She hesitates at first, before trusting me implicitly, lifting her arm above her head. I tie it to the bed.

"The other," I instruct.

She does so, never taking her eyes off mine.

When she's fixed I place, I unbutton the pink, cotton shirt she's wearing; the swell of her tits heaving with every laboured breath she takes. She's not wearing a bra and my cock stiffens at the sight. Her nipples are hard and I can't resist bending my head and taking each one between my teeth, flicking my tongue over the raised bud.

Grace arches her back into my invasion and moans my name. My balls tighten at the breathy sound she makes.

Sliding my tongue around her breasts, I trail a slick route to her stomach and down to the heady scent of her gorgeous pussy, removing her panties as I go.

Parting her slippery folds, I drag my tongue from the bottom of her glossy opening to her pulsing clit. She writhes against her restraints, her legs drawing up under the intense pressure. I press my tongue harder against her bud and insert two digits into her wet core. She clamps down on me, hard and fast.

"Colt! Please," she cries out, making no effort to mute her pleasure.

Staring up at her, I smile. Her skin is so flushed; I can make it out in the dim moonlight streaming through the window. She's tugging on the ties around her wrists and the sight of her, bound only for me, and my name on her lips while I control every move she makes, sends my pulse racing.

I draw my fingers out of her, slow, stroking, hooking them to tickle her sweet spot. Her body jerks again and her back arches further, trying to slide herself down the bed to dig me in deeper. I plunge back in. Out, in, out, in. She's all but screaming and I move up her body to thrust my tongue between her parted lips.

She moans against me, the vibration sending electric pulses to my already hardened shaft.

Removing my fingers from her pussy, and my tongue from her mouth, I slide my digits between my lips, sucking off her essence. "You taste fucking delicious," I tell her.

She pulls on her restraints and I release her from their hold.

Grabbing my shoulders, she turns me, throwing me down and mounting me.

Wasting no time, she removes my pants, strips me of my shirt and dips into me for a hard, rushed kiss.

With nothing now between us, she rubs the sodden folds of her pussy up and down my cock. I'm aching for her; so hard it hurts. I grab her hips and circle my pelvis into her, the friction hitting her clit while she continues to smear my dick in the flowing juices of her hot sex.

"I need to be inside you, Grace. I want to be buried deep in that tight cunt of yours."

Grabbing the base of my length, she angles herself above me, my swollen head grazing her wet entrance.

She slams down on me, gasping out loud, digging her nails into my chest while she rocks back and forth.

I let out a groan, feeling her walls lock me inside her wet heat. Grabbing her arm, I pull her to me, sinking my tongue between her plump lips, grazing teeth, grasping at the back of her head while she rides me, and I slam into her.

Taking hold of her back, I flip her over, sitting on my haunches and throwing her leg over my shoulder. With a firm grip on her thigh, I plough into her, balls tight and ready to explode - but not before I have her screaming my name.

I push on her pelvis with my palm, circling her clit with my thumb while I bury myself hilt-deep inside her.

She lets out a feral cry; her pussy clamps down on my pulsing cock and I feel her walls vibrate against me before I pump her full of my explosive release.

I fall down next to her, sated and beaming from ear to ear.

She turns to me, breathless and glistening. I place a gentle palm to her cheek before taking her lips to mine. Hot, soft, exploratory.

Smiling against my mouth, she says, "Colt, everyone will be wondering where we are."

"Let them wonder," I utter.

Sitting up, she smiles at me and I can't help but smile back while I rise beside her. I button her shirt, smooth down her hair, then reach for her panties, burying my face in them, inhaling before I get up to dress. I pocket the racy souvenir and flash Grace a cocky half-smile before she dresses and we make our way back downstairs.

Chapter 18
Grace

A glorious ache settles between my legs causing me to smile every time my pussy throbs. Which is every time Colt runs his fingers down my back.

His touch melts me, causes an intoxicating thrill to spiral around my very being.

On the way downstairs, he grabs hold of my hand, linking his fingers with mine. My stomach flutters and I can feel his gaze on me.

"Where've you two been?" A slim, pretty, blonde-haired girl swings round the bannister at the bottom of the stairs. She's beaming ear to ear and staring between me and Colt.

"Farrah, this is Grace. I was showing her some of the views."

"I bet you were," she smirks.

Farrah, the sister. "Hi," I mumble, trying to hide the heat creeping into my cheeks.

"Is that your friend outside, the one with the dark hair and gorgeous figure?"

Ah, another 'straight to the point' Harley, wonderful.

"Who, Cam? Yeah, it is."

She laughs at me, a beautiful sound if I'm honest - infectious. "Oh, Colt. You didn't tell her?" She glares at her brother before turning back to me. "No. Harley, is it?"

"She likes girls," Colt chimes in.

I give him a look using my brow that says, 'no shit, Sherlock,' and he shrugs.

"Put in a good word?" Farrah is animated and excitable. She wags her eyebrows at me and clasps her hands together in prayer.

Laughing, I tell her, "Sure, but I think she's just into guys."

"That's how it always starts." She giggles and runs off.

I turn to Colt, "Wow, bet she's a handful. I love her, she's so funny."

"Handful's about right, but I'd swap funny for annoyingly enthusiastic. She's only twenty though; she'll calm down... I hope." He smiles, so I know he's only playing. "Come on, I'll introduce you to Dad, and Bradley, the other sibling."

***

Colt

I couldn't be happier over Grace and Farrah's introduction. Yes, Farrah wanted the scoop on Harley, but I know my sister and her body language tells me she likes Grace.

She has her own group of snotty friends that I, personally, don't think are good enough for her. They're brats - brought up and fed on money.

My parents are rich, but my mom came from a standard class of living and instils a sense of worth and value into us - we haven't been raised wiping our asses with hundred dollar bills - we know the true value of working for what we earn.

My brother, Bradley, is an accountant. He spent his college years working in bars to pay for his education. My parents agreed they'd pay half if he worked for the rest.

They're doing the same for Farrah - she's studying to be a marine biologist. She teaches piano lessons and horse riding and she's damn good at both. Sadly, riding is how she met the bunch of pretentious, spoiled juveniles she hangs around with.

Leading Grace to my dad's office - I figure he'll still be glued to his computer - I knock on the door.

Sure enough, he's still here when he shouts at me to enter.

"Dad, you got a minute?" I poke my head around the door.

"Sure thing, son. What is it?"

Pulling Grace beside me, I tell him, "There's someone I want you to meet."

He smiles. "Ah, your mother told me you had a lady friend. Come in, come in, have a seat, both of you." Seating ourselves, Dad turns to Grace. "Can I get you something to drink, either of you? Brandy, whiskey?"

"No, thank you, Mr. Knight." Grace declines in a soft, affable voice.

"Oh, dear child, call me Rupert." He pushes a glass of amber liquid toward me, knowing I'll accept.

"So," he starts, "tell me how you two met." He nurses his glass of brandy between two hands.

I turn to Grace and she nods. "She's actually doing some pieces for me for the house in Kenosha."

Coughing out a giggle Grace, pipes up, "That's not quite how we met."

"No, I suppose you're right." I chuckle. "Jovan almost ran her over. I get out the car and she starts hurling abuse at me."

Dad chokes on his sip of brandy. "Did I hear right just then? You almost killed the poor girl?" My dad looks to Grace, laughing while she nods and grins at him. "Well, that's a tale for family dinners. How did it go from near to death to being loved up?"

Love?! *Steady, Dad.* We've only just started seeing one another. You can't love someone that quickly. Can you?

I look at Grace and she's turned a rosy shade of red and she's avoiding my gaze.

Clearing her throat, she answers, "He showed me his boat," and chuckles.

It's my turn to almost choke on my drink and Grace grabs my hand, giving it a squeeze and throwing me a sly smile. So much for dreading meeting my dad – these two will hit it off, no problem.

Dad beams from ear to ear and I think I see him blush, too. "Go on, now." He flicks his hand out tell us to shoo. "You two love birds go enjoy the party, It was lovely to meet you, Grace, you keep my boy on a leash, ya hear?"

"Yes, sir." She smiles between the two of us before we leave.

"Not as bad, huh?" I take her hand and lace our fingers together. "Not too intimidated this time around I gathered?"

"Your dad's less scary than your mom." She beams.

Her smile is perfect. I return it before pulling her to my chest and planting a wistful kiss on her lips. Her tongue caresses my bottom lip with the lightest of touches while her hand comes up to stroke my jaw.

"Careful, Grace. There are still many other places I can take you."

She smiles against my lips. "Promises, promises."

Growling, I go to lift her until a voice rings out behind me, "Put her down, bro. You'll get a name for yourself... oh, wait... you've been there, done that."

My jaw tenses. *Bradley.* Cocky little bastard.

Spinning, I clap eyes on the snarky fucker. "Bradley, this is Grace."

"I'm honoured, we all are." He looks at Grace and winks. "First time he's bought a plaything home, you must be a good fuck."

"Bradley!" I admonish, scowling at him.

He stumbles into the dining table, *drunk*, shocking. "Who's the hot little number in the garden. Brunette, pert ass, slamming body, fabulous tits? I'd love to slip my dick in that."

Grace tenses beside me. "That's my friend, Harley. I'll be sure to warn her away from you, you mouthy little shit."

I can't suppress the grin breaking across my face. Their loyalty to one another is refreshing. And hearing someone mouth back at my little brother is hilarious.

Bradley doesn't say another word, just staggers away grinning like an idiot.

"I'm sorry about him." I turn to Grace, grabbing her hand again. "He could never handle his liquor."

"I used to work in a late-night coffee shop," she smiles, "I'm used to drunken arseholes filtering in after hours."

Her smile is one of contented remembrance and I realise this is the first time she's said anything about her past without being prompted. Her smiles soon disappears, though - a painful afterthought, perhaps?

"Come on." I pull her toward the garden. "We'll grab a drink, then go somewhere private."

***

Grace

What an insolent, conceited little prick. If Colt weren't in the room - or related to the smarmy fucker - I'd have smacked him around the mouth. *How fuckin' rude.*

I don't care that Colt has a past - hell, everyone has a past, I'd be a fine one to talk - but to talk about my best friend in such a demeaning manner, and behind her back no less. Well, the bastard's lucky I didn't introduce my foot to his balls.

Outside, the fresh air is a welcome companion - the burning anger filtering with the slight breeze.

Looking for Harley, I spot Farrah talking to her - flirting with her eyes and hands; poor Harl none the wiser. Chuckling to myself, I tap Colt on the arm and point in their direction.

"She got there first, then." He grins.

"Wait here, I won't be a minute," I instruct him.

Power-walking toward my friend, she notices me and smiles. "Grace, this is Farrah--"

"We've met." I give Colt's sister an 'I know your game' kinda smile and ask if I can borrow Harley for a second - she nods.

Pulling Harl off to one side, I warn her, "Watch out for Colt's brother, Bradley. He's a filthy little fucker after one thing, and one thing only." I have to giggle when she salutes her understanding. "By the way, Farrah has the hots for you, but she's not a disgusting creep, so I'll leave you to it." I pat her shoulder, grin at her wide-eyed stare and wander back to my waiting man.

Not more than five meters away from him, I spy something that makes my stomach turn.

That slutty bitch, Collette has her hands all over Cam. What is it with perverted, promiscuous degenerates tonight? I feel like a goddamn babysitter.

Stalking over, I grab Cam and pull him away, throwing Collette a honeyed smile while she glares at me with her hands on her hips.

"What the fuck, Gracie?"

Once out of earshot, I tell him, "Stay away from her, Cammy, she's bad news. She's a dirty tramp and her rich, surgeon, old-man boyfriend is around here somewhere."

He nods at me, "I'm not gonna sleep with her, Gray-bo. I've watched her practically hit on everything here."

"Good." I smile at him and give him a little punch on the arm. "She's not good enough for you, anyway."

"Aww thanks, Gracie." He feigns shyness by batting his eyelids and skipping about like a school kid.

"Fool," I laugh.

Leaving him to it, I turn to see Colt in deep conversation with some middle-aged man, and I decide to head indoors for another drink rather than disturb him just yet.

Walking through to the kitchen, I spot Collette hovering around the canapés. I afford her a somewhat stoic glance before I grab a glass of champagne,

"Think you're something special, don't you?" Her voice is callous.

"I'm not letting you ruin my night, Collette. Stay away from the men in my life; you're poison and I won't let you taint my friends with your toxic shit."

"Watch who you're talking to, I'd hate--"

"You know what?" I'm sick of her shit already and I don't even know her. "I don't wanna hear it. Keep your snide remarks, your loose morals and your over-priced, under-rated plastic body parts to yourself. No-one's interested."

A muffled chortle sounds through her nose. "Once he's bored of you, he'll kick you aside like all the others."

"And you think that'll be your cue to get back in, huh? Way I see it, darlin', according to your logic, he's had you, too, and ditched your worthless arse, so go cry your crocodile tears to someone who gives a shit." I turn away from her, her face is insulting me.

"I know your game," she snipes, "you're after his money--"

"That's the pot calling the kettle black, sweetheart, don't you think?" I turn and laugh in her face. "Aren't you just fucking your way around this social circle to see who will pay for your next nose job?"

The sting from her slap shoots through my face and my glass falls to the floor, smashing into a thousand pieces.

Glaring at the overbearing bitch, I pull my fist back and launch it at her face, hearing her nose pop under the impact.

"Grace!" Harley comes rushing over to drag me away before I really do the slut some damage.

Bradley is with her, still drunk and still pissing me off every bit as much.

Collette latches on to him, her hand covering her nose. "Bradley, baby, I think she broke my nose. We should call the police. Will you take me to get it seen to?"

I can't believe what I'm seeing. She's pawing all over him like she wasn't just trying it on with about six or seven other guys before him.

Her nose has started to bleed, though, and it's dribbling down her sparkling, white top.

"Don't be fucking stupid, Collette, he's drunk," I remind them both.

"Don't talk to me, you barbaric fool."

How mature. Dozy bint. "Fine, whatever, but he's not taking you anywhere. I'll have Colt fetch your *boyfriend*. Can you remember which one he is?" Smiling, I head outside.

Hearing her mumble something indecent behind me, I smile wider before I walk out the patio doors.

Colt approaches me. "I've been looking for you, babe. Where you been?"

"I had a heart to heart with Collette. Speaking of which, where's her boyfriend, I think she needs to go home. She's bleeding."

"Sorry?" He does a double-take, glaring at me with wide eyes.

Shrugging, I tell him, "I ran into her palm, she ran into my fist, what more can I say?"

Laughing at me, he slides his arm around my shoulder. "Come on, we better tell Donny she walked into a door." He takes a moment to let something sink in before continuing. "Careful of her Grace, she'll wage a personal vendetta against you, now."

"Let her try," I counter. "I'm not some snotty, suburban, rich tart; I'm a London city bitch and I grew up having to take care of number one. Whatever she's got, I've had worse."

He smirks at me, but if only he knew the truth.

Chapter 19
Colt

Attempting a smile, I wonder what she means by that statement - concerned, my thoughts turn murderous over the notion someone hurt her.

And I'll kill them if they did.

I also worry Collette will try to dish out some of her childish, revenge bullshit. I've no doubt Grace could take care of herself, but I don't want to see her suffer at the hands of someone who sulks when she doesn't get her own way. Collette can be a vindictive bitch.

Walking into the kitchen, I stifle a laugh. Bradley is squinting at Collette's bloody nose while she dabs at it with a handkerchief. She's beginning to get bruising beneath both eyes, courtesy of the swelling and I can't help but feel a little delighted at her just desserts.

In pain and bleeding she may be, but she is fawning all over my brother like there's no-one around to see it - rubbing her thighs off his dick, stroking his arms, fisting his hair. The girl's got a broken fuckin' nose, for God's sake, and still she can't keep help but whore herself out.

Clearing my throat in an exaggerated manner, I say to her, "Collette, take your hands off my brother, go find Donny and get yourself cleaned up."

"Your *bitch* did this to me and I'm going to press charges," she snarls, scowling at Grace beside me.

"You'll do no such thing; you assaulted her first, I'm fairly certain Harley saw... " I turn to Harley and she nods her head.

"Like fuck she did." The airs and graces vanish and Collette's face turns an ugly shade of crimson.

I turn to my brother. "Bradley, go find Donny and tell him Collette's walked into a door. Stupid girl's too drunk to be wandering aimlessly around; she needs to go home and get fixed up."

"Just you wait, Colt. I'll--"

"You'll what, Collette, hmm? Try to have me shut down again? Fuck my brother behind my back? Or, wait, perhaps you'll try it on with my dad instead. Or trash my car, or put my apartment windows through, or badmouth me to every fuckwit who'll listen. Give it a rest, Collette, it's getting old."

She stares at me, mouth flapping open and closed like a fish out of water.

Donny appears at my side. "What the hell happened to you?" He sounds pissed off - doesn't want to leave the party, no doubt.

Looking between me and Grace, Collette frowns and mumbles, "I walked into a door." She pouts and averts her gaze to the tiled floor.

Letting out a hefty sigh, Donny stands aside. "Come on, get your coat, we'd best go home and sort you out."

Once out of sight, Harley high-fives Grace, and the two stumble about, giggling.

Grace turns to me. "I'm sorry about that, baby, but the bitch had it comin'."

"You've nothing to apologise for. I know many people who'd offer to buy you a drink after that." I return the smile she throws my way. "What d'ya say we get outta here, go back to yours and have an early night?"

"Sounds like a plan."

Turning to Harley, I offer, "You can stay if you want, I'll send Jovan back for you."

"If you don't mind," she responds.

"Not at all. I'll send him back here the moment we get in."

Heading for the door, Grace goes to say goodbye to Cam, kisses Harl and leads me by the hand to my waiting limo.

***

Grace

I don't think I'll be forgetting tonight in a hurry - for several reasons. All of which cause a cheeky smile to pull at my lips.

Colt has a quick word with Jovan to tell him what the plan for tonight is, then we climb in the back of the limo and he puts his arm around my shoulders while I cuddle into his chest.

I've still got adrenaline coursing through my veins and I need to release it.

I know the perfect way.

With a grin only I know is there, I trail my forefinger up Colt's thigh.

Shuddering under my light touch, he whispers in my ear, "Be careful, sweetheart. I'm not averse to fucking you right here in my car."

My insides clench at the words tickling against the prickling flesh of my head. I look up at him, bite my lip and wink. A growl rumbles in his chest and he presses a button on a panel above his head. The privacy window closes between us and Jovan.

Trying to control the moment, Colt shifts. I place my hand against his chest, pushing back, and I shake my head.

Through hooded eyes, he stares at me, a curved smile tugging at the corner of his mouth. He sits back and I move to straddle him.

His erection is pressing against my tender clit and sparks surge through my core while I grind against his solid cock.

Grasping the back of my head, he pulls me down, smashing his lips against mine in an onslaught of clashing teeth and wet, writhing tongues.

I slide my hand down his toned abs and cup his heavy balls. He hisses into my mouth and sucks my tongue between his lips.

I'm lost in the moment. His fervency stokes a fire between my thighs and I rip his shirt open, parting from his kiss to run my moistened lips down every hard ridge of his sculpted torso.

Staring at his beautiful face, I smile when he tilts his head back against the seat, his hands fisting my hair while I lower myself to the floor, unbuckling his trousers.

I part the material of his jeans and notice he neglected to replace his underwear after this evening's activities. His thick length springs free, resting against the rise and fall of his stomach. He looks to me again, swallows hard and implores me with wide, glistening eyes.

Taking the base of his shaft in my palm, I slide my tongue across his seeping, silky head. His excitement blazes a trail along my bottom lip and he throbs against me. His hands tighten in my hair and he groans, sinking his head back against the leather.

Driven by his lusty response, I glide my tongue from his balls to his swollen, bulbous head, circling my tongue around the tip.

"Grace...," he whispers on an unsteady breath.

Smiling against him, I part my lips and slide them down - deliberate, slow - licking, devouring each inch of his throbbing dick until he is buried at the back of my throat.

"Oh, fuck," he hisses through clenched teeth.

I draw him out of my mouth only to guide him back in, over and over, sweeping my tongue, sucking the essence leaking from him.

He's pulling at my hair with both hands, thrusting himself further into my eager mouth. I tighten my hold on him, gliding my hand up and down his moistened cock while I suck him in and out.

Pushing me away with amiable force, he reaches down, unzips my jeans and tugs me out of them before pulling me back toward him.

Lifting me on his lap, he impales me on his steel shaft, his hands positioned in the middle of my back, supporting me, angling while he thrusts into me, fast, deep.

I scream his name and claw at his shoulders, digging into the exposed skin where his shirt has fallen away, aware of every pulsing inch of him filling me, stroking my walls until I can't take the friction any longer.

Throwing myself against his chest - burying my head in his neck - I bite down on his shoulder before my body begins to convulse. My hips buck, plunging him deeper into my trembling pussy, causing fresh waves of euphoric bliss to crash through me.

Feeling his cock swell inside me, I rock back and forth, riding out my orgasm before he cries out, grips me tight and empties his seed into me.

His body loosens and I relax against him and a breath escapes his lips to warm the skin of my neck. His chest heaves against mine before his breathing evens out and he pulls me away, cupping my face.

"You amaze me, Grace Morgan."

I have no time to respond when he plants a tender kiss on my swollen lips.

***

Colt rouses me from the slumber I must've slipped into. My body isn't used to so much activity in so little time. I ache all over.

Offering him a sleepy smile, he helps me out the car, thanks Jovan and sends him back to Barrington.

Linking arms, I rest my head on his shoulder while we climb the stairs to my apartment.

I hand Colt the keys when he asks and he lets us both in. The flat is warm because we put the heating on before we left, and the autumn chill starts to seep out of my bones. The nights are getting colder and, even though I'm from England, I still don't like feeling the nip. Cosiness is what it's all about when it gets to this time of year – cosiness and lots of hot chocolate, sitting in thick jumpers that are at least three sizes too big.

"Do you want a warm drink?" I ask.

"Sounds good to me. How about we order something to eat, too?"

The man is a God send and I smile while I nod. "Pizza?"

"Pizza," he agrees, digging his phone out of his pocket.

I put the kettle on while he orders, then I spoon some cocoa powder into two large mugs and wait.

Entranced by the steam rising, I flinch when Colt wraps his arms around my waist and leans his chin on my shoulder.

"I ordered a large cheese with fries; you OK sharing?"

I can't hide the smile, even if plain cheese is a little boring. "Absolutely," I tell him. "You wanna watch a movie?"

He smiles against my neck. "Only if we get to burn off the pizza after it's finished." He flicks his tongue against my earlobe and pulls it between his teeth.

"You're insatiable, Mr. Knight." I chuckle while my skin puckers.

"You have no idea, Ms. Morgan," he purrs.

Slapping my arse, he tells me to get a move on with the drinks and I call him a cheeky bastard and tell him to pick a movie while I point him in the direction of the vast collection of DVDs we own between the three of us. I also add that it cannot be a chick flick – I fucking hate chick flicks. Horror and action are my preferences – give me a Bruce Willis film any second of any day.

"Con Air?" he shouts through.

Nicholas Cage – close enough. "Sounds like a plan," I yell back, lifting the two freshly-made mugs of hot chocolate before making my way into the living room.

He's certainly making himself at home. I take a moment to admire his tight arse while he bends to put the DVD in. He then sits on the sofa and acquaints himself with the remote controls before slipping off his shoes and tucking his feet underneath him.

"Comfy?" I ask him with a smile, placing our drinks on the coffee table.

He responds with a grin of his own, patting the seat beside him and manoeuvring himself so that we can cuddle in close.

"Who's your favourite actor?" I ask him, when I'm comfortably nestled against him.

Stroking my arm, he tells me, "I like a few, but I love Nicholas Cage, as well as Tom Hanks and Denzel Washington."

Commendable choices and I tell him as much. "Bruce Willis is my favourite; I've seen every movie with him in it."

"I approve." He kisses the top of my head and I can feel his smile.

"Well, I'm so glad about that." I tilt my head up and he plants another, warm kiss on my forehead. "Do you get time to watch many movies? You must be really busy running all your businesses."

"I don't watch anywhere near as much as I used to. I do work a lot; I barely have time for anything else."

That statement concerns me a little and I frown at him.

"Until you came along," he rushes, "I love spending time with you."

OK, I feel a little bit better now. "I'm not stopping you from doing your job, am I?"

He pulls me in tighter. "No, baby, of course you're not. I employ teams of people to make sure everything is ticking over as it should be." He hesitates for a moment and then carries on. "I only worked as much as I did because there was nothing better for me to be doing."

My heart lurches and I turn, kneeling in front of him. He looks deep into my eyes, so deep I'm almost scared that he can see right into my soul and for a flicker of a moment, I panic.

"I--"

He stops me from making a fool of myself by tracing his thumb across my bottom lip, then he draws me to him and kisses me with the softest of touches.

Heart racing, I run my hands up his chest and cup his face, deepening his kiss, probing his mouth with my tongue. He tastes smooth and delicious, but as I straddle him to get things moving, there's a knock at the door.

"Shit," I sigh. Damn the pizza delivery guy and his bad timing. "I'll get it."

Colt moves and I stifle a giggle at the large bulge in his trousers. "I'll readjust and then fetch us some plates," he offers, winking at me.

With a wide smile, I walk to the door and open it. There's no-one there, but there is an envelope taped to the door. *Strange.* I pull it off and unseal it while Colt wanders into the kitchen for cutlery.

Slipping out the contents, my blood freezes. My face goes numb and my whole body lurches. My legs buckle and I'm about to collapse.

Sprinting to the toilet, I reach it just in time before my legs give out. I launch myself over the bowl and hurl the contents of my stomach into it.

"Grace?" I can hear Colt's footsteps hurrying down the corridor.

Slamming the door shut with my foot, I reach up and lock it.

Colt knocks. "Grace, is everything OK?"

I can't find the strength to answer. My throat has closed, my body is trembling and there's nothing I can do to stop it. Hot tears gush down my cheeks, mingling with the cold sweat taking over me, my body still heaving from the shock.

I lean against the bath and look to the floor where I dropped the envelope; to the photograph that sends my crumbling mind hurtling back two years.

The glossy smiles of Garrett and Frankie stare back at me.

Chapter 20
Colt

I bang on the door. I can hear Grace crying and being sick and it's tearing at me. I don't know what's happened, I feel helpless and she won't let me in.

Instead, she keeps yelling at me to go home, that she's no good for me and I'll end up getting hurt. Sweeps of nausea churn my stomach at her words. *What is she talking about?* A few minutes ago, everything was great, and now...

I'm not leaving her. She needs me, and I her - more than I've realised before tonight.

"Grace." I bang on the door with my fists. "Grace, please. Open the door; I need to know that you're OK."

Ten minutes has passed and I'm still getting nowhere with her. But then her sobbing subsides and I hear movement before the door unlocks. I'm about to barge in, but she comes hurtling out. She runs straight into her room. I follow and watch her grab a suitcase from the wardrobe, shoving clothes and such like inside.

"Grace, what are you doing? Talk to me." I stride toward her, placing a hand on her arm, trying to quell my panic as well as hers.

She jumps and stares at me. Her face is tear-stained and so very pale and her eyes wide, red and puffy.

"You have to go, Colt. Steer clear of me," she gushes, her words quivering.

When she turns back to her packing, I notice an envelope sticking out of her pocket and my stomach tightens. Is this Collette's doing? Miles perhaps? I swallow, hard. "Grace, you have to tell me what's going on, why--"

"I don't have to tell you shit!" she screams.

I balk at the vehemence woven through her words. "Grace. Stop this, you're acting crazy." I spy the envelope again and I know I have to ask. "What's in that envelope?"

She stops. Her head turns to me and she looks petrified. Her eyes are bulging, and fresh tears course down her pallid cheeks. She shakes her head. "I can't... he knows... I need to get away--"

"Who's *he,* Grace? Tell me, please. I want to help. Who are you running away from?" I want so badly to touch her, to reassure her. But I don't know what's wrong, so I don't know how to help her.

"I can't tell you, Colt. I'm so sorry. You should walk away. I have to leave." Her words are hurried, frightened and shaky.

"No!" I grab her shoulders. "I'm not letting you walk away from me, sweetheart. Tell me what's wrong. I can help."

She shaking when she breathes, "You can't. No-one can help."

Spying the envelope again, and seeing that her guard is down, I grab for it and yank it free. It's callous of me, but I have to know what's causing this.

"No! Colt, don't." She reaches for me, but I move out the way.

It's a crumpled photograph and I unravel it to see two men smiling at the camera. One is portly in face, beady eyes, a greying beard and a bald head. The other is gangly, missing teeth, grim features.

Turning back to Grace, she collapses, falling into a crumpled, sobbing heap on the floor. I rush to her, crouching in front.

Taking a careful hold of her face, I urge her to look at me. "Has one of them hurt you?"

Folding herself into my chest, she bursts into a fresh bout of tears, heaving against me while her body convulses through her pain. I wrap my arms around her, stroke her hair and whisper to her that I'm going nowhere - I'll help her in any way I can.

I'm broken seeing her like this. I don't know what to do to bring back my brazen spitfire. She's damaged and I want to fix things for her, but I don't know how. It angers me that someone has done this to her - caused her so much pain she felt she needed to run away – broken her down in such a way she's sick with fear.

Her body trembles against me, but she pushes herself off my chest and looks at me.

"Why?"

That one word pulls at me with fierce potency and I realise, in that moment, why I want to help her. It's sudden and fast and it powers through me with all the finesse of a raging bull, but I can't deny it now. "I love you, Grace." And I do, I really do.

This woman makes me feel things I've never experienced in the past. Before tonight, her very being astounded me - her fire, her vitality, her passion. The chase was a game, but the prize at the end opened my eyes and careened into me full force.

My words pull a slight smile at the corner of Grace's mouth, but her inner turmoil takes over and she weeps.

"Move in with me. Whoever you're running from, he won't find you there. My building is secure; I'll protect you."

"Colt.... ." She puts her hand on my chest and my heart rate beats with rapid fury. "What about Harley and Cam? He'll hurt them to get to me. I can't leave them."

Her eyes are wide, imploring, begging me to understand her situation without giving me the details. "I have somewhere they can stay," I advise her, "a house in Westchester. It's nothing fancy, but they're welcome to use it as long as they need to."

Throwing her arms around me, she sobs into my neck. I stroke her back and her hair and tell her again, things will be OK. I just hope it's the truth.

Grace

He loves me. Colt Knight - playboy, millionaire, game-player - loves *me*.

His words choked me up, and I couldn't respond. I wouldn't have known what to say had it even possible. Do I deserve love?

I murdered someone. I'm a killer. Killers don't warrant the love of a powerful, gorgeous, caring man. They deserve punishment, misery... prison.

How do I tell this man what I did two years ago? Will he still love me, then?

He hasn't pushed me to tell him anything too detailed - he has no idea what I did - yet here he is, offering to help me and my two crazy friends on good faith.

I want to tell him what happened; I want him to understand what my life was like - what I needed to do in order to survive - what I did that night to save my own life. But the words catch in my throat and, instead, I want to be sick again. I don't want him to look at me in disgust or fear. I crave his loving touch, the glint in his eye when he stares at me with longing. If I lose that now, I'll break.

I nod at him. I'll need to think of a way to tell Cam and Harley without reliving the worst experience of my life. I can't lose them either - they are my world, my reason for being, the only two people in my entire life that have shown me compassion, understanding and unconditional love and support. Without them, I am nothing - I go back to being Grace Emery; poor, foolish, degenerate murderer.

Garrett isn't taking away everything I've worked this hard to achieve.

Moving toward my suitcase, something dawns on me and I freeze up all over again. Exactly how did Garrett find me?

***

Climbing into the taxi, Colt lifts my bags into the trunk and we set off to his apartment on East Lake Shore Drive.

It's not been ten minutes before we are pulling up alongside Colt's building. I'm surprised at just how close he lives to me and if my stomach didn't want to hurl its contents all over the car, I'd be more excited about it.

Handing the driver some notes, Colt exits the car, holding out his hand for me to follow.

The 1920's Penthouse building is beautiful and when we walk into the glossed-wood, parquet floored foyer, I forget for a moment who I am and why I am here.

The concierge greets Colt in a light, professional manner and Colt explains to him that I will be staying for as long as I need to, and to get a keycard made for me. Nodding his approval, the concierge welcomes me to the building with a warm handshake.

Grabbing my hand, Colt leads me to the elevator where he swipes his card over the I.D. system and we ascend. When we step into his luxury apartment, I am gobsmacked. It's gorgeous. Pristine-white walls, leather, chrome. Warm woods, rich colour. There's a variety of styles spread between the rooms I can see.

"I... erm... sleeping arrangements, would you... ?"

For the first time since finding that photograph, a smile plays across my features. "I think we're a little past separate bedrooms, if that's what you're getting at, Colt."

Beaming back at me, he takes my bag and me to his master bedroom.

The room is elegant. White-wood panels beneath warm, coffee-coloured walls, a cream suite with chocolate cushions, and a dark-wood, four poster bed. The walls are decorated with tasteful canvases in similar, rich colours and an off-white, shag pile rug lies in front of a white-wood framed fireplace.

"I'll put your things in the walk-in wardrobe." He walks toward one of two doors toward the back of the room, pointing to the other. "The bathroom is in there. Please, make yourself at home, Grace; I want you to feel comfortable here."

An overwhelming sensation surges through me and tears begin to slip from my eyes, coursing down my cheeks. Colt drops my bag and rushes toward me, grabbing me and pulling me into his warm body.

"I'm s-sorry," I stammer, "I don't deserve this."

Taking hold of my shoulder, he pulls me back, looking into my eyes. "Please, let me in, Grace. Maybe not tonight, but let me help you. I want to help you."

Nodding, I remind him, "We should call Harl and Cam, let them know to come here before they go home."

"I've already spoken to Jovan. He will tell them they're making a stop beforehand; that you want to see them."

Swallowing past the lump in my throat, I take a deep breath and prepare myself for the moment that could make or break everything good in my life.

Chapter 21
Grace

I've been wearing a hole in the lounge carpet for the best part of an hour when the elevator pings the arrival of my friends.

Colt rises from the sofa where he's been sitting, watching me, trying to get me to calm down. If only he understood the chaos screaming through my mind and the sickness turning my stomach.

Harl comes rushing through the lounge and straight for me, throwing her arms around me and pulling me close. "Oh, Gracie, what's happened?" She leans back, looking at me with tears in her eyes.

The guilt at the sight of her punches me in the gut. I've put my friends' lives in danger and I don't expect they'll forgive me for what I am about to tell them. I want to keep it bottled in, I don't want to lumber them with the shit I've done. I'm ashamed, a disgrace and I don't need to be dragging good people down with me.

But I have no choice. Garrett knows where I am - or at least someone does, and my friends have been exposed to the degrading life I once lived.

My moment of strength fails me and I collapse, Harl keeping me up with her arms while she settles me on the sofa. For so long, I've remained strong – at least on the outside. I've battled my inner demons and, although I've spent some years looking over my shoulder, I think a part of me never actually thought Garrett would find me. I thought the past was buried.

"I can't... I can't do this. You'll hate me; you'll never wanna see me again." I burst into tears and Harl holds me to her while Cam sits beside me, placing a gentle palm on my shoulder.

He rubs my arms up and down. "Gracie, we love you, we're here for you. Whatever this is you're going through, we're not going anywhere."

"Amen to that," Harl adds. "Come on, baby. You can tell us anything."

Sobbing subsiding, I pull away, drying my eyes with the back of my hand and staring at my friends. I know they mean well with their words, but they'll think so differently of me once I tell them. I'm shaking from head to toe and I can't stop it for the life of me; I feel so cold and the beginning of a headache is gnawing at the base of my skull.

Graceful Damnation

Colt, bless his soul, brings over a bottle of wine and three glasses, a bottle of whiskey for himself. He's having a laugh if he thinks wine's gonna cut it - I take the whiskey and pour myself two fingers before gulping it down in one. He pours me another and pushes it toward me, taking a seat opposite the three of us.

Running my hands through my hair and down my face, trembling and struggling to breathe, I take a deep breath. "Two years ago... I killed someone."

***

Colt

Shaking like a leaf, Grace knocks back a double shot of whiskey. I pour her another and sit back, praying she finds the strength to tell us what happened to her; what's causing her so much anguish.

I can't stand that she's going through this and feels the need to go it alone. I don't even know what this is, but I made a promise to her and I'm not about to cut and run over something that happened in her past. We all have a past, and something so dreadful made Grace run from hers. The thought alone makes my blood boil.

I told her I loved her, and I meant it. If something or someone is causing her pain, I want to know who or what, so I can chase the fuckers down and squeeze the fucking life out of them. I'm prepared to hunt, maim and kill for this woman.

What I am not prepared for, are the words that come out of her mouth;

"Two years ago... I killed someone."

The world stands still. Grace's eyes well up and tears slip down her pale face. But she doesn't break down - she sits up straight and stares at us one by one with doe-eyed expression.

Gulping down my whiskey, I resolve myself to hearing her out. The suffering she's gone through tonight comes from somewhere - and it involves those two shits in that picture; I know it does. I know you should never judge a book by its cover, but something about the look of them tells me they're bad news.

My brain is still telling me that someone hurt her and that someone needs to fucking pay.

Harley's face has paled and she looks ready to throw up, Cam is staring at her, wide-eyed with shock.

Taking another breath, Grace continues.

***

Grace

I tell them everything. It kills me, but I have to do it.

I go into detail about my old life, telling them about the death of my parents, how my aunty abandoned me because she couldn't cope, the foster homes I grew up in, the abuse and the bullying I received off the parents and kids. I tell them about the disgusting, insect-infested shelters I stayed in when no-one else would care for me, of the jobs I flitted through - getting fired for stealing food and money to survive.

It takes everything in me not to break down when I explain how I almost ended up sleeping with men for money. I have to stop on several occasions to calm my quaking nerves, and swallow down the bile clawing up my throat.

Taking another large gulp of whiskey, I continue, describing how I felt the first night on the streets. A cold, wet night; my body shivering from the freezing October air, made worse because of the mini skirt and halter top I wore underneath a meagre, fake-fur coat.

"My feet ached from the skyscraper heels I wore and all I wanted to do was sleep. But then a car pulled up, a decent car by all accounts and a man called me over to his open window." I gulp, hard, trying desperately to keep the stinging tears at bay. "He asked me how much and I told him the varying prices for hand jobs, blow jobs, sex with or without a condom. I felt disgusted with myself and so ashamed; I wanted to die." Both then and now as I relive the horrific nightmare.

"My body shook throughout the whole conversation with the punter, and not just from the bite in the air. I couldn't believe my life had sunk so low.

H-he asked for a blow job," I cringe at the memory, "and I was about to get in his car when a man ran up, yanking the driver's side door open and pulling the man from his vehicle. I watched while he kicked the guy in the face, smashing his nose and shattering his cheek bones; yelling and shouting about some money he owed.

He stamped on the man's knees, kicked him in the groin and pummelled his ribs with his fists. I tried to run, tried to scream, but fear rooted me to the spot." I clench my fists together because my shaking has worsened, to the point where my teeth are almost chattering.

Harley moves closer and wraps her arm around my shoulders before I continue. I can see tears in her eyes, and I can't bear to look at the others because I will break down.

Clearing my throat, I tell them, "The man stopped his vicious assault and stalked over to me, telling me his name; Garrett Phillips. He asked me why I put myself through this, that the street was no place for a woman like me and then he offered me a place to stay.

He took me to his flat, told me I'd have to share the one bedroom with him, but he didn't force himself on me, not at first. I felt I owed him for taking me off the streets."

This is where it gets difficult for me; where the real shit began. I swallow again, my throat is bone dry and so I take another gulp of whiskey, relishing the burn down my throat before I tell them what happened a week after moving in to Garrett's.

"His friends came over and Garrett thought I fancied one of them, accused me of flirting with him, taking advantage of his giving nature and all he did for me. He punched me in the face right in front of everyone." I hang my head with the shame and Harl chokes back a gasp, clutching me tighter. "When I fell to the floor, he smashed his foot into my ribs and kicked my hand with steel toe-capped boots, breaking my fingers." I pause, downing yet another double measure of the amber liquid Colt has poured me. My body is trembling and my voice quakes when I thank him.

They haven't run, and I'm thankful for it, but they don't know everything, yet.

I recount the moment I got the job in Ivan's coffee shop.

Garrett ruled my life, beat me almost daily, took what he wanted when he wanted from my body - regardless of my protests. But when Ivan offered me a job at his shop, I took it. I needed to cling on to a small part of my independence and he offered me the opportunity.

"Garrett beat the fuck out of me over it, until he realized he could use me to sell his drugs. And I agreed because I was too scared to say no."

The next part I have to divulge is the night I have tried for two years to forget. Two years of attempting to rid myself of Frankie's flailing body, his blood pumping from the gaping wound in his neck.

I can't drink any more whiskey; the sickly-sweet taste is clinging to my throat. Harl pours me a glass of wine when I pause to run my hands through my hair. I accept with a sad smile and tears in my eyes.

Turning to her, I notice her tear-stained face. She's stopped holding them in and she looks at me with so much sadness and compassion in her doe-eyes that I break down again and sob into my hand. She takes my glass off me and wraps me in her comforting embrace. Cam's arms encircle us both and he squeezes so tight I almost can't breathe.

Extracting myself, I look down to Colt's crouched form in front of me. He rubs my knees before placing a warm hand on my cheek. I lean into his gentle touch, closing my eyes, letting the last of my tears fall before I turn their worlds upside down.

Grasping his hand, I move it onto my lap, tightening my hold when I tell them, "Two years ago, I got home late from work. It wasn't the first time and Garrett beat me like he always did. He'd been taking drugs all day, him and his friend, Brass and cousin, Frankie. He fell asleep in his chair and I made my way to the bathroom to inspect the bruise on my face from his fist.

Frankie came looking for me, pushed me further into the bathroom when I tried to get away. He smashed my head off the mirror and threw me against the bathtub when I refused to suck him off." I pause, taking a deep breath, trying so hard to hold back more tears threatening to spill. "He slapped me and punched me, over and over, then he ripped my knickers away from me and tried to shove his dick in me. The fucker attempted to rape me." I can't look anyone in the eye when I say the words out loud. I feel so dirty and ashamed – still to this day.

Colt growls, an animalistic sound rumbling deep in his chest.

I stroke the back of his hand, taking a deep breath before continuing, "I've never been so scared in my entire life. When Garrett used to... ya know... I would lie there; I knew what he wanted and I was too afraid to fight back because I knew it was coming, regardless. B-but when Frankie... ." I take another deep breath and swallow hard. "I saw the glass shard from the mirror beside me and I grabbed for it." I turn my palm over, fingering the scar there - the constant reminder of what I did. "I stabbed him in the neck and I watched him die, and I did nothing to help him. I felt glad he was dying; he was a bad, bad man." I rush my words, trying to justify my actions while silently praying they don't leave me to face this alone any more. "He raped young teenagers and other women; he was a sick, twisted fuck. But it was me that took his life, and I had no right to do that. I killed him. I killed him and I ran."

I can't talk any more - I've said everything I needed to say and my body is drained. I slump against Harley and I cry. I cry until my eyes are sore and my throat is dry and still I carry on.

Colt's voice stills my sobs and with his words, I know I love him more than I could ever describe. "If he's after you, Grace, I'll kill him before he gets a chance to lay a finger on you. Do you understand me? If I see the fucker, I'll put a bullet in his chest."

Chapter 22
Colt

Every single one of my senses is on fire. Nerve endings ignite and burn a fiery blaze around my body. My muscles tense and I grind my teeth together.

I want to kill the motherfucker - rip him limb from limb and watch him bleed to death in front of me.

Grace struggles with the recollection of every devastating memory and I want to hold her so bad. But she needs to get everything off her chest and she needs to know her friends are behind her every step of the way.

When she tells us of Frankie's murder, my stomach plummets. Someone knows about it and now they're watching her, scaring her, but to what end?

Does Garrett know? He has to, where would the picture have come from? There's someone behind this and I need to find out who and put a stop to it before he gets his hands on her. And when I find the person responsible for bringing this shit back to haunt her, I will personally fuck them up so bad they need to breathe through a machine for the rest of their natural fucking lives.

Grace leans back against the sofa – she looks exhausted – I don't let go of her hands.

"Guys," I begin, getting Harley and Cam's attention, "Grace received a photo from someone. It was stuck to your apartment door, so we think someone's watching her."

Harley's eyes widen and she puts her hands to her mouth. "But... ," she utters.

"I have a place you can stay. You should go tonight, I'll have someone bring your things to you, but the place is fully kitted out."

"Thank you, Colt." She places a hand on my shoulder.

I force a smile. "I'll make sure one of my security detail follow you wherever you need to go. Don't worry; we'll get the bastard before he can do anything."

***

Harley and Cam leave for Westchester with Jovan and Dmitry, after they make sure Grace knows they are there for her every step of the way, no matter what.

My girl is exhausted and she soon falls asleep while I clear away our glasses.

Lifting her with careful ease, I take her to my bedroom, laying her on the crisp, white sheets. She stirs, but turns on her side before her breathing evens out again.

Removing her jeans, I place a blanket over her, then leave the room, closing the door behind me – I am wound tight and I need to vent some of my raging frustrations.

Heading for my gym, I grab a pair of shorts from the laundry basket. Slipping my pants off and them on, I strip off my shirt and begin my warm-up.

*

An hour later and my body is covered in a thin sheen of sweat, my breathing heavy and my limbs aching from the pounding I gave them on the treadmill.

Grabbing a bottle of water from the mini fridge, I down half before swiping a towel from my workbench and dabbing my head.

I sense her even before I see her beautiful face.

Turning, my gorgeous princess is standing in the doorway, wrapped in the blanket, her hair in disarray, but her cheeks hold a little more color than earlier this evening. And, despite the red rings around her eyes, she is still the most beautiful thing I've ever seen.

"I don't know how to thank you for everything you've done for me... for my friends." She lowers her gaze to the floor.

Striding toward her, I cup her chin between two fingers, looking deep into her eyes when I tell her, "You thank me just by being here. Before you, I just existed, I went about my day not really living, just reacting to whatever went on around me. You've given my life meaning. For the first time I have something to fight for, prove my worth to. I want to be the man you deserve, Grace. And you deserve so much. I love you; let me love you, let me be here for you every moment of every day."

A tear falls down her cheek and she smiles at me. It lights up her face for the first time tonight and I fall deeper for her with every passing moment. Only now, it doesn't scare me; not one bit.

Still looking at me, she trails her hand across my jaw and cups my cheek, bringing my lips to meet hers in a soft, lazy embrace.

Her tongue slides across my bottom lip with infinite slowness and I reciprocate with equal, heavy intensity.

Lifting her, she wraps her legs around my waist, the blanket riding up to her bare ass, her mouth never leaving mine. I grasp at her back and lead her to the bedroom where I want to make sure that she knows I'm not going anywhere – that I still love and want her as much as I ever did.

***

Grace

Placing me on the bed, Colt removes his bottoms before climbing next to me. I shift onto my side and he slips his tongue into the inviting warmth of my mouth, his hands grasping my jaw while he dips in deeper, grazing my lips with his.

"I love you, Grace," he whispers against me, pulling my tongue between his teeth and sucking. "But we don't have to do this... not now... not after the night you've had."

Pulling back, I look into his eyes - glistening under the moonlight seeping in through the window - and I place my hands either side of his face. "I love you, too. And I *need* this."

He recaptures my lips and moves his hands to undo each and every button of my shirt. Lying back, I arch my body so he can slip the material over my shoulders and down my arms. He peppers my flushed skin with delicate kisses and the intermittent flick of his tongue.

Sliding my hands across his back, I draw him in while he lowers his lips to my pebbled nipples. Throwing my shirt aside, he unclasps my bra, dropping it to the floor alongside my shirt, and draws one nipple into his mouth, tweaking the other between finger and thumb.

Paying the other nipple the same, warm, moist attention he takes hold of my damp, heated knickers and slides them down my legs. Once removed, he plants light kisses against the sole of my foot, moving further up my thigh before doing the same with the other.

The stubble on his jaw tickles my flesh and goose bumps skim across my sensitized body.

He lowers the bulk of his muscled frame, hovering above me, stroking my cheek with the back of his hand. "I want to make love to you, Grace."

Placing both hands against my cheeks, he angles himself at the heat radiating between my thighs and pushes into me.

I've never needed him more than I do in this moment, and I savour every tingling sensation in my body, knowing that he still loves and wants me, and needing for him to keep proving it to me right now.

Inching in with infinite slowness, he stretches me, fills me... consumes me. I clamp down on his hot, swollen length, gripping his steel with the strength of my slippery walls, pulling him deeper to feel every fervid thrust before he buries himself in me, over and over, with languid passion.

Back arched, I push my hips to meet his, tangling my hands in his hair, claiming his lips with a clash of tongues and the breathy whispers of our carnal pleasure.

I wrap a leg round his waist and pull him to me, my hand reaching down to claw at his back, trailing further to dig into the taut flesh of his thrusting rear.

Gripping my shoulders, he lowers his body and the coarse hair from his pelvis creates a delicious friction against my aching clit. He places his arms either side of me, cupping the back of my head with a tender touch.

"Don't stop," I moan into his mouth, "please, Colt... harder... make me cum."

A growl rumbles in his chest as he pumps into me, picking up speed when I feel the swell of thick shaft, body still grinding against my throbbing bud.

The beginnings of my release stir in my stomach and my toes curl as my grip tightens and heat radiates through my abdomen. My skin heats and prickles and when Colt litters kisses across my jaw to take my earlobe between his lips, I let go.

"Oh, God, yes...." My body bucks against him and my pulsing core grips his swollen length before he erupts inside me.

His hot, liquid seed gushes and he moans against my ear, his body convulsing while he empties himself into me, burying his face in my neck.

***

Colt

Dawn is breaking and I've slept for perhaps a couple of hours at most.

Grace and I made love once more before tiredness took over her again and she fell asleep, wrapped in my arms. I don't want her anywhere else - near me, I can protect her, love her.

I spent most of the early hours trying to figure out who would be behind digging into Grace's past and why, and I've come up blank.

It's obvious it's someone who knows her, but I've ruled out Cam and Harley because, if for no other reason, last night's reactions told me they knew nothing of Grace's former life.

There's no-one springs to mind who'd have a grudge against her. Miles hates me for paying him off, but I doubt he would want Grace to come to harm. I'll have him looked into just in case, though - we can't afford to take any chances.

And then there's Collette - but she and Grace only met last night, hours before the photograph turned up.

There's no way, even if Collette did possess the intelligence and know-how for something like this, she'd be able to pull it off so quickly.

I'll be sure to run through a list of Grace's past clients to see if there have been any disputes with goods or payment, but I can't see that leading anywhere, if I'm honest.

Getting up - careful not to wake my sleeping beauty - I traipse into the living room. I don't want to waste any time on this, so I make the necessary calls to have all the relevant people looked into.

I let Felix know I won't be at HQ for a couple of days - although, I don't go into detail why; just that I have some personal business to take care of. Any important calls I will take, but he can handle the 007 fundraiser next weekend.

I hope to have something by then - there's no way I won't be able to attend the fundraiser, but I will be upping the security detail and taking Grace with me. My angel will not leave my side, unless absolutely, irrevocably necessary... and even then, maybe.

I don't know what Garrett is capable of, but I won't be stopping to ask questions - if I see him, he's a dead man.

Dialling Dmitry's number, I amble around my kitchen, waiting for him to pick up. He's been stationed outside my house in Westchester since the early hours and I need an update.

I'll make Grace breakfast once this is out the way.

"*Da?*" Dmitry answers in his native Russian.

"Good morning, Dmitry. How was last night?" I place the phone between my ear and shoulder, removing eggs from the pantry.

"Everything good, Mr. Knight, *nyet problem.* Your friends, they are fine."

"Thank you. I have a favour to ask. Can you get a list from the guys and go to Grace's apartment for some of their things? I'm sorry to ask this of you, Dmitry, but we are keeping this all low key; there is no-one else I trust to do this."

"*Konechno,* Mr. Knight, I will do this for you right away."

"Thank you, Dmitry." Hanging up, I place my phone down and set about making pancakes with bacon, eggs and maple syrup.

Laying the table, I hear shuffling behind me.

"Mmm, something smells delicious," Grace inhales. I turn to see her closing her eyes and smiling. She takes my breath away.

She's showered. Her red locks pool past her shoulders in loose waves, the copper tones silky and highlighted against her black V-neck sweater and charcoal jeans.

She's got no make-up on and the natural beauty of her smooth, flawless skin radiates - sleep having restored the rosy glow to her cheeks.

Placing the cafetière on the table, I stride over to her and take her beautiful face between my hands. Embracing her lips with mine, I dip my tongue into her warm mouth, tasting her, savouring her.

"You look beautiful." I murmur against her lips. "I've made breakfast." I pull away from her, though reluctant, and lead her to the table by her hand.

"What have I done to deserve this?" Her smile makes my stomach flutter.

"A man needs no reason to treat his lady," I smirk, throwing her a wink and pulling out her chair.

Taking a seat, she beams up at and I plant my lips against her forehead.

***

Grace

Everything's moving so fast, I can barely get my head around it. Colt and I haven't even been on a proper date yet, but here I am, in his apartment where he's promised to take care of me until this nightmare is over. *Am I in over my head?* Should I be this comfortable so soon? What makes me so different to the other women he's been with? Does he just want to save me, am I a pity fuck?

I'm spending too much time in my own head and I have enough driving me insane without the add complication of over-analyzing a situation. I need to just take this for what it is – he's given me no reason to doubt anything he's said or done. I guess I'm just finding it a little unusual to trust someone I barely know after what happened last time... especially considering that mistake is now back to haunt me.

"You've tensed up," Colt whispers, "are you OK?"

OK, no more time in my head. I need to get a grip – I am stronger than this. Nodding, I tell him, "I'm fine, I'm just... ." *Do I lie?* "Scared." No, no more lying, no more running away and no more hiding. I'm fucking shitting myself and it's probably clear across my face and, let's be honest, understandable.

He shifts on the sofa and turns me to him. "You're safe with me, baby. I won't let him hurt you, I promise."

I appreciate his words, but he doesn't know Garrett like I do. He's not just some London thug – he spent his life fighting and getting what he wants. He might be a fat, lazy fucker now, but, once upon a time, he used to be a martial arts nut with an obsession for knives. And he's not stupid, despite what drugs might have done to him. If he's found me, he'll be biding his time; watching me, planning his next move. He's waited too long for this moment of twisted revenge and he won't just run in blind because he knows where I am now. I've seen what he's capable of; I know the mind games he plays in order to fuck with your head before he delivers the final blow.

"Grace?"

I blink hard, my face is moist from tears I didn't realise I'd shed and my body shivers from the cold taking over it.

"We haven't been on a date, yet?" It's random, I know, but I need the distraction – and not the way Colt is staring at me with all the sympathy and concern in the world. I don't deserve it, but I know he will continue to give it freely.

"What?" He looks at me, bewildered.

"We haven't been on a date; not a proper one, just you and me."

I think he knows what I'm doing because he wipes away my tears with the pad of his thumb and gives me a soft smile. "We have plenty of time for that," he soothes, "but first, I wanna make sure you're safe."

Pulling me back into him on the couch, he puts a strong, warm arm around my shoulders and pulls me close; inhaling the scent of my freshly-washed hair before kissing the side of my head.

Releasing a sigh, he says to me, "I've got people looking into all possibilities of who could've pulled this off. Can you think of anyone with a grudge?"

I shake my head, but can't string together a coherent sentence for fear my quivering voice might continue to give away my anxiety.

"I have one of my security guys coming here any moment; his name's Harris." He rubs my shoulder. "He'll go everywhere with you when I can't. I'm sorry it's come to this, but I want you safe, Grace, and if I can't see to it personally, then I want someone I know and trust watching your back."

"I get it, and thank you." I place my hand over his and squeeze. "I just want this to be over."

"I know you do, baby." He kisses my hair again. "I won't stop until I know who's behind this, and Garrett is out your life for good."

I shake at the mention of his name and Colt clutches my chin, turning my face to his.

"You don't have to be scared, sweetheart; nothing's gonna happen to you while I'm around." He brushes my lips with his and I close my eyes against the tender touch.

The intercom announces the arrival of Harris and Colt sends the lift down for him.

Within minutes, Harris is striding from the elevator doors. Holding a blazer over his shoulder, he cuts an imposing figure - at least six and half foot of pure, broad muscle with a black goatee, bald head and deep-set, piercing green eyes staring out from under thick, even eyebrows.

He's wearing black trousers and a black polo-neck jumper, and packing with a shoulder holster - two guns strapped on either side.

Swallowing past my dry throat, I look at Colt.

"I'm taking no chances, Grace," he whispers in my ear, "I want you protected at all times. Harris has a permit to use those things and he's a deadly shot. Don't let it scare you; he won't let anything happen to you."

Harris walks up to us and Colt stands. I follow suit, and Harris thrusts a large hand toward me. "Ms. Morgan, I trust you know who I am and why I'm here. I won't let the sly bastard get anywhere near you. He'll be sucking shit through a straw if he tries."

Harris is Scottish. Glaswegian, actually - his accent is broad, strong.

"Thank you," I utter, not knowing what else to say under the circumstances.

I don't need to think of things to occupy any impending awkward silences when Colt's phone sounds out. He grabs it and beckons Harris to follow him to his office.

"I'm gonna fill him in, babe, I won't be long." He kisses my cheek and walks off, answering his phone.

***

Colt

"Dmitry, what is it?" I ask the Russian, worried that he's calling me.

"Mr. Knight, there is package left for Ms. Morgan outside her apartment door." He sounds concerned.

"Is it safe?"

"I've not yet checked, but it is small, perhaps too small for dangerous explosive."

He can read my mind. "Bring it with you, Dmitry; I want to look at it before I tell Grace."

"As you wish, Mr. Knight. I come now."

Hanging up, I tell Harris what Dmitry said.

He cocks a brow. "I'll meet him in the foyer, check the package out myself."

Nodding, I thank him. The day is not going to end well when I tell Grace about this - and I will have to tell her, she deserves to know. I just don't want to break her any further. I hate seeing the light in her eyes replaced by fear and vulnerability. I know she's a strong woman – I've seen it for myself – but we all have that one thing that brings us to our knees.

Grace is mine. But for all different reasons, and every one of them good. She's giving me the strength where hers is failing and I will not let her down, but I won't keep her in the dark, either.

***

It doesn't take long for Dmitry to reach us. Harris met him downstairs and phoned up to tell me what the package contains. The thought makes me sick and I don't want to tell Grace any more - I fear her reaction, but I can't keep it from her. It will only serve to make things worse if she finds out any other way.

I meet Harris and Dmitry at the elevator. I can feel Grace's eyes on me while I take the package from the Scot.

Walking over, she looks at me - her eyes dipping in questioning fear.

"Dmitry found this outside your apartment," I advise her. "You don't have to look, I can get rid of it, but I thought you at least should know."

Shaking her head, she holds out her hands for the small box. Her face is deathly pale and she swallows hard while she rests the package on the table in front of her.

Taking a seat behind her, I place my hand at the small of her back. "Don't touch it, Grace, it could contain more evidence than what it already does."

Wide-eyed, she looks at me before returning her attention to the parcel and, with agonising slowness, she lifts the lips of the box and peers inside. Her hand clashes to her mouth and she buries her head in my chest, trembling, sobbing against me.

I take one more look at the bloodied, glass shard in the box and instruct Dmitry to get it out of my sight.

Chapter 23
Grace

Catapulted from my sleep, I place my hand over my racing heart. Staring at the weapon I used to take someone's life has crushed my resolve. The bastard is winning – he's breaking me down, because this is the first nightmare I've had in a long time. I can safely say I haven't missed them. I'm sweating buckets and my heart won't slow down. Colt brought me in here after I saw the glass shard and I think he stayed with me until I fell asleep. But he isn't beside me any longer and, right now, his comforting embrace is very much needed. I'll find him, but first I need to shower because I'm drenched and it's disgusting.

Stepping into the bathroom, I turn on the shower and grab a towel to place on the hook outside the glass doors. I get under the water and close my eyes beneath the inviting heat. Scrubbing at my face and body feels almost like I am ridding myself of the dirt of my past. I open my eyes and watch the water swirl down the plug hole with a smile.

I *can* do this. I *will* do this. Garrett took away too much of my security... too much of the person I used to be before my life got turned upside down. I can't blame him for all of it, but I can certainly blame him for holding me back. I can blame him for the bruises that marred me daily, for the beatings and the sexual violence. I can blame him for the broken bones and the nasty names, and for the life he pulled me into. But I can thank him, too. I can thank him because the fuckin' shit he's put me through has made me the person I am today. Maybe he had a helping hand, maybe I never quite lost myself during my time with him, whatever, I don't care which way I look at it. But when this over, when the people in my life now hold my hand through to the end of this goddamn tragedy, the biggest thanks of all... will be me thanking fuck that he's gone and I'm still standing.

I step out of the shower with a new resolve – how long it will last, is anyone's guess, but it's the here and now I'll concern myself with.

Walking out of the bathroom, I spy a gorgeous, red dress laid out on the bed. There's a note attached to it in Colt's neat handwriting;

Wear me xx

Hmm, strange. Nevertheless, I dry myself off, blow dry my hair, leaving the waves loose, and move to put the dress on. However, I've a tingling sensation in the pit of my stomach about this and, so, I make an assumption and put on some lacy lingerie before slipping into the dress.

I don't want to put shoes on, it doesn't feel right indoors, but then again, this dress wouldn't feel right without heels. Oh, sod it. I grab some black stilettoes from the bundle of shoes I brought with me, and put them on.

When I step out of the bedroom, I am blown away. Tears spring to my eyes and I cup my hands over my mouth.

The whole living area is lit with sparkling candles of varying shapes and sizes. The dining table has rose petals strewn across and around it and holds something that looks and smells delicious. Colt is standing beside it in a smart, black suit and the most gorgeous, genuine smile I have ever seen on him.

He holds out his hand for me and I walk over, placing my fingers in his. Pulling me close, he kisses me softly and utters, "Consider this our first official date," then he presses a button on a remote I'm only just noticing, and soft jazz fills the room.

I am absolutely floored by his gesture, so it's a good job he leads me to my chair, pulls it out and sits me down. My legs are shaking.

Grabbing an open bottle of wine from the centre of the table, he pours me a generous measure, then sets the bottle back down. I notice his tumbler is filled with what I imagine is whiskey, and when he sits down, he takes a small sip.

I still don't even know what to say; I can't string together anything intelligible. Instead, I whisper, "Thank you."

"You're welcome, baby. You deserve it." His smile lights up the room even more and my heart melts.

When we finish the three course meal, Colt takes me back to bed where he makes tender love to me until we fall asleep, wrapped up tight together.

***

It's been three days since I laid eyes on the glass shard and I'm still trying to remain strong and determined to get over this.

Lying on the bed, naked and wrapped in Colt's arms, there is something here keeping me going. Shifting in his arms to face him, I stroke the three day-old stubble on his cheeks. His eyes flicker open and he smiles at me, a dreamy expression that I can't help but return.

"Hey, sleepy head," I drone.

It's going on for eight and darkness has already swooped in. We made love twice this afternoon and fell asleep while the sun set over a gorgeous backdrop of oranges and pinks.

I'm savouring this moment because Colt needs to go into work tomorrow, and I don't know what I will do without him here.

Harris is ripped to fuck and huge as hell, but it's the warmth and security of Colt's embrace I'll miss. Not to mention the umpteen mind-blowing orgasms he gives me in one afternoon - they help occupy my mind from an otherwise gruesome memory.

I've been in touch with Cam and Harley and told them about what happened. They're doing well, but they worry for me - I hear it every time Harl comes on the phone; she tries so hard not to cry and I feel fucking awful for putting them through this. I wouldn't even blame them if they did disown me after this is over, but I hope with everything in me that they don't.

I'm going to see them tomorrow - Harris is taking me in Colt's bulletproof Prado, but I'm still scared shitless of leaving the apartment.

Colt assures me I'll be safe. The underground carpark is secured to high heaven and no-one knows I'm here, so no-one would think to look twice at a blacked-out Toyota leaving the building.

Stretching, Colt gets off the bed and struts, naked, to the bathroom. "You coming?" He turns to me and tilts his head in its direction.

Sliding off the bed, I sashay over to him. He spanks my arse when I walk past and into the marble-tiled en suite. I giggle and hurry forward, covering my backside with my hands.

Colt follows me and turns the shower head on and the steaming water bounces off the stone tray. Stepping inside, he holds out a hand, pulling me toward him and closing the glass doors behind me.

The water is lush - hot enough to turn my skin pink; just the way I like it.

Facing away from Colt, I run my hands over my face and through my hair, letting the water run in hot rivulets down my body.

Colt reaches around me and grabs the soap from its dish. With gentle finesse he rubs the soap over my shoulders, across my back and around to my stomach. Placing it back, he massages the suds into my skin, his hands soft and warm.

Both hands cross over my abdomen before sliding up to cup my breasts.

"Mmm." I lean back into him, closing my eyes, my hands covering his while he kneads my aching mounds, pinching my hardened nipples.

Gripping one of his hands, I snake it down my belly to the smooth skin of my damp pussy. He circles two fingers around my clit, my fingers mimicking his every move.

"Stroke yourself for me, darlin'," he whispers into my ear, warm water dripping down my neck from his lips.

I slip past his fingers and glide my own across my slick entrance, feeling the heated moisture between my thighs.

"That's right, feel how wet you are for me, baby. Slide a finger into your pussy; feel how tight you are; imagine it's my cock you're clamping down on."

My body shudders at his words and my sex clenches with avid hunger. I do what he says and slide my middle finger into the heat of my drenched opening when he parts my slippery folds.

Chest heaving against my back, he utters, "You're so fuckin' hot, Grace."

His hard, heavy shaft presses between my arse cheeks and I stifle a moan - a carnal pleasure races through me, hot and intoxicating, knowing I've caused his reaction.

I dip my finger in and out of my wet core, picking up speed while he strums my throbbing clit.

"That's right, baby, fuck yourself for me." His words are laced with want, his voice low and heady. "Don't stop; make yourself cum. Faster."

With my free hand still over my breast - his now opening my insatiable cunt, the other teasing my pulsing clit - I pluck my nipple between finger and thumb, tweaking, pulling.

"Oh, God... ." My body ignites, the heated water biting at my flushed skin.

My legs begin to buckle, but Colt holds me up. "Cum for me, angel."

His words overthrow me. My body explodes; a mind-shattering orgasm ripping through me with lightning speed, tearing from my throat in an animalistic scream.

*

Wrapping me in a towel, Colt carries me from the shower into the bedroom and lays me on the warm sheets.

Without a word, he takes the towel from me and begins to dry me in gentle, sensual strokes, my body quivering when he rubs the course material over the most sensitive parts.

When it comes to my face, he dabs the cotton over me before pulling me in to kiss my lips with such softness I barely feel it, but it's enough to send a current of a thousand delirious pulses racing through me. I tingle under his touch.

"Get into bed, baby, I'll fetch us a bottle of wine," he murmurs into my ear.

Diving under the covers, I grab the TV remote and put on some soppy romcom - I can't usually stand chick flicks, but then again, I'm not used to the wave of soppy emotions streaming through me - they've obviously turned my brain to mush.

Colt walks back into the room and I could throw myself at him and fuck him all over - not only has he bought wine, but a huge bag of Doritos and cheese dip - this man is my champion.

"You, Mr. Knight, are an amazing fucking mind-reader."

He throws the crisps at me and I waste no time ripping the bag open and shovelling a handful into my mouth. Colt laughs at me, sitting beside me and offering me the dip.

"Hnk hoo," I manage.

He puts his arm out and I slide my body up next to him, snuggling into his chest. He hands me a full glass and I swallow the contents of my mouth before sipping at the ruby liquid.

This is my tranquil haven - I'd give anything for a lifetime of moments like this.

***

I woke up super excited. Harris is taking me to see my two best friends this morning - it goes a little to suppressing the pang of disappointment that Colt is back at the office.

He's already gone. I woke up to a quickie and breakfast in bed before he left - my kinda morning.

With a couple minutes to spare before Harris buzzes up for me, I grab my laptop to check my emails. There's a couple of follow-ups from previous clients, a message from Harl telling me how she's ready to burst at the seams pending my arrival and another from Cam to tell me Harley is driving him mad with her incessant chatter about my visit - but he's looking forward to it, too.

I have three emails from prospective clients and I make a note to delve into those later tonight.

A message pings through from 'unknowncityboy666@gmail.com' - could be another enquiry, so I open it.

My stomach lurches and I lean over the side of the sofa, vomiting onto the tiled floor just when the intercom buzzes Harris's arrival. Stumbling over, wiping my mouth with the back of my hand, I hit the speaker. "C-come up, quickly, please." I sink to the floor, put my head in my hands and burst into tears, heaving with every wracking sob. *Why is this happening? How is he doing it?*

The elevator doors slide open and Harris is at my side almost immediately. "Ms. Morgan, are you OK, what happened?"

Lifting my head, I can't string together a sentence. I point to the sofa where I threw my laptop aside. Harris strides over, lifting the machine and staring at the image depicted.

From the white glow of the screen I note his face paling, eyes wide.

"You haven't called anyone, yet? Not the police?" he inquires.

I shake my head - I know I can't go to the police; I'll be arrested, deported, imprisoned.

Sitting down, Harris taps away at my keyboard and, moments later, his phone pings. "I'm going to forward the email envelope to Colt, see if we can get someone to track the IP address. This is good news, Ms. Morgan; he's slipped up."

"B-but not the picture?" I stammer.

Harris shakes his head. "No, Ms. Morgan; the less this gets bandied about, the better. We'll discuss it with him tonight."

Nodding, I stand, bracing myself against the wall when my legs buckle. Harris marches into the kitchen and returns with a glass of water. "Go steady, Ms. Morgan. He's only trying to scare you; he can't get to you here."

" He's doing a bang-up fuckin' job. And please, Harris," I implore, "call me Grace."

Smiling, he bows his head in understanding. "Do you still want to go to Westchester, Grace?"

Nodding, I reply, "Yes, please." I shouldn't - I feel exposed. But I miss my friends so much, and Harris is right, he doesn't know where I am. Garrett's using scare tactics, but he can't touch me from the other side of the world.

***

Pulling up outside the white-wood property with the wraparound porch, Harris advises me to wait a moment while he surveys the area. I've been peering over my shoulder for most of the journey, feeling sick every time I spot similar cars twice round.

I note the blacked-out Merc a few cars down - I know it belongs to one of Dmitry's guys because Harl has told me.

"We're good to go, Grace."

Releasing a breath, I exit the car and race up the pathway, banging on the door - not stopping until Harl answers. She throws herself at me and Harris has to catch me before we go arse over tit on the concrete.

"I've missed you," she squeals.

It's only been a few days, but it feels like forever and I can't let go of the tight hug I have my friend trapped in. Her happiness is genuine and I could cry all over again because of it.

Cam comes bounding across the hallway and throws himself at us. "Graybo!" he cries.

Ushering us inside, Harris takes one more look up and down the street, mutters something into the two-way pinned inside his jacket and shuts the door.

Entering the Tudor kitchen, with its light wood and illuminated glass-windowed cupboards, we sit at the breakfast bar. Harl's phone rings and she rushes to grab it before excusing herself.

"That's the fourth time today," Cam moans.

Looking at him I ask, "Who is it?"

"Colt's sister." He slumps, elbow on the counter, chin in his hand.

"Farrah?" I shouldn't, but I smile - feisty little minx managed to get her number after all.

But wait, what's this? Cam is sulking over Harley's friendship with Farrah? "Why the long face, Cammy?" I have to hear what he has to say - this is priceless.

"Huh, what? Nothing, I've just been bored with her phone permanently attached to her ear." His words are hurried and he's sat up straight - I'd say he's on the offensive.

I find the entertainment value in this, and I do feel a little guilty for that, but I can't wholly sympathize with Cam because it's not like he's celibate, or saving himself for Harl - it's about time my girl got herself some.

"What do they talk about?" I hide my smirk by pulling my bottom lip between my teeth.

Shrugging, he answers, "Fuck knows, I don't listen."

I can so tell he's lying - he's heard something because his cheeks have gone a delightful shade of pink. A shy Cameron - who'd have thought.

"Sorry about that." Harl comes bounding back into the kitchen beaming from ear to ear.

"Who was that?" Again, trying to hide a smile.

"Erm... Farrah, Colt's sister. We got on well at the party and thought we might hang one night, or something." A blush creeps into her face.

Oh my days, I've hit the 'I've seen it all' jackpot today. Cam showing a jealous streak... and rosy cheeks, and Harl is lusting after another woman. Amazing.

"So, what's going on at Chez Love?" Harley's attempt at changing the subject does not go unnoticed.

Humouring her all the same, I wiggle my brow. "How do you think?"

"Eww!" she exclaims. Figures - apparently she's into pussy now.

Cam throws a bucket of water over our bonfire. "Have there been any more... occurrences?"

My brain goes screeching back to the last thing I saw before I left the apartment and my body ices over. So much for this visit trying to put those things to the back of my mind.

"Are you OK, Grace?" Harl places a hand on my shoulder. "You've gone pale. What's happened?"

Pulling my smartphone from my jeans pocket, I tell them, "I received a photograph from an unknown email address." Scrolling through the emails, I can't stand to open the attachment, but I also don't want to subject them both to what I saw. I hesitate and Harley notices.

"Grace, you can show us; we love you and we want to help you."

She says that now, but wait until she sees the picture. I still can't hand the phone to her, though, and my hands are shaking so badly, but she grabs for it and I don't have the strength to hold on to it.

I can't look at her as she taps the screen to open the envelope. I feel so sick and I jump when she gasps. Closing my eyes, I fight back the threatening tears while I bury my head in my palms.

"Is that... ?" she starts.

I nod, trying to swallow past the bile rising up my throat. "Frankie's body."

Chapter 24
Colt

Fuck work - I've been trying to hound everyone I know to get a location on the IP address Harris gave me. I have no idea what she's received, but it sickens me to think. I need to go to her.

Standing to leave, my phone vibrates. "Colt," I answer rather brash until I realise it's her. "Hey, baby." Grace's sweet tone on the other end dances through my ears. "Is everything OK?" I sit back down.

She misses me - she's frightened; I can hear it in the quaking of her voice, but she's trying so hard to be brave, and she laughs when she tells me Harley has taken a shine to my sister - they've been on the phone to one another none stop, and Cam is jealous. Poor lad; if Faz has set her sights on Harley, she won't quit. She's headstrong that one.

After checking in, we say goodbye ten minutes later. I feel better for having spoken to her, but I'm still concerned - she tried to instil confidence into her words, but I noticed the quiver.

Spying some paperwork relating to the 007 Fundraiser, I decide to treat my lady to something elegant for the occasion, before I can leave, there is a knock at my office door. "Come in," I call.

Lucinda sways in, her white blouse unbuttoned to a level unbecoming a professional business woman. Her black bra shows through the thin material and she isn't carrying her folders against her chest like usual - they're down by her side while she puffs her chest out. The woman is nothing if not desperate, but she looks dishevelled. While her attire is a little revealing, it's also unkempt which is unlike her. She has a faraway look in her eyes, masked intermittently by her usual look of lust.

"What can I help you with, Lucinda?" I divert my attention back to the papers in front of me.

Placing her hands on the desk, I look up while she squeezes her arms together, enhancing her small bust. She's going for her usual, brazen persona, but something is still ringing different – the usual light isn't in her eyes, but she still stands there, pushing out her breasts and I've had enough.

Letting out a breath through my nose, I grind my jaw. "Lucinda, you seem to have forgotten how to dress in a manner appropriate for the office. Kindly see to that, then tell me what it is you want."

Refusing to acknowledge my first request, she asks, "I need to know how work is progressing on the Kenosha project. I'm crunching the monthly figures for accounts and I don't know where we are."

There's a note of disdain in her voice - she pissed off that she's not been kept in the loop over a project she considers hers, when, in actual fact, it's *my* damn house. And then there's that something else bothering her that I can't put my finger on, and actually care little about.

"I'll email you the figures; I'm just about to head out."

"Where are you going; don't you think you've had enough time off?" Her face drops, her hands along with it and she scrunches her face up, glaring at me with a mixture of annoyance and shock. Her face is paler than usual and I notice, now, that she's wearing very little of the make-up she usually does. Something is wrong with her, but it doesn't give her the right to talk to me like *she's my* boss.

"Watch your tongue with me, Lucinda. Remember who the boss is here. I need to drop something off at my apartment for Grace, so if you'll excuse me, I need to be going." I'm hoping she gets the message.

I don't give her the opportunity to bite back, though. I head out, but I do hear, "Fucking the boss, eh?" before the door closes behind me.

People in glass houses and all that.

***

Before heading back to the apartment, I stopped at Karen Millen and spent a good hour picking out a dress for Grace – a white, box pleat design with black, geo lace panelling and an embellished collar – and teamed it with a Tiffany & Co silver, Paloma Love Heart bracelet. She will look perfect this weekend and I cannot wait to see her in it.

To further surprise her, I have bought the biggest bunch of flowers I could find - a delicate, exotic spray of lilies, orchids, tulips and roses. I battle with them to get into my car, but before I can leave to head back home, my phone rings.

"Yes?"

"Boss, it's Harris."

"You have news?" I emailed Harris about the IP address and set him on to a guy I know in computers. He must've heard back.

"It's from Chicago."

The bouquet drops from my hand and I ask him to repeat himself. "Are you certain?"

"Hundred percent. Whoever sent that picture, they did it not far from her home; in a café around the corner."

I close my eyes, feeling sick to my stomach. *Does he know where she lives? Fuck!* I grit my teeth together and clench my fists. The bastard is in for a rude awakening the very moment I get my hands on him. I mentally plan his destruction the whole journey home; how I'll find him and how I'll make him disappear so no questions are asked.

He'll regret the fucking day he tried to mess with Grace.

*

Parking up in the underground garage, I get out my car and all but stomp my way to the elevator. My blood is numerous degrees above boiling and I'm contemplating how to tell Grace... or even if I should. She's been through enough and this will only cause further panic. I look forward to the day that this is fucking over and she doesn't have to be put through it any longer.

"Mr Knight."

The concierge's voice stops me in my tracks; he sounds a little flustered.

I turn to him and see him fiddling with his hands behind the desk. "What is it, Jacob?" I try to remain patient, but I need to see Grace's beautiful face in order to instil some calm back into me.

"Sir, Ms Morgan is still out, but there's a package been left for her." He grabs something from beneath him.

My stomach knots when I see the small parcel he puts on the desk in front of him. I walk closer and notice that the handwriting is the same as before. *It's from him,* he knows where she is and the thought both scares me and fills me with unbridled rage. *How fucking dare he?* I clench my jaw and grind my teeth together, balling my fists at the side of me.

"Who left this?" It takes everything in me not to grab Jacob by the lapels and get in his face, but this isn't his fault. Nevertheless, he recoils at the severity of my voice and backs away when I move closer.

"I-it was y-your Design Head, sir. Ms Gould; she left it with me after I refused her entry to your floor."

Lucinda? What the fuck has she got to do with all of this?

If I thought I knew rage before, it's nothing to the blind fury consuming me right now. My vision dances with black spots and my body quakes with the anger swimming through my blood. *I'll fucking kill her myself if any harm comes to Grace because of her jealous meddling.*

Snatching the parcel from the desk, I turn and head back to my car. I need to pay Lucinda a visit and she better have a goddamn stellar excuse for this shit because I am ready to wrap my hands around her throat.

I don't even register the drive to her apartment; my mind is focused solely on Grace's safety and wondering how the bitch fits into this mess because I am damn sure gonna find out. I practically rip the car door from its hinges when I park up and get out.

Climbing the stairs to Lucinda's apartment, I bang my fist off her door. She doesn't answer after a moment or two, so I do it again. She's either not in or purposely not answering. She better hope it's the former as I try the handle.

The door's unlocked and I step into her apartment. It smells musty; like she hasn't been home in a few days, and another odour hangs in the air... something off, like rotting food left in the heat for too long.

Wandering through her home, I noticed the mess. Vases are smashed on the floor, small tables are turned over and the curtains have been pulled down from the window. There's been a struggle here. When I walk into the bedroom, I begin to piece everything together. Clothes are strewn across the bed and a lot are missing from the wardrobe; the empty hangers left dangling inside. There's a half stuffed suitcase on the bed and two little drops of blood on the cream carpet.

However, it isn't that that I can smell. The scent is sickly-sweet and is strongest in here. I spy a couple of flies hovering near a small box on the nightstand.

I am sick to death of seeing these ominous packages, but I moved toward it regardless, my stomach knotting.

I recoil at the sight of the bloodied stump of a finger nestled inside. It's too large to be a woman's and it's been here for a few days, minimum – I saw Lucinda mere hours ago, with all her fingers intact. *Why would she leave this here and try to take off?* I don't understand it… and who the hell does it belong to? And where the fuck is she?

It goes someway to explaining her involvement, but it doesn't tell me everything I need to know. I wonder if Lucinda's life – or body parts – is also in jeopardy and part of me wants to call the cops. But I can't, because I don't know how deep this goes, or how Grace will be affected by any of it.

No, this is best kept quiet for now.

I dig my phone out of my pocket and instruct it to call Harris. He answers after only a few rings.

"We might have a problem," I tell him. "Lucinda's involved and I think I know why." I explain what I've found here and instruct him to meet me back at the apartment when Grace is ready to leave. "Find her, Harris," I tell him before hanging up.

I can't tell Grace about this – not yet. Harris needs to confirm a few things first and find that conniving bitch of an ex-employee, but I won't hang around while he does that. I need to get us out of Chicago for a few days.

If this involves what happened to Grace, then hacked off body parts means shit's getting real.

Using an item of clothing from the floor, I put the lid back on the box and take the whole thing with me. Something isn't right here and I'm gonna get to the bottom of this.

Grace's life depends on it.

***

Grace

It's getting late and I need to be heading back, because Colt will be home shortly and, since talking to him, I've missed him more and more.

Cam and Harl have been a huge comfort to me, despite sending each other glaring daggers across the room. I don't think Cam is handling Harley's change in sexual preference very well and I almost feel bad for him – if only Harl had said something to him sooner. But maybe this is fate's plan.

I don't know. Either way, they need to sort their shit out or it's just gonna go from bad to worse between them, and I would hate to see them fall out when they've been friends for so long.

Harris pulls into the underground carpark and Colt is already waiting for me – I guess he's missed me just as much and the thought tugs a smile from my lips.

Until I see his rigid expression and tense posture.

He holds up his hands and signals me to give him a few moments with Harris. After a brief conversation, he hands the bodyguard a small box and Harris leaves without another word.

"What was that?" I ask Colt as he opens the car door for me.

Shaking his head, he tells me, "It doesn't matter, sweetheart, it's nothing for you to worry about."

Do I believe him? Do I fuck. But I don't have time to mull it over because I notice several packed bags behind him when he pulls me in for a tight cuddle.

"Are we going somewhere?" I eye the bags with one raised brow, then turn my attention back to Colt.

"Grace, these last few days have been a test for both of us and I want to take you away." He looks sincere, but there's also something else he isn't telling me. "I've booked us a few days at a luxury spa before I have to attend the 007 night."

OK, fine, he isn't telling me everything, but a few days away at a spa with this muscled picture of perfection is just too delicious a thought to badger him about his silence. I'll go with it, but I'll want answers afterward.

Chapter 25
Colt

There's no way she believes me – I can see it in her eyes. I can't say I blame her, either; my words lacked conviction because I'm still battling between fury and fear, and I fuckin' suck at lying.

But she's not pushing it and, as we get into the car, I'm thankful for that.

The drive to the private airport is quiet, but comfortable. Grace relaxes and even takes a nap. When she wakes up, I ask her about her visit to Westchester and she tells me all about it with a smile on her face. She's so relieved that Harley and Cam are standing by her because I hear it in her words when she talks about them.

To be honest, I'm glad, too. There's no way on this planet I would have left her side after what she revealed to us, and I didn't doubt that her friends would stick with her through it either, but it likely won' be an easy thing for them to live with. However, it's much more for Grace. For two years, this nightmare has hung over her head, and I can see the relief, also, that it's out there now – that people know about it and it's not just her burden any longer. Even if she is going through shit right now.

I hope she doesn't blame herself for any of this. She did what she had to, otherwise she might be dead. I can't even say I wish it never happened, because she might still be trapped in that degrading life... and I might not ever have met her. And that might sound selfish, but I'm glad I met her, because I can protect her better than anyone – I can make sure she's kept safe and loved for the person she's grown into despite everything.

I admire her more than she could ever fathom, and I smile at her while she continues to tell me about the situation between Harley and Cam... and my sister. It's hardly a shock – I said before that Faz is a determined girl.

The airfield comes into view and I wake Grace up from the nap she's slipped into again. She looks around, dazed before she notices where we are.

"Where are we going?" she asks me, her tone of voice still heavy with sleep.

"One of the best spas in the US," I tell her, "Boca Raton Resort." I return her smile, watching her eyes light up. She's heard of the renowned Waldorf Astoria resort, then. She must have; she's got no opinion coming from her parted lips and that's a bit unusual of her.

I pull up as close as I can to my private plane and get out the car, moving to Grace's side and helping her out, too. Dmitry is already here and Harris won't be far behind, so, for the time being, the Russian and I load the luggage on to the plane while Grace gets settled into one of the plush, leather sofas.

Dillon, the air steward, offers her champagne before take-off and she accepts with a polite smile.

Hidden from her view, I mimic her enthusiasm, watching with something close to pride and wonder while she takes all this in her stride. I'm glad that I can both please and protect her the only way I know how.

A hand snakes its way over my shoulder while I stand near the cockpit and I turn to see the air hostess, Octavia stood behind me. A sweet smile emblazons her face and she bats her eyelashes at me.

Dammit! I knew fucking the staff would come back to haunt me, and I failed to make proper arrangements to have a male-only team in my rush to get Grace to safety. I pray that my past mistakes don't bite me on the ass during the three-hour flight. Thankfully, I have the option of shutting the whole world out of the private cabin Grace and I will be seated in. There's something I want to experience with her and I could do without any unwelcome interruptions.

Being gentle about it, I move Octavia's hand from me and walk away from her, closing the door to the cabin behind me.

Grace smiles when she looks up and I am completely captivated by the innocence behind her eyes. She's mouthy and brash and not one bit shy and she's gone through some shit, but there's still an angel buried deep inside and I see it when she looks at me with all the gratefulness and courage she can muster.

Taking the glass of champagne from her, I place the flute on the table and grab hold of her hand, lifting her to her feet. She blushes, and it's the first time I've ever seen her do it. I pull her into me and tilt her chin with my fingers. She places her hands on my chest when I dip down and cover her sweet lips with mine.

Melting into me, she opens her mouth further and I slip my tongue in, slow and exploratory, tasting the vintage Brut on her. She trails one hand over my shoulder and grasps the base of my neck, but she doesn't pull me in like I expect. She tickles the skin with light fingers and tugs at my hair while her other hand remains on my chest.

My cock stirs, fully awake with the unhurried, deliberate pace of our moistened kiss. She purrs a little and the vibrations shoot right down to the head.

Reflexively, I crush her to me and delve deeper into the sanctity of her mouth, eager to taste as much as I can before--

"Ahem, sir?"

Breathless, I pull away from Grace and she tries to hide the rosy pink in her cheeks from Harris.

He doesn't look perturbed in the slightest.

"We're ready for take-off," he informs us.

I nod, and seat Grace back down before buckling in beside her. "Harris," I shout, just before he disappears from sight. "Make sure we are not disturbed, unless I say so."

"Yes, sir." He closes the door behind him and I swear I see the ghost of a smile on his lips.

With such a soft caress, Grace runs her hand up my thigh and licks her lips. She's thinking the exact same thing as I am and I love her more for it, but we will have to wait until we're in the air.

She doesn't seem to think so when she cups my balls and gently massages them.

I throw my head back against the sofa and close my eyes, relishing the pressure on my dick when she slides her hand across my already-hard length. She doesn't know what she does to me, and when the button on my pants pops open, I have to struggle not to launch myself at her and take her right here.

The higher we climb, the rockier the ride becomes, and the more her hand jostles my cock. If this carries on, I'll cum before I even get inside her.

She reaches into my pants and pulls my shaft free, but my groan of pleasure is drowned out by the noise of the plane. When she leans forward and slides me between her damp lips, I grip first the leather and then her head, hissing a more audible, "Oh, fuck," as she sucks me in.

I feel her smile against me.

She sucks me with such force that I feel her saliva drip down my length before she laps it up with her tongue, swirling the appendage around my swollen head before she plunges me back in her warm mouth.

Fuck this – I can't wait for the plane to reach altitude – I need her, now.

Unclipping my seatbelt, I shift on the sofa and move Grace off me – albeit begrudgingly because now my cock feels abandoned, desperate for further contact.

Without a word, Grace slips off her jeans and panties and positions her legs either side of mine, hovering over my swollen shaft. I can feel the heat from her hot cunt and she grabs the base of my dick, positioning it at her slippery entrance.

With torturous slowness, she dips down. My head penetrates her tight pussy and I groan while she gasps, but still she lowers herself with such languid movements. I can feel every single ridge of her walls grazing my cock as she takes me deeper. Her eyes are closed and she's drawn her bottom lip between her teeth. She looks fucking sexy as sin and I can't help myself – I rip open her blouse and suck one uncovered nipple between my teeth.

She draws in a sharp breath and grasps the back of my head with her free hand, fisting my hair to the point of pain and I enjoy every fucking minute of it.

When I draw her other hardened bud into my mouth, she slams down onto me and we both cry out. I let go of her nipple and grab her hips in both hands while she wraps hers around the back of my neck.

Gyrating her hips, she moves back and forth on my cock, rising and falling, twisting and circling and it feels so fuckin' amazing. It looks pretty goddamn hot, too – watching my length disappear into her pussy and reappear again, glistening with her excitement – it's the biggest fucking turn on.

I thrust into her, over and over while she works her hips and already I can feel the swell. I'm ready to burst and I don't know how much longer I can hold on.

She loosens one hand from my neck and cups her breast before massaging her stiffened bud between thumb and forefinger. Her eyes are still closed and I want to tear my gaze away because I'm going to cum, but I can't. I want to see her come undone.

"Touch yourself, Grace," I whisper, my voice hurried and hoarse.

She does – she snakes her hand down her stomach and strums her clit with two fingers. Her face contorts into a mask of pleasure as she builds up the rhythm and her walls clamp tight around me. She needs to finish soon because I can't take the pressure for much longer; she's so tight and hot and my cock is throbbing.

Her body tenses above me and I glance at her curling toes. She's close and, if I time this perfectly, we can go off together.

"Tell me when, baby," I urge her and her rubbing quickens while her breathing comes in short, sharp gasps.

"Oh, God," she breathes, digging her fingers into the flesh of my neck.

She throws her head back just as I release my load inside her with a groan. She screams my name and my body shudders right alongside hers as she rides out her climax, pulsing around me and coaxing out everything I have to give her.

Completely spent and breathing hard, she collapses on top of me, burying her face in my shoulder and smiling against me while she nips at my skin. Her body is still quaking and her cunt is still gripping me, tight. If she's not careful, I'll be ready to take her all over again.

***

Grace

A glorious ache settles at my core and I don't have the energy to move off Colt. He senses this, because he lifts me off and scoops me into his arms, turning to place me full on the sofa and nestling cushions behind my head. From an overhead cupboard, he grabs a blanket and covers me with it before kissing my forehead and whispering how much he loves me.

Adjusting his clothing, he zips himself up and heads for the door to the cabin. I miss him already, and the last thing I remember – before slipping into an exhausted oblivion – is his face at the moment we came together.

*

It's turbulence that wakes me; though, it's not that bad. I was only dozing, anyway – I can't properly sleep or nap anywhere other than a bed. I'm too conscious of the fact that the sofa is only slim and I might fall off if I toss and turn in my sleep.

Colt's still not back from wherever he went and I look at the time on my phone, noticing that I've probably only been asleep for about twenty minutes; given the time that we left.

I sit up and stretch out the aches that are actually throbbing through my entire body. Whether it's the sex or the sofa, I don't know and I don't care. I'm still riding the buzz from earlier and that's the only thing on my mind right now.

Standing, I stretch some more, grab the blanket to cover my bare skin after Colt tore my shirt and since I'm bottomless, then head for the cabin door, intent on finding somewhere where I can get a non-alcoholic drink, because there's nothing that I can see in the room.

I open the cabin door and see the door to the cockpit ajar, so I peer in. Colt is leaning over and talking to the co-pilot and some tramp in a stewardess outfit is pawing at him. When he turns to remove her hands from him, he's got a look of complete disinterest on his rigid face, but she's not getting the hint.

I'll help her out.

Striding over before she spots me, I grab the fingers she's using to trail Colt's shoulder and ask, "Something *I* can help you with? It's looks as though you're boring my boyfriend."

Boyfriend. I haven't used the title, yet. In fact, we haven't really put any kind of title of definition on our relationship, so it makes me glow inside when Colt smirks in my direction.

With a *hmpfh,* the tart walks away, swinging her long ponytail behind her and trying to sway her arse to match. She just looks like a dickhead in my opinion, but I could be biased.

"Boyfriend?" Colt moves us out of the cockpit and then grips my waist with both hands and pulls me close, nuzzling his nose into the side of my neck. "I kinda like the sound of that."

My stomach somersaults and my pussy throbs to remind me that she's won. She got what she wanted and she's keeping a good hold of it, and it's not something she'll soon let me forget when the throb turns into a pleasant ache.

"That OK with you, then?" I look at his beautiful face from under my lashes and return his smile with a shy one of my own.

"Abso-fucking-lutely," he tells me, leaning down to snake his tongue across my lips.

I suck it between my teeth and he growls against me, cupping my arse and pulling me closer to him.

He's hard again and, on autopilot, I pull him back into the cabin and shut the door.

Chapter 26
Grace

Dressed in a fresh, zip-up hoodie and gloriously sore, I step off the plane and inhale the sweet air before heading for the waiting limo. Colt is all but holding me up, while Dmitry and Harris follow close behind.

It's dark already, so I don't suppose we'll do much when we get to the spa, and I really wouldn't mind a hot bath, some over-sized comfy PJs and a cappuccino in a stupidly large mug.

The drive flies by because I'm in and out of a tired stupor, but when I exit the car and take in my surroundings, I am fully awake and in complete awe.

The place is magnificent and looks like paradise. Mediterranean-style buildings line the entire area and there are palm trees and exquisite water features as far as the eye can see, lit up beautifully with extravagant lighting structures.

This place must have cost Colt a small fortune and I am at a loss for words when I turn to thank him. He knows, though, because he smiles at me and takes hold of my hand, walking me toward the lavish reception area.

*

It's not long before we're shown to our gorgeous room. The bed is huge and every ounce of the fawn and white décor screams opulent luxury. A huge bay window looks out upon a crystal-blue sea and the lights around the resort make everything look so goddamn spectacular. I am so in love with this place.

My fatigue is completely overtaken by my enthused excitement and I throw myself into Colt's arms, peppering his face with kisses. "Thank you," I purr, "this place is amazing."

It might be somewhat premature – I haven't even seen what the resort has to offer – but I very much doubt that I will be disappointed.

Wrapping his arms around my waist, Colt lifts me off the ground and carries me over to the bed, throwing me down on to it.

There's not much I take note of in the room, aside from the waiting champagne on the bedside table. I pull my lip between my teeth and watch while he unbuttons his shirt. God, he's so fucking sexy and my body – despite the dull ache still echoing from the inside out – wants even more of him.

I'm still dressed when he starts to pull off his jeans; I'm too enthralled with the show before me to worry about my own clothes right now. He stands in front of me in just his boxers, and the low light from the bedside lamps shadow each and every delicious curve of his toned body.

Muscled perfection. And he's staring at me as though he could devour me at any given moment. Fine, I can put on as good a show as any. Rising to my knees, I tamper with the zip on my top, fingering it, staring at him and fluttering my lashes. He licks his top lips and gives me a subtle nod.

With desperate slowness, I take the zip down. I have only a bra on underneath, so his eyes widen when he gets a good enough view of my cleavage. I leave the zip half way down and get off the bed, to which he growls and comes to move closer.

Holding out a hand, I shake my head and he stops in his tracks. He's not the only one who can play control freak and I'll enjoy this every bit as much as he will.

Spying some chiffon drapery around the frame of the bed, I remove it and twist it around my wrists and fingers. It's silky smooth and an idea forms in my head. I use my finger to tell him to come closer and get on the bed – it's time for a little payback after what he did to me at his parents' place.

He doesn't complain, not even when I tie his wrists together, then loop the fabric through the bedframe, securing him in place. Instead, he shifts further down the bed in anticipation of my next move.

His large cock is bursting to get free from its confines and I smile, but I don't take my eyes from his when I slide my jeans down my legs and step out of them, returning my attention to the zip of my top. I take it all the way down and shuck it off my shoulders. His appreciation for my satin blue lingerie set is evident in his darkened, hooded gaze.

I climb onto the bed and straddle him, just above his knees, so no part of my body is touching where I know he wants me most. He's rock hard and his dick is still twitching beneath the material of his boxers.

Good.

With the lightest of touches, I trail my fingers along the outside of his thighs and watch him pulsate beneath me. The power is immense and I can't hide my sly smile. He isn't smiling, but his lips are parted and his breathing is heavy. He still hasn't taken his eyes off mine.

Dipping low, I flick my tongue across the ridges of his taut stomach. He's hot to the touch and his skin puckers beneath my light assault. I tuck the tips of my fingers beneath the waistband of his boxers and the head of his cock grazes them when it throbs. He sucks in a breath and, this time, he closes his eyes.

I lean over him, making sure that my breasts are close to his face when I reach for the bottle of Cristal champagne, but he opens his eyes too late to notice and curses under his breath.

I pour some of the vanilla and nutmeg-tasting liquid into my mouth and savour the flavours before I lean in and dribble some into Colt's waiting mouth. It trickles down his chin and neck and, swallowing the rest, I trail my tongue down after it before I tip small amounts down his chest, chasing those and stopping at each nipple and circling them before nipping with my teeth.

He wants to move so bad because he's getting restless underneath me. But I'm not finished with him yet.

I put the bottle down at the side of the bed and return my attention to his body. Some of the champagne has pooled in his belly button and I suck it out of him before hooking my fingers in the waistband of his boxers again.

Slowly, I take them down, but he's so long and hard that he's out within seconds. The heat pools off of him, as does the musky aroma of our previous session. I find the scent intoxicating and I slide the tip of my tongue up his length, lapping at the small bead of pre-cum seeping from him.

He tenses beneath me and jostles his hands, seemingly desperate to be free. *Tough shit, hot stuff,* this is my turn to make him squirm under my control.

Snaking one hand down his stomach, I reach his cock and grip the base in my palm, bringing him up to my hungry lips. With deliberate slowness, I slip him into my mouth, sliding down, twisting my tongue around him until he's almost at the back of my throat.

He tastes so good and I love when he pulses against me. I bring him halfway out, parting my lips and circling my tongue around his head. Chancing a glance at him, I delight in watching him squeeze his eyes closed and fist the sheets beneath him. Then I plunge him back in, using my hand to create a rhythm up and down his shaft in time with my sucking.

Tensing, he thrusts his hips up and arches his back, riding every movement right along with me. His grip tightens and he hisses, "Stop, Grace. I'm going to cum."

Music to my ears. I pick up speed, applying more pressure around his length. Using one hand, I reach underneath to cup and massage his balls; they're so taut and his body is trembling and slick with sweat. He swells in mouth and I look up at him. When he catches my gaze, he erupts, flooding my mouth with his hot, thick load.

"Untie me now, Grace." His voice is heavy and urgent.

I swallow his seed and lean over to undo his bonds.

The very moment he is free, he throws me underneath him. His cock is against my stomach and he is still so hard. He looks at me, so deep and needy, then he crashes his lips against mine. He still tastes of champagne.

With mastered finesse, he angles his hips between my legs and slams into me.

"Oh, fuck!" I cry out and into his mouth, lifting my hips and wrapping one leg around his.

He grasps my wrists and pulls them above my head, holding them in place with one hand. With the other, he pushes himself up off the bed and looks down. I follow his gaze and can see him sliding in and out of me. It's fucking hot, and I can't tear my eyes away until he looks back up and reclaims my lips, reaching up to lace his fingers with mine.

His tight body presses down on me and the friction from his pelvis grazes my clit. It sends delirious tremors the entire length off me and a tingling begins in the soles of my feet. It climbs up my body and heats my core, desperate to explode.

"I love you," Colt whispers against me.

I scream his name, returning his declaration when my body ignites from the inside out. I dig my nails into his back and ride the exquisite waves as they crash through me, one by one, sending me skyward to someplace heavenly.

***

No more. I can take no more as I sink further beneath the hot water in the enormous bathtub in our suite. The bubbles smell delicious and the heat is soothing every inch of my aching body.

Colt has already got out. He's on the phone to someone from his staff – even at this late hour – while he orders us some room service online. Food is very much needed right now and my rumbling belly reminds me that I haven't eaten for hours.

I'd love to stay in the tub for the rest of our time here, but I'm all wrinkly and I need something to eat. I can already smell whatever's arrived by the time I get out and wrap myself in what I can only describe as the softest cotton wool ever.

Heading into the bedroom, I spy Colt through the half-open door, pacing the adjoining living room. His phone is glued to his ear and he doesn't look impressed. I know I shouldn't, but I edge closer, intend on hearing some of his conversation. I pick out words like "finger" and "Russell" and realise it's not about me and my situation, so I back off and get dressed in my flannel pyjamas. They might not be the sexiest thing going, but, my God, they are so comfortable – exactly what's needed when you just want to chill out and eat crap in front of the TV while you're curled up with a hot man… who just blew your mind more than once.

I walk out the bedroom and Colt tells whoever is on the phone that he's got to go. Then he saunters over to me and kisses my forehead.

"Work stuff?" I ask and he hums against my head.

"I can't get out the casino night, I'm afraid." Again, he doesn't look impressed.

I didn't even know he was trying to. "Well, that's OK," I tell him, "we can still go; we'll just have to up security, or something."

Shaking his head, he replies, "No, Grace. I don't want you anywhere near there." His brow knots.

"What's going on, Colt? What's happened that I don't know about?" I'm not stupid; I can see in the worries lines creasing his brow that something's gone on. It'll be the something he's kept from me since we left for the airport. "What happened while I was with Harl and Cam?"

He takes a gentle hold of my arm and pulls me over to the sofa where I sit at his request. He then disappears into the bedroom and reappears moments later with a small box in his hand. Immediately, my stomach plummets and I'm not sure I wanna know what's in there. The last *surprises* delivered to me haven't been great and doubt this one holds much promise.

He hands it to me. "I'm so sorry, Grace; I didn't want anything to ruin this time away together, but this came for you today, while you were out."

Gulping, I look up at him, but he tells me he doesn't know what's inside. My hands shake when I take it from him and place it on my lap. As if Garrett hasn't done enough to scare my shitless and remind me of what I did. I don't think I can take much more of this; especially considering we don't have the first clue as to his whereabouts, but, apparently, he's on top of mine.

"You need to open it, baby," Colt urges me.

He's right, but it doesn't make me feel any better knowing it.

The tape covering it is unbroken, so I use my fingernail to rip at it. I take a deep breath before I find the courage to lift the lid.

I drop it almost instantly and the blood-stained, silver heart pendant falls to the ground. Sickness claws its way up my throat and I don't even make it to the bathroom. I fall to the floor and vomit across the polished porcelain.

"P-pen… ." I can't even get my words out; I am so choked up with fear. "Penny," I finally stutter, swallowing down bile. "It's Penny's." I cover my mouth with both hands and cry my eyes out.

Chapter 27

Colt

Penny.

Grace told us about the friend that helped her escape and my body shakes with rage. I'm gonna find that bastard and I'm gonna cut him a second smile, ear to ear. I can't even see straight and I dread to think about what's going through Grace's mind as she trembles on the floor.

I sink to my knees and pull her close. Her body is wracked with fearful sobs and I hate myself for making her open that fucking box... because it's only going to get worse when I tell her the rest of what I know.

"Grace, baby?" I try to pull her back, but she clings to me and I know this is going to be one of the hardest things I've ever had to do. "I need to tell you something else."

For a split second, her breathing hitches and I feel like the biggest prick on the planet. She leans back and looks at me, sadness filling her eyes and I can tell she wants me to make this all go away, but I can't. I will, whether it fucking kills me or not, I will, but right now I can't.

"Lucinda dropped that off at my apartment."

Her eyes narrow and the tears stop. She has murder in her gaze and I don't blame her. She must be wise to the fact that something happened between me and Lucinda, and she's wondering – like I did – what the hell she has to do with all this.

"I went to her apartment to confront her," I continue, "but she wasn't there. I found something... a finger."

Her face pales and her eyes widen. "The phone call...," she murmurs and I nod, unaware that she'd heard me.

"It belonged to a man she was seeing. I think she was being blackmailed." Part of me feels for Lucinda, because she doesn't know what I do. "The finger was severed after death, but I don't think she knows."

With an audible gulp, Grace slumps back against the sofa. "How did *she* even know?"

This is where things became clearer for me, when I spoke to Harris earlier. "The man, Russell Alcott, was a private investigator. Harris had someone check out his place, and he'd been tailing you. He discovered your routes back in London and he contacted Garrett."

Her hands fly to her mouth again and her face turns whiter.

"Harris got rid of the evidence, baby. You don't have to worry about that, he--"

"But what if they told someone?"

Her fear is understandable; it mimics my own. "I don't think they would have." I can't explain why I think that, but I believe that Lucinda would want to keep this as quiet as possible. Especially considering what Garrett is using against her. If he can get to Russell, he can get to her, and perhaps he already has – maybe she realises that Russell is dead, or at least as good as, and tried to run.

"Do you think Lucinda told him where I was staying?" Her voice cracks and I want so badly to make this all go away.

"I don't know, baby, but it's not a chance I wanted to take. When we get back, you'll stay with Harley and Cam while I get to the bottom of this and find the fucker." I grit my teeth. "Harris has someone out looking for him."

She straightens and looks right at me. "Is he in Chicago?"

I bite my bottom lip until I taste blood and nod at her. "I think so."

***

Grace

A migraine has settled in every angle of my head and I'm sweating through sheer terror. Garret is in Chicago. I can't even begin to piece together a rational thought. My life is spiralling out of control before my very eyes and I don't know what to do. Part of me wants to run again, but if he found me once, he'll keep finding me until I go crazy or worse.

I'm struggling to see a way out of this, and if not for Colt, I don't think I would have the courage to go on. It's cowardly, I know, but I can't escape this. I am physically sick with fear and I can't stop trembling.

When I saw that pendant, my heart stopped. If he's killed Russell, he will have killed Penny and I fucking hate myself for putting any of this on her. She did nothing but help me when I needed it most and, because of what transpired that night, she could very well be dead and it's all my fault.

Colt helped me into bed over an hour ago, and I've done nothing but toss, turn and cry into the pillow. He's on the phone making call after call, trying to find out everything he can about where Garrett might be holed up. I've not known him long, but I've never seen someone so angry... at least, not when it's not directed at me. He is almost fuming and a very small part of me almost sympathizes with Garrett, because if Colt finds him, he won't come out of this alive.

I shouldn't feel that way; Garrett is a fuckin' cunt for doing this, but I'm not as heartless as he is and I kinda pity what will happen to him. Kinda.

***

I try so hard to enjoy this time away with Colt. He pays for everything – massages, special treatments; the whole package – and it is so appreciated, but I can't fully immerse myself. Even my personal masseuse mentions how tight and knotted I am and it's no surprise.

Colt's surprised me with romantic dinners, a walk along the beach where we ended the night with a candlelit meal under the setting sun – everything a girl could dream of from the man she's grown to love irrevocably. I've felt like such a bitch for not being able to enjoy every minute the way I should have. Colt knows – he understands; all he's done is apologize for showing me the package, but it doesn't make me feel less guilty about not showing my appreciation for this trip.

He hasn't found much out in the way of Garrett's whereabouts. He's narrowed it down to within twelve blocks of my apartment and the realization alone makes me sick, but that's as far as he's got with it. He's even hired other security detail and they're working around the clock to locate him. I pray they find him soon, because we're going back today and my stomach is curdling with the thought.

Aboard the plane, I can't sit still and Colt tries to comfort me. His touch is welcome, but my nerves are shot to shit and I down two glasses of champagne before we've even taken off.

The flight feels like the longest in my life and, when we touch down back in Chicago, I have to run to the toilet to be sick. It pains Colt to see me this way, I see it in his glassy expression, but there isn't much more he can do – he's doing everything in his power already.

We don't drive to Colt's apartment. Instead, we head to Westchester, having filled Harley and Cam in on the situation. Harley cried and I felt like even more of a bitch for subjecting even more people to my bullshit past life. Cam tried to stay strong, but I could hear his fear when his voice quaked. I'm so hoping they don't decide to change their minds and hate me for any of this, because I need every single one of them even more right now.

Pulling up outside, I can already see Harl looking out the window. As soon as she sees the car, she disappears, reappearing at the front door with the saddest smile I've ever seen from her.

"Grace," she soothes, holding out her arms and enveloping me in a tight hug.

I sob into her shoulder because I can't understand why these people still love me, but I am so thankful that they do.

My body sags, and between Harl and Colt, they help me into the house.

Cam is on a shoot he couldn't get out of, so when Colt leaves to see to his casino night, it'll be just us girls. As much as I love Colt – and will miss him when he leaves – I'm looking forward to spending the evening with Harl. We've got a lot to catch up on and I need her spontaneously adventurous new lifestyle to distract from the pain of mine.

Colt's reluctant to leave me, though. He holds on to me for what feels like forever and, when we part, I miss the warmth of his body. It's like one of those disgustingly romantic chick flicks when we stand on the doorstep to say goodbye; each of us refusing to let go of the others' hand. Except, this isn't so much out of love as it is fear... on my part at least – fear that if he leaves me now, I might never see him again because Garrett will come and kill me in my sleep. Fear that I'll never get to touch him again, or look into the depths of his beautiful eyes. Fear, even, that something might happen to him in order to hurt me even more.

A tear slips down my cheek when his fingers leave mine and he walks to the car. My heart feels hollow and my legs feel like they can't hold me up on their own... without him. It's a horrible feeling to be so shit scared that you have to depend on someone else just to feel safe and loved. But it's also comforting to know that someone out there is willing to kill for you, just to make sure you're protected.

Closing the door, I drag my feet back into the living room and slump down next to Harley on the large sofa. She hands me a can of beer and I chug down about a quarter of the can before I pop it on the coffee table in front of me, followed by my feet.

"How's Farrah?" I cut to the chase because I don't want to sit here in my own pity party and dwell on what might happen.

There's a gleam in Harley's eye when she turns to me and says, "She's good. We've struck up a really good friendship."

"Yeah, I bet." I smirk.

She tuts at me, but the smile doesn't leave her face. That's fine; she'll give me the details when she's good and ready to admit that she fancies a female.

More poignantly, I ask, "How's Cam?" I'm a little disappointed that he's not here, but I understand that he couldn't get out of his shoot and he'll be home soon, no doubt.

This time, her face kinda hardens before it softens. "I don't get it, Gray. I spent so long wanting him, then I meet someone I like…," she tails off and her face blushes – I fucking knew it. "He just doesn't want to accept it. He keeps asking me what I see in her, and he's got really touchy-feely all of a sudden."

"You know the saying, babe. You don't know what you got 'til it's gone." I shrug my shoulders.

"He's getting to be a bit of an asshole about it, though. We bicker at one another and it drives me insane. I swear, he took this shoot today, just to get away from me."

"Oh, sweetheart, I bet he didn't. He's in demand and he gets paid well. I'm sure it's not you, but you just need to sit down and talk it out with him."

She shrugs this time, then glugs back her beer. "Maybe," she says.

Chapter 28
Colt

The moment I left her standing there, my heart ached. It's not been long, not long at all, but the things I feel for that woman already, they both scare and excite me. She's the one for me – the one I've been waiting for to open my eyes and I don't care how cheesy or clichéd that sounds. She owns every inch of me in ways she doesn't even realise yet, and I will protect her – because I protect what's mine; and she is mine, every bit as much as I am hers.

When I get to the casino, I go straight to the office. Everything is prepared – the tables are set up, the buffet is out and the entertainment has arrived. All that's left for me to do is open the event and mingle. I'll be as quick as I can because I want to get back to my angel. I miss her already.

I make a few calls to see if we've gotten any further with locating that sadistic son of a bitch, but we haven't. It doesn't please me to learn this, but I'll be back with her soon and I am confident that my professional team can handle one drug-addicted lowlife and any delinquent mates he deems fit enough to bring to the party.

The event kicks off and I am pulled from table to table, sorting out issues and meeting and greeting some of the high-flyers that are attending. I've had no time to check in with Harris or Dmitry, but they would be in touch if something happened.

Still, it doesn't mean I don't want to be kept up to date. I head back upstairs to my office, but no sooner am I in the door, then it closes behind me. I turn to find Lucinda and she looks like shit. Her jaw is bruised and she has the same clothes on from when I saw her last, except they're dirtier and there are a few drops of what I assume is blood on the collar. It's likely come from the small cut above her lip.

"What the hell happened to you?" I try to pour some kind of sympathy into my question, but I can't because of how involved she is in what's happening to Grace.

Shaking and pale, she walks over to me. "Colt," she whispers, tracing a trembling hand across my chest.

I brush her off and step back. "What the hell do you want, Lucinda and where the fuck have you been?" She smells like she hasn't washed for days and her hair is bedraggled mess. I remain quiet about what I found in her apartment, though, because she doesn't know about it by the look of things, and she's still tied up in whatever shit she's in.

"For old time's sake," she mumbles, though the usual lust isn't in her words; it's replaced by something like panic or fear and she can't look me in the eyes.

"What the fuck is going on?" I push her off me and hold her away at arm's length. "What is wrong with you?" I still don't want to give away what I know because I want to give her the opportunity to come clean on her own.

Her eyes glass over and she opens her mouth to say something when a piercing scream rings through the casino. I snap my head in the direction of the monitors and see black smoke billowing from near the main entrance. People are running, panicking and crying out and my staff are trying to regain control among the chaos.

Looking back at Lucinda, I scowl at the tears rolling down her cheeks. "You fucking bitch," I scream at her before running down the stairs.

I reach the bottom and turn to the staff members near to me, instructing them to make their way to the fire exit behind me. They hurry over, but someone screams out that it's locked and all hell breaks loose. Flames start to lick at the drapery on the walls and the fire spreads so quickly around the building. Someone shouts out that they've called the fire service, but everyone is still panicking.

Men and woman are crying and yelling around me, pushing past each other to try and find an alternative route out of the building. I see one woman lying on the ground, her neck clearly broken and shoe and boot prints all over her face and chest.

"Get upstairs," I try to yell above the shrieking noise.

There's a fire escape in my office, which isn't as easily accessible from the outside – it should be unobstructed.

Herding those nearby into a group, I point to the stairs and call over to one of the security guards, instructing him on where to take them.

The heat is almost unbearable as a good portion of the room is ablaze. Smoke is making my eyes water and it's become a struggle to see everyone now that the lights have gone out and the emergency lighting has kicked in.

Panicked faces swarm me and I try to get as many of them as I can to head upstairs. My guys are dotted around, attempting to do the same, but I see bodies falling all around me; consumed by the smoke and some having caught fire. The stench of burning flesh permeates the atmosphere and I can feel my lungs becoming constricted with the fumes.

Coughing and spluttering, I try to make my way to the front of the building, but it's too far damaged. Burning bodies litter the floor and I know it's too late for anyone caught down there. I take a few precious seconds to watch my business get eaten up by the roaring flames, before I turn and run for the stairs.

The fire exit in my office is wide open and already I can hear the wail of sirens getting closer and closer. I can hear large groups of people at the bottom, but before I can escape myself, Lucinda reappears from outside.

"I'm sorry," she murmurs before a sharp pain throbs through my stomach.

Looking down, I see the end of a knife sticking out of my gut. Sticky blood covers my shirt and Lucinda's hand and, when I look back at her in complete, wide-eyed shock, she's crying and mouthing her apologies.

She shakes her head and stumbles passed me and back into the office when she launches herself downstairs, her sobbing growing louder.

There's nothing I can do as my legs buckle. Then I hear her pained screams and I can only imagine what the stupid bitch has done to herself. I can't even feel pity when my limbs turn to lead and my vision swims. The fumes have started to creep into my office and my eyes are stinging so bad.

Stumbling outside and down the fire escape, I hear people gasp when I fall down the last few steps. I crumble to my side and stare at the throngs of people around me with their black, smudged faces and ruined clothes. Most are a safe distance away, but some have collapsed on the floor, struggling to breath and my own breathing becomes harsh and scratchy.

I cough up thick mucus and it dribbles down the side of my face before someone runs toward me, dropping to their knees.

"It's OK, Mr. Knight."

I vaguely recall the voice… it's someone from my staff, but my mind is heavy from the pain in my stomach and I can't think straight.

He tells me again that things will be alright, then he places something over my mouth and I suck in sweet, welcomed lungfuls of air.

After a few gulps, I try to wave the guy away – others need it, and my watery vision is fading in and out. I hear disembodied voices and feel pressure on my stomach. Fuck, the pain is intense. I think someone is calling my name, but I can't be sure. My body feels light and I'm kinda welcoming the oblivion creeping up on me – the pain is fading with it.

Someone tells me to stay… or something, I can't make it out, everything is merging together – the voices, my surroundings. Before long, the only thing I can see is bright stars against an ebony backdrop.

***

Grace

Talking everything through with Harl helps. She assures me over and over that she and Cam aren't going anywhere; they both love my crazy arse and are hoping this is over soon so we can all get back to our normal lives where we drive each other insane, shoot each other on computer games and drown our sorrows putting the world to rights in Potter's. It sounds absolutely perfect.

A bang outside captures our attention and Harl drops her third can, soaking both of us. "Shit!" she exclaims. "Sorry, Gracie, but what the hell was that?"

I have no idea, but I see Dmitry emerge from his spot with his hand on his gun. This can't be good and my heart rate spikes. I swallow, but my throat has gone dry. "Turn off all the lights," I whisper to Harl, and between us we do just that.

Dmitry pulls out a radio, but before he can say anything, a shot rings out and he drops to the floor.

The next sight that greets me freezes the blood in my veins. My skin prickles and my body shakes with uncontrolled fear.

Garrett steps out from the shadows with a dark smile on his face.

This isn't happening; he cannot be here.

His dark grimace is focused on me, whether he can see me or not; it's penetrating my soul and I am reliving every single fearful, tortuous moment of my life with that man.

"Grace?" Harl's voice shakes and her fingers find mine before she grips my hand. "Is that… ."

I can only nod and I don't know whether she notices or not, but words won't come.

"Let me in, Grace." His voice sends shivers through my entire being.

Where the hell is Harris? And has anyone called the fucking police?

A racquet erupts at the back of the house, but I'm too scared to move to find out what the hell is going on out there. More shots ring out and Harl lets out a scream, grabbing my hand even tighter, but never taking her eyes off of Garrett.

He's standing in the street and I can see people's curtains twitching, but he doesn't even care. He just remains there with a smirk on his face like everything he's ever lived for since *that* night is coming to fruition in this moment,

A smash echoes through from the kitchen and I know someone has kicked the back door in because it I hear it splinter against the cupboards behind it.

"Gracie."

I tense at my name on Brass's lips and sink back into the sofa. Harley is shaking next to me and, even without the light, I can see how pale she's gone. She looks at me then back at the living room door, never letting go of my hand.

Brass emerges from the darkened corridor, brandishing a knife. The moonlight and streetlamps from outside bounce off the wicked blade and my heart catches in my throat. Harley whimpers beside me, but I won't let anything happen to her – this is all on me; it's me he wants.

"Long time, no see, babe. Been keepin' well?" he taunts me, bandying the knife from hand to hand. "Tut, tut, naughty Gracie; been keeping secrets that are back to haunt you." His sneer is still just as disgusting as I remember it.

He moves to the front door and unlocks it, allowing Garrett entry and that's the moment the world begins to fade to black. I'm trembling so bad and I think I'm gonna hurl, but I can't afford to show weakness now.

Standing, I point to Harl while I look Garrett dead in his expressionless eyes. "Let her go, I'm the one you're after. I'll go willingly with you; the police will be here any minute." I'm rambling, but I don't care. If we leave now, Harley will be safe – providing he leaves her here in one piece.

"Oh, Gracie. I don't give a fuck about the police." He smiles at me and I can see he's lost some teeth since the last time I saw him. "I've missed you, ya know? Come here and give your old man a kiss."

With heavy limbs, I go to him, praying that he'll just let Harley go once he has me. But I'm not that lucky. As soon as I am within arm's reach, he grabs me by the back of the neck and pulls me to him, turning me around and holding me by the throat while Brass stalks over to Harl.

"No!" I scream, though it's constricted with the pressure around my neck.

Pulling a gun from somewhere in his jeans, Garrett trails my cheek with the barrel. "You murdered my cousin, Gracie. It's only right I get some payback for that since the police won't ever find you for it. I wanted *this* pleasure all to myself."

I cringe when he licks the side of my face, his fetid breath stinking of stale whiskey and cigarettes. The stench takes me right back to that horrific night.

"How about we have a little fun with your friend before I slice her open?"

Harley is crying, her pale cheeks are stained with a thousand tears – all of which I am responsible for. She looks at me with wide, imploring eyes and I wish so bad that I could help her. I struggle in Garrett's grasp and receive a gun-butt to the head.

I drop to the floor and the room spins, black stars dancing in my vision. He kicks me in the ribs and sends me reeling. I tumble onto my back and he stamps a heavy boot into my stomach. Curling up, I cough and splutter, pain throbbing through me. Harl's cries grow louder and I hear her murmur my name, begging them to stop. I wish she'd shut up, or it'll be her they take this out on and she doesn't deserve it.

***

Colt

The pain in my stomach is throbbing like a son of a bitch and there's a sharp pinch coming from my arm when I move it. I look toward it, first noticing the oxygen mask attached to my face, and then the drip feeding God knows what into my arm – painkillers most likely, because my head is fuzzy and I can't properly open my eyes.

"Mr. Knight?" A voice the other side of me startles me.

When I turn, it's only then that I notice I'm in a hospital – it begins to register in my muddled brain.

A man stands from a chair beside me and walks toward the bed I'm lay in. "Mr. Knight," he says again, "I'm Detective Godson, do you remember what happened?"

Of course I fucking do. That two-faced slut distracted me from my business being burned to the ground and then stabbed me in the fucking gut. Pain throbs through me as a not so tender reminder. I nod.

He carries on talking, but I'm drifting in and out; trying to piece together what the hell happened and why. The cop mentions a name, but I don't recognise it. Only when he tells me the guy was British does it catch my attention.

"Do you know him?" he asks.

Shit, he's taken my wide-eyed stare and tense body language the wrong way.

I need to get out of here, Grace could be in danger. *Fuck!* Why didn't I just stay with her? I will die if something has happened to her. I need to get rid of this asshole without raising suspicion, so I shake my head as best I can. If I don't speak, perhaps he'll fuck off and come back later when he thinks I've got a better grip on things.

Thinking quickly, I flutter my eyes, pretending that I'm drowsy and can't carry on with whatever line of questioning he has up his sleeve.

He puts a hand on the side of the bed and tells me, "Rest up, Mr. Knight. I'll come back in the morning."

YES! Now hurry the fuck up and get out so I can leave this place and go to Grace before it's too late.

***

Grace

I blink against the blinding pain in the whole of my body, telling myself over and over how I survived the beatings once upon a time.

Crouching beside me, Garrett grabs me by the hair and pulls my face up close to his. He spits at me then head-butts me. My nose cracks and blood gushes down my mouth and chin. *Don't scream, don't cry, don't ever give him the satisfaction.* I didn't before and I won't now, but by fuck the pain is excruciating.

Through blurred vision, I see Garrett nod toward Brass and I know this won't be good. I have to stop this, I have to grow a set and finally stand up to this barbaric son of a bitch. Reaching up, I grab Garrett's arm, bring it to my mouth and bite so hard into his hand that he squeals like a pig.

I don't let go. I tear into his flesh until I taste blood. Once, twice, three times he punches me until I release him, spitting out the chunk of flesh I took with me along with one of my back teeth.

"Mother-fucking slut," he cries, standing and clutching his bleeding hand while he delivers another kick to my already throbbing ribs.

Another crack echoes and this time I cry out.

"You sound just like that bitch from the café. What was her name?" He sneers at me. "Oh, yes. Penny. She screamed like a girl, too, and begged for her life."

Oh, God, no. My nightmares have been confirmed. Why? How? How did he even know? My heart aches and the emotional and psychological pain from his confession overtakes all else. Hot tears slip down my cheeks and I try to hold in the sobs while I gag from the coppery tang at the back of my throat.

"It didn't take her long to talk; I saw the guilt all over her face when I walked into the café the day after you murdered Frankie; I only had to mention your name and she went a lovely shade of white. I knew she'd helped you leave me."

I don't want to hear this. I don't *need* to hear this; the blame already eats me alive… to hear this is going to destroy me.

"I followed her home." The sick son of a bitch is grinning from ear to ear. "She didn't see it coming when she opened the door and I backhanded the bitch around the face. She was a crier… sobbed through the whole story of what she did for you, right up until the point when I aimed a gun at her chest and pulled the trigger."

A strangled cry escapes me and my chest hurts. I try to roll over onto my side, but Brass pulls me up and throws me on the sofa. I squeeze my eyes closed and grit my teeth against the burning, agonizing pain searing through me. Harl moves closer and wraps her arms around me and I try not to wince against the aching spasm that lances through again.

***

Colt

I slip by the nurse's station a lot easier than I thought I would. Godson is still hanging around, but he doesn't notice me either – there are a lot of people on this wing and I'm thankful they're taking up all the attention.

My arm throbs where I ripped the cannula from me and my stomach is going from lancing pain to aching throb. My legs are still weak, but I'm getting the fuck outta here and saving my woman. She needs me – something in me is gnawing at me; convincing me that bad things are going down because I don't even know how much time has passed.

Leaving the hospital entrance, a draught breezes across my skin, and it's then that I realise I'm wearing a god damn hospital gown. Fucking bollocks.

I spy an ambulance nearby and there's a fluorescent jacket hanging up inside along with a pair of paramedic's trousers. I slip them both on and put the wallet and phone I grabbed from my room in the pocket, all the time clutching and wincing at the thumping in my gut. *Now I need to find a goddamn car.*

A cab pulls up nearby and I thank God that the driver's timing is perfect. I stumble over and receive a bemused stare from the guy in the front seat. I tell him the address and that I will pay double if he gets me there as fast as possible.

Despite the speed, the drive is the longest of my entire life. I caught a glimpse of the dashboard clock and realise I haven't been out too long, thank fuck. I try calling Dmitry, Harris and Grace, but no one answer and my body goes ice cold as endless possibilities batter my brain.

Please be OK. She has to be… she just has to.

***

Grace

Garrett finds something to wrap his hand in, then he stomps over to me and punches me in the face. Harl screams and throws herself at him and I try to stop her, but it's too late. Garrett punches her, too, and she drops to the floor.

Seeing the hate in his gaze, and despite the pain, I throw myself at him before he can hurt Harley any more. We both go down, but he's stronger and not suffering from several broken bones. He overpowers me and sits atop me while Brass hauls Harley back up and throws her on the sofa again. She's sobbing so hard and clutching her face.

"I'm gonna enjoy tearing you a new one, Gracie. You can go meet that fucker you've been shagging at the pearly gates. He should have gone up in smoke by now." He spits in my face again and I turn my head, trying to avoid the majority of it while my stomach churns at his words.

What the hell has he done to Colt?

I spy the gun beneath the coffee table and make a grab for it, but he sees it a split second before I can curl my fingers around the butt, and grabs for it himself.

Aiming the gun at me, he snarls, "This has been a long time comin', sweetheart. I covered up your crime because I wanted the pleasure of ending your life. And tonight, I'm gonna get it." He thumbs the hammer, but before he can pull the trigger, a voice startles him.

"What the fu--"

Garrett raises the gun and shoots. I twist my head just in time to see Cam smash into the wall behind him and slide to the floor, leaving smeared blood down the cream-coloured paint. Harl screams.

"NO!" I cry, grabbing for the gun.

I prize the weapon from Garrett's fingers, turn it and shoot. A bloody hole erupts in his head and he drops backward. Brass looks between me and Garrett before he reaches for his own weapon. I fire three more times. One bullet sails passed his face, but the other two catch him in the chest.

He, too, drops.

I scramble from under Garrett's deadweight and stand, hunched over. I fire another round into his stomach, then I turn and empty the gun into Brass, clicking away on an empty chamber until Harley comes up beside me.

She takes the gun and tries to lead me to the settee, but I won't go. I hear sirens in the far distance, but none of that matters right now. Instead, I turn to the door and stumble over to Cam.

His shoulder is bleeding, but he's alive and I grab him, laughing and crying all at the same time, apologizing when we both hiss against the pain.

"I think we need to discuss the things that happen when I leave you two alone," he forces out, trying to smile, but wincing.

I laugh again, just so relieved that he's OK.

Harl drops down beside us and smiles at him, putting her hand on his good shoulder. "You look like shit, Cammy," she giggles, still clutching her swollen, bruised face.

"You don't look too hot yourself, Harbo," he manages through gritted teeth and a smile.

"Grace?!"

I turn my head toward the front door to see Colt standing in the doorway, silhouetted by the moonlight. Wearily, I stand and stagger toward him, throwing my arms around his neck. It's only when I'm in front of him that I see he has black ash covering his face, and he's doubled over in pain... wearing a paramedic's uniform. But he gets his question in before me.

"Is that... ?" He looks toward the carnage in the living room and I nod. "Are you OK? My God, Grace, what the hell did he do to you?" He looks me over and I wince when he touches me absolutely anywhere.

"I'm OK," I tell him. "It's nothing short of what he put me through on a daily basis. I'll heal."

"Oh, baby," he cries, hugging me, but wincing and apologising when we both flinch. "I saw Dmitry outside; I called an ambulance."

"Is he alright?" I dread the answer because I saw the shot. It was a kill shot and Colt's solemn shake of his head confirms my fears. I feel utter devastation because this is my fault. "Are you OK?" I'm crying and I can't stop the tears while wipe at some of the soot on his face. "What are you wearing?"

My eyes go to where he's clutching, and I open the jacket he's got on. A blood-stained bandage is wrapped around his bare stomach and I freeze, tears running hot and freely down my face. "Wh-what... ?" I can't even finish because my voice is shaking so badly.

"The casino's destroy--"

"Fuck the casino, Colt, what the hell happened to you?" I can't stand any longer and I fall to the ground, pulling Colt down beside me and crying into his chest. "What happened?"

"Lucinda stabbed me while one of Garrett's lot burned down my building." He rests his chin against the top of my head and sighs, tensing again with the pain, I imagine.

I look up at him in shock. "What?!" *Oh my God, the nightmare never ends,* and I hear Harl and Cam gasp behind me. "Are you OK? Did anyone else get hurt?"

His silence tells me everything I need to know and I collapse in a sobbing heap against him as the first of the police cars pulls up.

"Ssh," he soothes, "he can't hurt us any more. It's over, baby. It's all over."

Epilogue

Grace

Dressed in a beautiful, white gown with a deep purple sash around the waist, I stare out of the window across the vast expanse of the city. The lights from hundreds upon hundreds of buildings – both big and small – twinkle in a spectacular display.

A warm hand circles my waist and pulls me against hardened muscle.

I turn in Colt's grasp and smile up at him. He really is beautiful and, when I wrap my arms around his neck, I admire the biggest sparkle of all – the gorgeous, 18 carat white gold, princess cut engagement ring that he slipped on my finger after I came out of the hospital a few weeks ago.

Tonight, Colt's parents are hosting an engagement party for us – now that I'm fully healed and able to move again. His mother called me personally to congratulate us and apologise for her frosty behaviour toward me the first time we met.

After that night, the police caught the guy who set fire to Colt's casino – an acquaintance of Garrett's; he didn't tell the police that, but I recognised the name.

Apparently, he wasn't very forthcoming with information surrounding his presence in Chicago without any kind of legal paperwork. Perhaps Garrett didn't tell him – he had an army of goons that would do whatever he said providing he hooked them up with their next fix. He'll be deported and thrown in prison, no doubt.

The reason for Garrett's appearance wasn't uncovered either – though he had legal documents... or probably faked – no-one uncovered any solid trail for him. The intrusion and subsequent deaths were put down to a robbery gone wrong and I don't even know what Colt said to the police to explain his departure from the hospital to be with me. Whatever it was, it worked.

Lucinda's body was recovered – among fourteen others – from the devastated casino. I am sorry about that. As much as I didn't really like her, she didn't deserve to be brought into this, even if she did instigate their coming here. She didn't know what she let herself in for and I can't lay any blame at her feet, not after Garrett blackmailed her using Russell – who we think he killed, because his body hasn't been found.

I checked the London news every single day. Penny Gordon's body was found in her flat. She'd been shot in the chest; her killer still at large – or so they think. I cried for days and I cry still to this day because she was the only friend I had back then. She helped me when she didn't have to and I will be eternally grateful that I got to have her in my life. Every year I will say a prayer for her, on the anniversary of the day I finally escaped – and one more for the day her kindness killed her.

Cam healed – well, the physical wound did. He's still milking it for everything it's worth. And he does still wake up in the night sometimes, sweating and wondering where he is, but he's on the mend. We're all there for him. In fact, we're all there for each other and it's something I didn't think I'd ever get to experience again.

Not just because I thought I would lose everyone after I disclosed the biggest secret of my life, but because I honestly thought I would die that night. I think I fought back because I didn't see a way out and I didn't want to make it easy for him.

My true strength came out and I finally battled my demons and came out on top. He can't hurt me now.

I hate him with everything in me, but I have to thank him, too. It brings me peace because, if not for him, yes, I would probably be dead in an alley somewhere with a needle sticking out my arm, but I also would never have found what I now have.

I wouldn't have come to Chicago and met the two craziest people I've ever known. I wouldn't have known the level of friendship that I do now, and I wouldn't have met the one man who's made me feel like the most cherished, loved and protected person in the whole of this vast city.

Moving closer, I plant my lips on his and savour every single taste.

"We should get going, future Mrs. Knight." He smiles against me and I smile back. "You don't want to piss off the in-laws before we're even hitched." Pulling back, he winks at me.

"Then lead the way." I widen my grin and hold out my arm for him to take, which he does with his own smirk.

"Sir, the limo's ready for you." I lift my head and smile at Harris.

The bruises on his face have almost gone and the scar on his neck – while still quite angry-looking – isn't half as bad now. He should be proud of that war-wound. Brass shot him and grazed his neck, but we think he couldn't see very well in the dark and missed anything vital... luckily.

"Thanks, Harris." Colt places his hand over mine and walks me out of our apartment.

Settling into the limo, he tells Harris to take the scenic route to his parents' place, then he looks at me with a sexy gleam in his eye.

"Are you trying to take advantage of me?" I purr.

"There'll be no trying." His lip curls at the corner and then he's on me, kissing my neck and fondling my breasts with one hand, while he uses the other to hitch up my skirt and slip my knickers down my legs.

Dropping to his knees, he smiles up at me then disappears under the chiffon material.

I let out a gasp when his warm tongue glances across my clit before he laps at my moist entrance. Seconds – that's all it takes for me to get wet for him... because of him. He tongues me relentlessly, pushing in and out of my pussy, strumming my throbbing bud with his thumb.

"Fuck, Colt... ." I paw at the seat beneath me and try to balance my legs over his shoulders. I'm already quivering.

He slips a finger inside me and drags it against my pulsing walls, over and over while he flicks the tip of his tongue up and down my clit.

I throw my head back and scrunch my toes when the first wave of heat blasts through my stomach. "Oh, God," I breathe, gripping Colt's head under my dress. My body trembles and one leg falls from his shoulders.

He gathers me under my knee with his arm as he reappears before me, his face glistening with the aftermath of my pleasure. He doesn't release my leg when he uses his free hand to slide his large cock from his trousers.

He bends down and pushes his thick shaft into me. I'm gloriously full with him when he moves back and forth, hitting every sensitive spot deep inside me. I can't get enough of him and I snake my other leg around his waist, drawing him in, urging him deeper.

"Fuck, baby, you'll make me cum too soon," he groans.

I don't care. "Harder, Colt."

He groans again. "You know what it does to me when you say my name like that."

He pounds into me, hard and fast, just the way I want him until his balls slap off my arse.

"Yes!" I cry, digging my nails into his back and lifting my hips to meet every one of his frenzied thrusts.

"Shit, baby, I'm gonna…." He fills me, in every single way.

His hot seed gushes through me and I let go of my own release, calling out his name and biting his shoulder between screams.

Shuddering above me, he makes no attempt to move. His weight is my comfort and I can feel him smiling against the flushed skin of my neck, prompting one of my own.

"Colt," I utter, "we need to sort ourselves out; we're almost there."

With a *hmpfh*, he gets up, adjusting his still-impressive cock and tucking it back into his trousers. He retrieves my panties and slides them back on me, kissing my legs as he goes. I giggle like the excited, little girl that I know I am; the one that he makes me.

Smoothing down my dress, and checking my hair and make-up in my compact mirror, I'm satisfied that I don't look like a recently-fucked mess just as we pull up outside Colt's parents' enormous house.

Harley and Cam are waiting outside for me – surprise, surprise. Harley throws me a knowing grin when I get out of the car.

"Took your time," she chuckles, linking my arm. "Come on, girly, let's get you plastered one last time, before he makes an honest woman of you." She laughs in Colt's direction and then instructs Cam to make sure he gets him nice and drunk, too.

I'm laughing all the way into the house before I tell Harl that I love her to bits and couldn't imagine my life without them all.

Before I'm dragged away to the shots I can see already lined up in the kitchen, Colt grabs my arm and spins me toward him.

"Behave yourself, future Mrs. Knight. I want my way with you again later." He licks at my top lip and I quiver.

"You're insatiable," I giggle, giving him a quick kiss.

He pats my arse before turning me back toward Harley, and then he whispers in my ear, "And I'm gonna spend the rest of our lives together showing you how true that is."

I walk away without looking back, knowing he's watching me and knowing that his words – and his eyes – hold more than the truth. They hold the rest of my future within them.

THE END

Want to know more about what happens with this crazy lot?

Check out Harley's story in…

Harley's Kiss

Due out Summer 2020

About the author

Blair lives in the middle of England with her puppy dog (who's no longer a puppy), close to family and friends.

Her passion started, and continues, with reading – mostly Erotic Romances, but also Paranormal and other sub-genres.

When she doesn't have her nose in a book, she can be found shopping, be it online or around town, in a tattoo parlour, adding to her collection, or at home with her family or friends enjoying a movie, or gaming online.

Her hobbies include photography, gaming, painting, designing and making her own jewellery.

Unfortunately for Blair, she must finance her hobbies through full-time employment.

When she finds herself with a spare five minutes, she enjoys going out with her friends, taking small breaks around the country, and cooking.

Keep up to date with new releases and giveaways by visiting:

http://www.facebook.com/BlairColemanAuthor

Other books by Blair Coleman

Standalones

Allegra's Song